THE DOUBLE HUMAN

Tor Books by James O'Neal

The Human Disguise
The Double Human

THE DOUBLE
HUMAN

James O'Neal

A Tom Doherty Associates Book New York

James
O NEAL

This is a work of fiction. All of the characters, organizations, and events portrayed in this novel are either products of the author's imagination or are used fictitiously.

THE DOUBLE HUMAN

A Tor Book
Published by Tom Doherty Associates, LLC
175 Fifth Avenue
New York, NY 10010

www.tor-forge.com

Tor® is a registered trademark of Tom Doherty Associates, LLC.

ISBN 978-0-7653-2015-5

First Edition: June 2010

Printed in the United States of America

0 9 8 7 6 5 4 3 2 1

To Donna. Because she told me to.

Acknowledgments

Special thanks to: Bob Gleason and Eric Raab for guidance on a number of issues; Meg Ruley for her sharp insight and unending support; Justin Golenbock for his efforts to publicize my novels; Matthew Kuhn for his help in explaining the mysteries of websites; Florida statewide prosecutor William Shepard for his incredible support through all my novels; and Buch Buchanan for outstanding editing and proofreading skills.

THE DOUBLE HUMAN

ONE

Tom Wilner watched in silence as each family walked through the entrance to the housing development on the southern edge of the Lawton District, his waterproof windbreaker beading up with droplets from the constant drizzle. His service pistol felt like an anchor on his hip.

Steve Besslia said, "This is a shitty assignment."

Tom Wilner shrugged. "Watching people move doesn't sound that tough to me."

"I know, I know, you don't have any Iranians shooting at you or Bosnian car bombs but just standing here with our thumbs up our asses is boring."

"Do you really want the alternative to boring?" Wilner had seen it and was perfectly content with boring.

"I don't know, Willie," started his friend Steve Besslia. "None of 'em look too happy to be down here."

Wilner cast a sideways glance at the uniformed cop and said, "Would you like it?"

"What'd ya mean? I *am* here."

"I mean forced to relocate like this. I don't blame them one bit; especially when there are no jobs down here, no entertainment and it's too cold and rainy to even go to the beach."

"Government is paying for the move, providing free housing and a stipend for two years. You and me moved on our own, work sixty hours a week and pay for our housing."

Wilner shrugged. It didn't matter that Florida was no longer the sunny garden spot it had been when he was a kid. He liked it here. This was where he was raising his kids and they had all lived together as a family. For a while at least.

A young woman with brown, stringy hair stomped up to them and looked at Besslia. "You the Nazi assigned to shoot us if we complain?"

Besslia shook his head. "No, ma'am, I'm here to shoot the gators if they try and grab a kid."

The woman's eyes widened. "What kind of hell have they sent us to?" She hurried away, shouting, "Sara, Kenny, where are you?"

Besslia smiled and said, "Used to be the tourists around here that you could mess with. Never thought new faces would be so rare." He looked at Wilner. "At least you don't get those kinds of comments as a detective. No one even knows who you are unless you badge 'em or draw your weapon."

Wilner shook his head. "You know it's not like the old days. Not enough people to cause too much trouble. They're always happy to see a cop; particularly this close to the Quarantine Zone."

Both cops' V-coms started beeping in unison, so they knew it was a police call. Their newest communication units incorporated police radio, video communicator, mail service and a GPS locator service as well as a host of information services available to the police and public.

Wilner flipped his open first and heard the bland, clear, un-accented voice of a dispatcher.

"Any unit in southern Lawton District. Call of assault on or near the Eastern District boundary just north of Miami Quarantine Zone." The message repeated twice more.

Besslia said, "Let's go."

"One of us should stay here as assigned."

"You kidding? When's the last time we got a call like this?"

Wilner looked up at the dark sky. It was difficult to tell day from night anymore. He had not seen the sun in three weeks. He didn't bother answering the patrolman, instead he started jogging toward his government-made issued hive, which was a hydrogen-powered vehicle.

Besslia trailed him, jiggling and clanking his duty gear, his heavy pistol slung low on his leg for easy access while riding his big Hive-bike.

Wilner knew the only populated streets in the area where the assault was taking place and cut under the decaying remnants of the old Interstate 95. He used his V-com to tell Besslia to cover the approach from another angle, shouting, "Steve, cover the back, I got the front door." He punched the accelerator and felt the newly issued vehicle respond well. Sometimes the pro-duction hives were sluggish, which earned them the nickname "Hindenbergs." When the government started competing with the private carmakers, the one thing they eliminated was speed and fuel regulators. His tires screeched as he turned onto the unmarked road where several old but clean apartment build-ings stood. Most of the residents either had government subsi-dies to live in such an unpopulated area or worked at jobs in the southern part of the Lawton District. A few were smugglers who specialized in crossing the border into the Miami Quaran-tine Zone.

As he approached the front of a four-story building he caught sight of a woman jumping up and down, waving her arms.

Wilner jumped the old crumbling curb and brought the big cruiser to a halt next to the front door. Before he was even out of the vehicle, the woman was shouting, "He's killing her, he's killing her."

"Where?" Wilner drew his big, 11-millimeter, police-issued autopistol.

The woman, panting now, gulped out, "Second floor."

Wilner didn't wait for any more information; he was inside the lobby of the building scanning for stairs. He had not grabbed his backup weapon. He now kept an unlawful energy weapon in the car. In the marines they had called the handheld version of the weapon a "flasher" and now that was the street name for any powered, light-beamed guns. Events of the past few months had taught him the value of the extra firepower and the truth was the streets were full of these surplus military weapons.

He took the stairs two at a time and then slowed by the second-floor door. He raised the gun in front of him and caught his breath.

He felt his pulse slow and then he burst through the door. The long, wide hallway was empty so he started moving forward quickly, scanning the rooms, most of which had no doors. About half of the apartments had someone in them. He heard a noise and froze. It came from in front of him. Instinctively he crouched and edged forward, gun up and following the movement of his eyes.

At one of the last apartments with an open door, he peeked around the old wooden frame. Another sound came from inside.

In the back of his mind, Wilner wondered where the hell Besslia was. He should have pulled up by now.

Wilner couldn't wait. He slipped into the open apartment silently and slid along the wall, the next room in the sights of his duty pistol. He turned and eased down the hallway toward the open bedroom door. Shadows moved inside the room at the end of the narrow hall.

His pulse increased now as he consciously tried to control his breathing. He paused momentarily at the door, then stepped in with his gun pointed at the figure crouching next to the bed.

The scene stunned him for a second. After all he had seen—combat in Iran, ethnic conflict in the Balkans, murders here and over in the Quarantine Zone—this image froze him.

A man with short graying hair looked down at a naked woman, laid out neatly on the bed with a slight trickle of blood leaking out onto the white sheet from her neck. Wilner couldn't see his face clearly. The shocking part was the loving care with which the killer was now stroking her hair. It had a hypnotizing effect.

Before Wilner could bark out an order to freeze or just fire his gun, the killer's head snapped up and he pounced with incredible speed and surprise, throwing his whole body at Wilner as the gun went off. The bullet flew wide and high and the killer's momentum bounced him off the larger detective, springing him down the hallway.

Wilner, stunned, shook his head clear, took one more quick glance at the body on the bed and followed the killer.

He raced down the hallway after the fast, agile man but as he came toward the front door of the apartment he ducked a chair that flew at his head.

The polymer chair fractured into a few large pieces on the wall just above Wilner's head. Holding one piece, the killer swung hard and knocked Wilner's gun to the old, rotting hardwood floor.

Wilner twisted and threw a low kick into the man's leg, then grabbed a piece of the chair himself and aimed at the killer's head. Instead, he struck the man's shoulder, the jagged edge ripping his old cotton shirt and drawing blood.

The killer sprang back, turned and darted down the hallway to the stairs.

Wilner stood up, a little unsteady, scooped up his pistol and stumbled as fast as he could toward the stairs. By the time he was out the front door he saw Besslia pulling up on his Hive-cycle.

He stepped out to the front of the porch and froze.

At the bottom of the steps the woman who had directed him to the second floor lay on the ground, now still in a soaking wet dress, her arms and legs poised neatly along her body. He saw the blood mixing with a puddle next to her neck. She had the same kind of wound as the woman upstairs.

This bastard was quick.

Besslia was off his bike and running toward Wilner when an old pickup truck thundered from the rear of the building, blasting through the front yard of the apartment building and bumping over the curb into the street.

Wilner raced to his car in seconds. As he jumped in he shouted, "Call it in, Steve. Two dead. Chasing old truck, I don't know the make. Prewar for sure." He didn't wait for a reply.

The tires of his hive screeched as soon as they made contact with the street. He flicked on his concealed blue lights and siren. Not that there were many cars to chase out of his way. In fact he had not used the lights in more than a year.

It took a minute to catch up enough to see the truck's tail-lights as he headed south. He got on his V-com as he tried to close the distance with the ancient, gas-powered pickup truck.

"Dispatch, this is UPF 536. I'm in pursuit of a suspect headed south on Highway Six." He checked to make sure he had called out the right road. He knew it used to be called U.S.-1 years ago but now it was just called the "Six."

Wilner hoped the call would go to the National Guardsmen on the quarantine border. He figured that was where this guy was headed. With Besslia staying at the scene, there would be no UPF backup for miles around. Wilner's right arm ached where the killer had struck him with the broken chair but it wouldn't help him escape. The UPF detective was pissed.

The truck took a hard right turn, almost flipping on one side. Wilner took the same turn. Just as the truck was coming up on one of the checkpoints manned by the military, the killer swerved hard along the canal. The door flew open and the killer jumped out of the moving truck and rolled into the wide canal.

Wilner slid up behind the truck and hopped out.

National Guardsmen were already firing from their checkpoint on the bridge into the water with their assault rifles, making artificial waves with the volume of fire.

Wilner scanned the surface of the canal, not wanting to get too close to the bullets piercing the water. He saw no sign of the fleeing man. Just the water ripped by rifle fire.

After a minute of sustained fire he heard a sergeant calling, "Cease-fire, cease-fire," to the six guardsmen who were still pointing their weapons in the direction where the killer had last been seen.

Wilner stepped up to the edge of the canal, his pistol hanging in his right hand, pointing down at the ground. All he saw was the dark, muddy water of the last canal in the southern United States with no clue to the fate of the killer he had just chased.

TWO

Detective Tom Wilner held his badge up high and had already holstered his pistol as he approached the National Guardsmen on the bridge.

A young Latin sergeant stepped down to meet him. "We heard the chase over the general frequency. We were ready."

Wilner said, "You don't usually shoot at people going into the zone, do you?"

"Nope, not unless it's something like this. These boys needed to cut loose."

"Ever see him surface?"

"No, sir. But after the fire we laid down, I don't think we ever will. We had to puncture his lungs and stomach. He'll be dragged by the current until something eats him." The younger man turned his dark eyes up to Wilner. "He really stab some ladies?"

"Looks like."

"That's probably why we were okayed to fire. With the new transplants coming in from up north and the Midwest they don't want no mention of this kinda stuff. They got us really cracking down on Quarantine Zone violations too."

Wilner nodded. "Makes us look like the Wild West. They want people to feel safe."

"Safe in Florida? I have a couple of guardsmen who say they've seen more action here than they did in Syria."

Wilner chuckled. "I doubt that."

"How do you figure?"

"Any of them asking to go back?"

Tom Wilner shook his head as he pulled up to the apartment building where the chase had started. Someone had at least placed a sheet over the woman's body in the front of the building. Steve Besslia sat on the stairs to the building speaking to another uniformed cop.

As he came closer he heard the unmistakable voice of the UPF district commander.

"Willie, what happened to the killer?"

"Hey, boss," said Wilner, turning to meet the shorter, fifty-year-old man who had run police operations in the Northern Enclave and Lawton District for the past eleven years shortly after the tax revenues had forced all the police departments to combine and form the state's only law enforcement agency.

"What happened?" His years as a captain in the army in several different wars showing by the impatience in his voice. The thick burn scar on his left cheek was a testament to the combat he had seen.

"I answered the call. Saw a man with the body upstairs. We fought a little and then I chased him."

"What'd he look like?"

Wilner shrugged. "I didn't get any kind of look at him. Shorter white guy. I might recognize him if I saw him again."

"When did this woman die?" He pointed at the sheet-covered body.

"During the chase. The guy was fast, boss, real fast."

"Coming from you that means something." He rolled his fingers in a hurry-up motion. "What happened to this creep?"

"He bailed out in the canal next to the Quarantine Zone and the guardsmen laid down a sheet of fire."

"They got his body?"

"Nope."

"You sure he's dead?"

"Nope."

"Why not?"

"Because I've seen too many guys slip away from firefights. I never think it's over until I see a body. I just wanted to check on things here, then I was gonna take Besslia and start searching the canal on both sides."

The commander nodded. "I even brought out crime scene on this one."

Wilner stared in surprise.

"The new policy is to make it at least look more like regular police operations. They figure with more people, tax revenues will increase. They don't want people scared off."

Wilner said, "I'm gonna take a look around before I go search for the killer's body."

"You're the detective on this so you can take charge. I'll send Besslia and a couple of patrolmen to look for the body now."

Wilner nodded and started to walk through the scene. It wasn't like the crime scenes he had watched on old video broadcasts or movies. There was no yellow tape to keep people away.

There were hardly any people to keep away. No one wanted to get mixed up in a UPF investigation and no one wanted a criminal mad that there might be a witness. There weren't many cops either. They were spread too thin over an area that used to cover five counties and seven major cities. The climate change and a couple of terror attacks had shifted most of the population north. Away from the borders and as far from the dreadful Miami Quarantine Zone as possible.

The first thing he did was stoop and peek under the sheet at the woman who had flagged him down. She was about thirty, with a pretty face and short brown hair. He knew where the wound was. He touched her cheek and moved her head to see the single puncture wound in her neck. It had to go deep to kill her in those few seconds the killer had to act.

A patrolman stepped up behind him and said, "Did you get him?"

"We'll know in a little bit." The patrolman wasn't squeamish seeing the dead woman. All of the UPF cops, even the women, had been in the service and most, like this guy, had seen combat. A single, clean corpse didn't do much to spook him.

Wilner started checking for witnesses and other evidence inside the apartment building. He positioned a second patrolman at the front of the apartment, which held the first victim. Wilner took a few minutes to see if he could figure out why she was a victim. It looked like she lived alone. He found an identification card for the district hospital. She had been an emergency room nurse. Wilner looked at the photo and then stepped into the room to see her face. He recognized her. He'd seen her in the hospital several times over the last year and remembered her smiling, happy to see cops coming inside, a safety blanket added to the second-rate security guards.

Her sleek, pale, nude body held no clue to her bright personality. This was one of the few murder victims Wilner had ever known as a cop. The poor woman's delicate face looked almost peaceful. Wilner wondered how she had been unlucky enough to fall victim to a killer like this. Had she known him? Where had she met him? Perhaps the hospital.

If Besslia found his body it wouldn't matter, the case would be closed and he'd be told to move on to something else. But if his body wasn't recovered Wilner needed someplace to start.

He gently pulled a comforter up over her body. The crime scene techs, if they showed, wouldn't be too thorough. They wouldn't care if he moved something like that. He just didn't think it was right to leave her so exposed.

He looked through the rest of the apartment but found nothing. Just outside the door he saw the remains of the chair that the killer had almost managed to crush Wilner's head with. He looked at the piece he had used to strike the killer. He bent down and picked it up. Even though DNA wasn't used much anymore due to the cost and the degraded database, there might be a fingerprint or something they could use to identify the killer. It was all he had right now.

THREE

His whole body shook from the chill of the canal water. He was lucky he'd evaded the big, fast cop and the wild gunfire from the National Guardsmen on the bridge had not struck him. He had crossed from the Quarantine Zone over this same bridge, paying off the National Guardsmen in U.S. suds he'd won in the casino near the border. A casino that catered to residents of the district; a fact that only the guardsmen at the checkpoints seemed to appreciate. No one wanted to admit that illegal travel from the zone into the United States occurred every day, but it did. The army never thought to ask why none of the guardsmen wanted to be rotated out of an assignment in dreary, cold, damp Florida. They had no idea that most of them were getting rich just watching the checkpoints.

Now those same men had tried to shoot him. He was lucky he could hold his breath so long. He laid at the bottom of the fifteen-foot-deep canal, clutching the bumper of an abandoned car as the bullets popped on the water's surface above him.

Now, as he waited for the three UPF patrolmen to move

down the banks of the canal, his teeth began to chatter. Luckily they had been too lazy to get their feet wet and he had remained motionless here, hidden by vegetation hanging wild from the Quarantine Zone side of the bank.

Still, the trip back to his old stomping grounds had been worth it. If he hadn't met the friendly little nurse at the casino and become enthralled by her he would have been content to stay in the lawless Quarantine Zone where no one worried about missing women. As the population shrank in most of Florida, the Quarantine Zone grew as more and more immigrants came from the decimated Caribbean Islands. Since tourism had virtually ceased and air travel was a thing of the past, the fragile economies of most of the islands had collapsed, bringing the governments with them.

Anything produced in those areas was being done cheaper by the Chinese, even rum. Gosling's Rum was now manufactured in Beijing and exported to the United States. So was sugarcane, bananas and tank-raised lobster. Anarchy resulted in Jamaica, the Bahamas and even the Cayman Islands, which were now just an empty, burned-out shell of the former banker's heaven.

He would've stayed on the streets of the zone if not for meeting the nurse. Her cute smile and weakness for blackjack had attracted him. But he had been unable to lure her to his spacious house a few miles from the border on the edge of the Everglades. It had used to be miles from the giant wetlands, but the swamp had been slowly regaining its territory for the past decade. He knew it was only a matter of time before he'd have to move closer to the zone population center.

Even now he didn't regret his trip. The excitement would carry him for a while, even if he didn't get to spend the time with his new love that he wanted to.

The other lady, the one out front who wouldn't shut up, gave him no real satisfaction. He had stuck her in the neck to quiet her but couldn't leave without placing her arms and legs in a comfortable position for her. She had technically still been alive when he did it, her mouth moving as she gasped and tried to say something.

It would be completely dark soon and he'd slip back into the zone. But he'd remember the big, plainclothes cop who he had tussled with. Something about the cop had interested him. He knew he'd have to do something about him.

Wilner returned to the canal about two hours after he had lost the killer. The crime scene had been processed—at least as much as two disgruntled crime scene techs, who weren't getting a cash tip, felt like processing. He had given them the chair the killer had handled and they had photographed everything. They had followed him over to get fingerprints from the truck too.

Wilner knew they weren't going to find the body. If they were it would've happened by now. His stomach tightened looking down at the murky water. The whole situation reminded him too much of Tiget Nadovich and the explosion that enveloped him. That was on the edge of the Everglades, but they never found his body in the long, swiftly moving current of the Zone River. No trace of the Serbian was ever found. Not much was ever found in the Zone River. At least not on the U.S. side of the border.

His whole life had changed during that time. He had faced the Serbian and his crazy family, met Shelby Hahn and learned the truth about the other hominoid race and the truth about his own children. Now, four months later, everything seemed to remind him of those troubling questions.

A small crowd had gathered a hundred yards back from the canal on the Quarantine Zone side. It wasn't much different than what would happen on the U.S. side of the border if there were more people.

Wilner decided to take the opportunity to talk to them to see if anyone saw anything. He wouldn't get another chance to gather potential witnesses. Not in the zone. But hardly anyone cared about the UPF or district problems.

As he turned away from the canal and started walking toward the crowd, several men broke from the group and hurried back into the zone, away from any possible conflict with an official from the United States.

Wilner was careful to walk slowly and ease up to the group.

"I'm Tom Wilner and we're looking for someone."

"You a cop?" came a male voice from the crowd.

"Unified Police Force."

"That don't mean shit over here."

"I understand, but the man we're looking for is a killer. He stabbed a nurse. You don't want him to get loose in here."

Another voice said, "We handle our own problems."

Wilner could make out a few faces in the dim light. There were five women and eight or ten men. One of the larger men stepped forward. "We didn't grant you permission to enter the zone."

"I didn't know you had the right to grant it."

"You keep us out of the district."

"That's the government, not me."

The big man stepped forward. "I'm the government here." He started to reach for Wilner.

Wilner already had his hand resting on his stun baton. He yanked it from his rear pocket, flicked his wrist to extend it, then struck the man on the side with it. The pop as it sent a charge into the man made the others step back. The large man dropped to the ground, panting and moaning.

Wilner didn't even look at him. "I don't want to be here. But I don't want this killer loose over here either. Did anyone see a man running this way?"

Now most of the crowd was backing away from Wilner. Two men grabbed their fallen buddy's arms and dragged him away in the sand.

One woman stepped toward him. "Did the killer stab the victim in the neck?"

Wilner nodded. She had a slight Spanish accent. Her dark eyes caught the light from the checkpoint behind him.

"He has struck here in the zone but no one could do anything."

"How many times?"

"I've heard of two. We nicknamed him 'the Vampire.' "

"Did you see anyone fleeing tonight?"

She shook her head, her long black hair swaying as she did.

"I appreciate you talking to me."

She smiled. "I'm Mari Saltis."

"How long have you lived in the zone?"

"Twelve years. I wasn't a citizen yet when they closed the border."

"Where are you from?"

"Colombia."

Wilner looked at her. "You don't want to go back? Colombia has a working government. It's secure."

"It has no freedom. The secret police. Here, I'm needed."

"What do you do?"

"I'm a teacher." Now she looked at the surprise on Wilner's

face. "I know you don't think of the zone as having any orga-
nization, but we do. And educating our young people is vital to
our survival."

"I'm sorry, I didn't mean to offend you."

She smiled again. "It is nice to hear some manners." She
took out a pencil and scratched out a note then handed it to
Wilner. "I live two blocks south of here. I run the school for
girls a mile from here. Come and see me if you have any questions."

Wilner nodded. "Thanks, Mari, I will."

Ten minutes later he was back at the canal, the teacher's
pretty face still in his head.

He called out to Steve Besslia. "Anything at all?"

He shook his head.

Wilner shouted, "I'm gonna cross and check the bank on
the other side."

Besslia nodded and waved as Wilner slowly tromped through
the mucky bank of the canal toward the checkpoint bridge to
probe under some of the foliage that dipped down into the
water.

He told the guardsmen what he intended and no one volunteered to come with him.

He didn't think he'd find anything, so he didn't mind going
by himself.

He saw the big plainclothes cop walk up and yell to the patrolmen. Then the big cop crossed the bridge and started walking down this side of the canal. His heart started to race. He
gripped the handle of his combat knife with the spike folded.

Should he use the spike or the blade? He smiled at the idea of three in one day. This was definitely worth the trip.

In a way he was disappointed he wouldn't get the chance to think about the big cop and enjoy the buildup. He had found as he got older that he enjoyed the buildup as much as actually seeing the life drain out of them. When he was young it was too fast. Sort of like sex was. Quick in and quick out, no appreciation or anticipation. Now he liked things to last.

He felt the heft of the good surplus German army knife in his hand. The gravity-operated blade was his best bet. He decided to wait until the cop was right next to him to open it so he wouldn't tip off his position. The other three cops were down the canal all bunched together. He thought he might be able to stick the plainclothes cop in the neck, let him slip into the water and then be up over the bank and into the zone before anyone knew what had happened.

He might not enjoy it as much but he'd be safe and he'd have a hell of a memory.

He smiled, knowing that he had never taken any of it lightly. He remembered his first victim. It was more of an accident than intentional and he was so young he didn't appreciate it until he was older. But it was one of his most precious memories.

This could be a good one.

FOUR

Steve Besslia wanted to impress these two new patrolmen as well as Tom Wilner. He had been through the academy with Wilner and had seen how good a cop he had become. He deserved his detective job. He'd saved Besslia's ass on the force more than once. It'd be nice to do something for him for a change.

He glanced up and saw his friend now using a broken tree limb to poke though the thick brush on the zone side of the canal even though the body probably wouldn't be over there. Not the way the current was running. He had watched the leaves and garbage drift to this side of the canal and away from the bridge.

He focused back on the water, hoping to do some good work today. He wanted to make an impression. The last good thing he had done involved the use of illegal flashers fighting some kooks who had threatened Wilner's family. He and his partner prevailed, but they couldn't tell their bosses exactly what had happened. He wasn't sure he believed it himself.

Today he could brag about his good work. If he found that damn body.

Tom Wilner was using a long, straight, solid tree limb that felt like it weighed a ton. But it was better than bending too far over and risk tumbling into the cold water of the canal. The canal had been the old county line back in the days when Florida was divided into counties. After Congress had declared all of Florida south of the old Broward County line as the Quarantine Zone, the canal had been widened, razor wire had been laid down and all the bridges sealed off in an effort to keep everyone south of the line from coming into the country. It took a permanent force of more than a thousand National Guardsmen to protect the border.

Those efforts to widen the canal made it harder to find the killer's body. As he poked and moved along the bank, Wilner wondered what motivated the killer. He had a host of other unanswered questions such as: Who was he? Where had he come from? How many previous victims did he have? The woman he had just met, Mari, said she knew of two others in the zone. And that was just hearsay. There was no news broadcast in the zone. Things could happen without anyone but a few witnesses knowing of it.

Wilner found himself thinking about the Colombian teacher. Her rich black hair and dark, intelligent eyes reminded him a little of Svala. She obviously cared about others, having decided to live in the Quarantine Zone. He'd find a reason to talk to her again soon.

He went back to considering the killer. This was his first serial case. The other murders he had investigated involved single or gang killings. There hadn't been a report of a serial killer in Florida since the first of the Islamic terror attacks in Miami. The added law enforcement after the tanker bomb that took out three square blocks in the center of Miami and killed three thousand scared away a lot of the criminals. Then, when the anthrax was blown through the Dadeland Mall's air-conditioning and caused sixty-five hundred people to die, the army was sent in. After the mass migration and fear of the bioplague, it was easier just to abandon the southern tip of Florida rather than save it.

Wilner didn't intend that to happen to the Lawton District. This was his home now. He had a responsibility to his children. He didn't want something like this to scare off the new arrivals. He looked ahead on the bank and continued to probe with his long tree limb.

He shivered from a combination of the cold water and his excitement as the big cop moved closer. He had the combat knife upside down, ready to let the blade drop open. The cop had a stick but was still leaning down toward the water slightly. He already had the plan to spring up, jab him in the throat and then pull him in as quietly as possible.

He looked back toward the bridge; the guardsmen were paying no attention. Two of them were talking to a man in an old Chevy who obviously was seeing if he could cross over into the zone.

The cop was now less than five feet away and the anticipation set his nerves on fire. His heart felt like it was shaking the water. He held a low, hanging branch and was ready to shoot up like a knife-tipped missile in the next few seconds.

———

Wilner had an uneasy feeling about this whole situation. This killer had been sharp and fast. Although the guardsmen had good firepower and poured it on quickly, he now doubted that the killer had been hit. He could be anywhere in the zone or the district. Hell, could he still be hiding nearby?

Wilner looked up at Besslia and the other patrolmen. Their side of the canal was cleared of brush and easy to search now that they were quite a way down the bank. He decided he'd check another fifty or so feet, then he had to get home. It was getting late and the new nanny didn't live with him. She had her own life. After his experience with the last housekeeper, Mrs. Honzit, he didn't think he could ever trust an outsider to live in the same house as him again.

Just as he was about to check the next ten-foot section of the bank his V-com beeped. He stood as he pulled it off his belt and flipped open the screen. He grinned as he saw the image of his two smiling children before they even spoke.

"Hi, Daddy," they sang out in unison.

"What are you two nuts doing?" he asked, a wide grin across his face.

"We missed you," said Emma, his eight-year-old daughter.

"I miss you too."

His son, Tommy, asked, "When are you coming home?"

That always made his heart hurt. Their mother had left the family more than a year before and now he knew it was hard for them to understand that Mommy was dead and not coming back. Hell, it was hard for him to understand. He quickly glanced at his watch and said, "You know what?"

"What?" they both asked, their dark eyes reflecting a light inside his home.

"I'll come home right now." He dropped the stick he was using to probe and started marching with purpose back to the checkpoint. He had spent too much of their young lives on long surveillances or patrols.

He wasn't sure if he was disappointed or relieved. The big cop had given up his search and was now crossing the bridge back to the district. He knew his escape would be easier now but he had liked the idea and challenge of seeing his knife stick into the cop's neck.

Now he had a project; he had to find out who this cop was. Find out all he could and maybe let the buildup work him into a frenzy. He could still experience the thrill of seeing his face when he stuck a sharpened implement into his neck.

He watched from under the cover of the tree limbs as the cop met with the patrolmen and then they all pulled away in hives and on Hive-cycles.

It would be an exciting time tomorrow.

FIVE

Tom Wilner pulled his government-built and -issued hive into the driveway of his house in the Eastern District. This was considered the family area of the district. Emma and Tommy had playmates here and would actually go to their houses to study and do things that kids have done for thousands of years.

Wilner paused as he noticed a car very similar to his parked in the driveway of the empty house next door. He knew who it was and wasn't sure if he was happy or annoyed that he had a visitor. He locked his pistol in a metal box welded into the frame of the car under his front seat. It had taken a couple of months to convince himself that he was past the trouble he had seen because of his wife and the Serbians. He no longer felt as if he needed to take his weapon into the house with him. Not that it had done much good against anyone in that group. But he didn't like the kids to see him with a gun. They were already skittish enough when he left the house.

He used the hand scanner at the front door to unlock the

various locks that had been installed since his wife was killed. As usual, the first sounds he heard were the kids rumbling toward him. He bent down and took one in each arm. He could always tell when they were happy and had good days and knew he wasn't entirely the source of their squeals now.

He looked up toward the family room and saw his visitor get up from the couch.

"Hey" was all Shelby Hahn said as she smiled and stepped toward him.

"I didn't expect to see you," said Wilner.

"I was in the area and wanted to say hello. I hope you don't mind."

He stepped to her. "Don't be silly."

She embraced him and laid her head against his shoulder. "I'm sorry I had to lie to you. I'm sorry you can't forgive me."

He pushed her away and looked down at the kids. "Hey, you guys, go find Miss Lynn."

Shelby cleared her throat and said, "You were running late so I sent her home. I didn't think you'd mind if I played with the kids for a little while."

It was right then that Wilner knew his night would be as perilous as his day.

Steve Besslia sat across the table from Johann Halleck. Between them were the remnants of a dinner from one of two casual restaurants in the Western District. Their plates of processed turkey loaf and synthetic vegetables had been tasteless but filling. The vitamin-enhanced vegetables made from a combination of real vegetables, polymer and animal product had become so accepted that unless someone said it was a real vegetable no one knew it was.

Besslia raised his vodka and synthetic orange juice. Vodka was so simple and easy to produce that it was real, but virtually all mixers were man-made. He looked at his tall friend and finished telling him about his day.

"Then we chased the killer toward the zone where the guardsmen on the bridge shot him." He took a swallow of his drink and continued, "We never found his body."

"Why do you sound so disappointed if they stopped him?" Johann's slight accent pointed toward his European childhood. His blue eyes and light hair also pointed to his ancestry.

Besslia looked down at the table. He had only known Johann for a few months but they had become good friends. He hesitated, then said, "I just feel like I have something to prove."

Johann laughed. "You stood up to members of the Simolit family and lived. You have nothing to prove, my friend."

Besslia smiled at the comment. "I couldn't really tell anyone about that or about your family."

"Another sign of good judgment. A man of his word."

"It's just that everyone knows Tom Wilner is a big-time war hero, plus he kicks ass on the job."

"So you're envious of him?"

Besslia considered the word and just shrugged. "Maybe."

Johann took a swig of vodka and said, "I have been many places and have much experience built up in three hundred and fifty years of life."

Besslia stared at him. He was always amazed when any of these young-looking people mentioned their real age. He and Wilner had learned about the two great families of an undocumented species several months before. The Hallecks and the Simolits had an uneasy peace. No one knew how many there were. Outwardly they looked just like humans but they were hearty. They lived incredible life spans, recovered from all but the most catastrophic injuries and had a DNA structure just slightly different from humans. They had kept their identity secret and blended into human society. They had no superpowers but time, and discipline had made them tough. His friend, Tom Wilner, had unknowingly married a member of the Simolit family and assumed he had fathered their two children. Over the course of a brutal investigation the truth had come out. In the end, Wilner's wife, Svala, had been accidentally killed and her lover, Tiget Nadovich, was assumed to be vaporized in an explosion.

Johann continued. "Men like Wilner are rare. Brave, smart and, most important, decent. He's raising those children even though they cannot be his. He loved his wife even though she had betrayed him. He works hard no matter what. The only difference between him and you is a military record that happened to take notice of his actions. Steve, you have not faltered. You are a decent man and that's all any one could ever hope to be."

Besslia smiled and threw back another gulp of vodka, then said, "Thanks, Johann, you know how to make a guy feel better."

Tom Wilner just kept his mouth shut like the marines had taught him. He stared at the beautiful face of Shelby Hahn as she explained her current bombshell.

She said, "I'm sorry, Tom, but I had to take the assignment. I'm not sure it's good for either of us if I stay down here much longer. We need some distance and time."

Wilner nodded. He didn't disagree.

"Aren't you going to say anything?"

"What's to say?"

"That you want me to stay." She stared at him.

"I'm sorry. I've lived with too many lies. I can't say that. Not right now."

"You still think I misled you."

"You did."

She paused and considered it. "You understand why."

"I understand you have an obligation to your family to keep their secrets. But you know about my family. You knew a lot you could have told me. I just happened to discover it."

She looked down.

He hated to be so blunt, but he had no room for false sentiment or uncertain feelings. Shelby had been forced to tell him that she was a member of the Halleck family; a relative to the human race just as he was grappling with the knowledge that his wife at the time was a member of the Simolit family. He had found it difficult to completely trust her after that and it had shown in his unwillingness to continue their relationship. Now she was putting it all on the table.

"I may be in Pennsylvania for up to a year."

"Helping with the relocations?"

"You make it sound like a Nazi program."

"That is what you're doing, right?"

"I'll be making sure no terrorists, or Simolits, slip in with the regular people. The Department of Homeland Security is the only agency that can do that kind of stuff anymore."

"I heard the government might try and re-form the FBI so there's more than just one federal law-enforcement agency."

She shook her head. "No way. After the things that have happened and the attacks that hit New York and here. No one wants that kind of bureaucracy back." She looked into his eyes and wrapped her arms around his neck, then kissed him on the cheek. "You have no idea how much I wish we could start over."

Wilner returned her embrace, but his mind was on the killer and what he would be doing tomorrow to find him. He also looked forward to a trip to the zone to visit Maria Saltis again.

SIX

It was just after nine in the morning when Tom Wilner walked through the doors of the Unified Police Force station. No one cared if the detectives kept a particular schedule. They were so understaffed that even with the reduced crime there was plenty to do. A detective needed to be out on the street. That was a code that had carried over from the earliest days of professional police work.

Near the turn of the century a series of devastating hurricanes had spooked people and slowed the migration to the-then Sunshine State. The ensuing insurance crisis made new houses unaffordable. Then Hank, a monster category-five storm, blew up through the Gulf and destroyed the coastal areas from the south in Naples for almost one hundred miles. With the wars and the economy tanking, almost no effort was made to rebuild and the area was essentially abandoned.

Then the terror attacks in Miami and Jacksonville showed the state's vulnerability and started a stampede north. Once the climate started to change and the cloud cover became constant and the cold drizzle fell from the sky without end, Florida was a near wasteland. Without a tax base and no work to attract people, the only way for any government to survive was to cut and economize. Now they were left with forced relocations.

As he plopped into his chair, a relic left over from the early part of the century, his V-com on his belt beeped. He flipped open the video unit and saw his boss's face.

"You in the office yet?"

"Yes, sir."

"Come in here and see me."

Before Wilner could give him a good marine, "Yes, sir," the screen went blank. Wilner liked that about his boss; he was direct and no-nonsense.

Down the hallway and past an administrative assistant, who looked like she was a teenager, he entered the open door of the UPF district commander and automatically took one of the chairs in front of the wide oak desk.

"You did a good job yesterday chasing that freak."

"Thanks, boss."

"Any word on the body yet?"

"Nothing. I'm gonna look into a few more things and if the guy is not dead I want to identify him as fast as possible."

The commander nodded. "I don't want this popping up again. Not with all the media about the new residents and how they don't really want to be here anyway. If that corpse doesn't show up somewhere in the next few days, have a good idea where you're going with the case."

"Yes, sir."

The older man looked up, his extended forehead wrinkled. "How's everything else, Willie?"

"I got a handle on the bank case and the guys selling fake pig meat in the Western District."

"I mean at home."

"Not bad. The kids seem to accept that Svala is gone. They really miss Mrs. Honzit."

"Did you tell them what happened to her?"

"No. I just said she had to leave." He still struggled with the idea that his housekeeper and nanny had been a member of the Simolit family sent to keep an eye on his children. It was chance that he had stumbled onto their plan to make South Florida a "human-free" zone and foiled the plot. Mrs. Honzit was killed in the struggle to keep the plan alive.

The district commander said, "I doubt you'll be called up for service right now. It looks like Germany is staying put and not advancing any farther into Poland."

"The Tehran nuclear blast made them think twice."

The commander chuckled. "Who has such ancient labs that work on making a nuclear weapon under their main city? I wasn't sorry to see the city destroyed. You ever in Tehran?"

"Once after the Second Iranian War. We caught transports from there on our way to Bosnia."

"That regime didn't last too long after we pulled out."

"That's why I doubt they'll ever send us back in. Twice was enough."

The commander nodded. Wilner knew the tubby commander was one of the first recruits of the new draft laws and had worked his way up to a captain in the army. He had fought in Indonesia and took part in the Central American conflict. That was back when the United States had the manpower to fight a couple of small wars. Before they started using the court system and immigration to fill the manpower needs of the U.S. military.

"What's your plan on the killer?"

"I want to find out more about the victim upstairs. That was his target. The second woman was just in the wrong place at the wrong time."

"Thank God the media isn't jumping on this. If we had any local reporters we'd be in trouble. The Northern Enclave reporters are all in the center of the state for Disney's incorporation as a separate county."

Wilner nodded. He didn't care what the largest employer in the state did. They could be their own county; it had little effect on the Lawton District.

"I'll start by going by the hospital where she worked and see what they might know about her. Maybe the killer picked up on her there."

"You think he stalked her?"

"By the way the body was positioned, I'd say he planned it and this wasn't his first time."

"Any other murders like this?"

"I checked our files but without the old FBI databases or former local police departments I doubt if I could find anything here. It's also possible he's been preying on people in the Quarantine Zone and none of those would ever be reported."

"You got anyone you could ask down there?"

"A couple of informants who might clue me in. I'll cover all that in the next few days."

"Excellent. You know, I never worry much when you're on the job. I'm happier than you the marines didn't call you back. Then I might have to promote your idiot friend, Besslia, to detective and nothing would get done."

Wilner didn't hesitate to say, "Steve's a good man. He wouldn't let you down."

"I'd like to see him come through once in a while too. He's

lucky we got no applicants to ride a Hive-cycle up and down the district in freezing rain or he might be an evidence custodian."

Wilner knew his boss wasn't too serious. At least he hoped he wasn't.

Steve Besslia had on his heavy, weather- and water-proof boots as he stood in the gray mud on the banks of the canal that separated the United States from the Miami Quarantine Zone. The zone had been formed when immigration to the country had been banned and people still poured into the southern tip of Florida. Then the sighting of bioplague victims—or, as the correct term, victims of the Gleason-Raab disease—had forced the government to send the military to seal off the former Dade County. Many U.S. citizens were able to return but after a time limit the southern end of Florida was permanently sealed and became the fifth of the country's seven Quarantine Zones. New York was the largest, the dirty bombs having made Manhattan virtually unlivable anyway. South Dakota held the bioplague victims. The others were either concentration camps for jihadists or areas hit by some lasting terror attack.

Besslia liked being so close to the border because it made things interesting. It was also one of the reasons he had met his friend, Johann Halleck. Johann and his other "family" members were here in response to the move of many Simolit family members.

Besslia just wanted to make sure the killer who had run from Wilner was really dead. He admitted to himself he'd like the attention if he found the body, but he did want to make sure the creep didn't kill anyone else. Anything beat riding in the rain and issuing speeding tickets to any of the few drivers still on the road.

After working his way up the U.S. side of the canal he crossed the checkpoint into the zone. The National Guardsman barely acknowledged him as he nodded hello, his dark uniform clearly identifying him as a member of the UPF.

He took his time working along the bank of the Quarantine Zone side. The heavy vegetation clogged the side with a solid wall of vines running from the trees a few feet from the bank of the canal. Besslia could see Wilner's footprints from the night before. How he edged along the canal. As Wilner's long footprints ended he noticed the dirt disturbed. He squatted down and examined the thick soil. The rain had softened up some of the marks but he could clearly see a handprint and as he followed the trail into the bushes he saw a gap in the vines where they had been torn apart. He probed the vines, then stepped through the gap. It opened into a low, empty field. The weeds were also parted near the edge and Besslia followed the trail until it died out into an open area of sand and low grass.

Someone had escaped. He wondered how strict and alert the checkpoint was. As he marched through the field in his heavy boots he noticed a car, then two people on bicycles ride past from the bridge. He paused, sat down in the weeds and was shocked to see the guardsmen pass people by in both directions with little or no confrontation.

Besslia knew he had to get to Wilner. It looked like their killer was alive and in the zone.

SEVEN

His eyes popped open like they did every morning. He had welcomed every day for all these years in a rush of light and adrenaline. He didn't understand the haze of sleep that others spoke of because he woke with a start and then dropped like a rock every night. No matter his activity for the day.

Once, years ago, before the collapse of much of civilization, when he had tried to hold a "regular" job at a department store in the area that used to be called Fort Lauderdale, he would occasionally lay awake in bed and think about his interactions with people during the day. They were unusual to him. He had spent his life tucked away, empty of contact with anyone other than his family. His father had always called him "impetuous," but it was so much more. Nothing the old man could ever understand. It was an urge that ran through him like an electrical current. It pushed him in directions few could imagine. And he had little control over the urge.

He remembered the first time he had felt the urge to act out violently. The first time he had acted on an impulse. But the act itself had been so fast, so unpredictable, that he couldn't control it.

She had blond hair and the most perfect white teeth he had ever seen. He recalled every detail of her beautiful face. She was tall and had a lithe, long body with an athlete's legs. He'd been sitting on the intracoastal seawall wondering about the world when she had sat down near him. Not so close as to speak to him but close enough so he could see her clearly as she tipped her head to let the east breeze blow her light hair out of her face. Her clunky running shoes dangled over the white cement wall near Fourteenth Street in Pompano Beach where his family had lived. He hadn't heard anyone even mention the city of Pompano in years. It was like it never existed.

But then it was a typical beach town on the southeast coast of Florida.

He kept stealing glances at the girl on the wall. She was about twenty. Then something occurred to him. Why not talk to her? She was pretty. What would she do? Slap him? He stood up and walked along the wide seawall and then plopped next to her.

"Hello, my name's Leonard," he blurted out. Why not? It explained who he was.

She looked over at him and smiled. "I'm waiting for my boyfriend," was all she said, then she looked out at the water again.

This is exactly how his father had said people acted: rude and mean. He had no real experience at the time. This was one of his first times slipping away from his parent's house without them. Then he noticed the girl's neck; long and lovely with a muscle pulling as she continued to look in the opposite direction so she wouldn't have to face Leonard.

He was mesmerized by it. He wanted to touch it. To

squeeze it. Then he remembered the broken metal skewer next to the wall where he had been sitting before. An old bar-beque skewer with a flat, solid ring on one end. He slid off the wall and raced back to find it. He didn't even know why he needed it but the urge inside him said, "Find the skewer."

He snatched it up from the weeds and gravel alongside the low wall. The metal base fit in his palm and the seven inches of steel skewer felt like another finger popping out of his fist. He walked back to the girl, who turned her head again as soon as he approached. Then, without thinking about it or hesitating, he held up his fist and plunged the skewer into the girl's neck. It disappeared all the way into her long, beautiful neck until he felt his knuckles stopped by her skin. She was frozen for a second. He leaned back and saw that the other end of the skewer had just broken the skin on the other side of her neck.

The girl wheezed as she started to shake slightly.

The skewer came out amazingly easily. He just sat and watched in fascination as the girl slowly turned her head to see what had happened.

Blood started spurting from the hole in her neck. The red liquid shot out like a sprinkler as she rotated around. By the time she was looking at Leonard, he was sitting silently, the deadly skewer resting on the sea wall on the other side of him.

She tried to speak but nothing came out.

He saw her mouth was also filling up with blood. His urge subsided as he watched the girl.

He wanted to touch her. To explore her somehow, but he had so little experience. She reached across and clutched at his shirt as her balance began to falter. Her hand went to his face and he felt the need to touch her. He started to run his fingers through her hair and unhooked a black, plastic hair clip. He held it, looking at the shiny finish, then dropped it as he focused on the girl toppling into the murky intracoastal waterway.

It had all happened in a matter of seconds.

He'd been lucky and later realized it. He'd never even looked around to see if there were any witnesses.

But there had not been anyone around to see the attack. The news media covered her disappearance and then went wild about her body being found two miles down the intracoastal a few days later. Back then there were local channels and this was big news. He never told anyone.

The police pleaded for tips. Her family offered higher and higher rewards for information. Stories ran even ten years later about the unsolved murder of the girl sitting on the seawall.

That was the kind of experiences he had had before working for the department store. The whole job confused him. He was nice to customers, but they never seemed nice back. He had thought about acting on his urges again with one of those department store customers, but knew it would be easy for the police to figure it out.

He had many more instances where he acted on his urges over the years. A young mother from Davie. The grocery store clerk who needed a ride. It was always their necks that made him act.

Since the establishment of the Quarantine Zone he'd been much more active. Now he could move among groups of people and blend in, always staying anonymous and never leaving real clues to his identity.

Now he stretched and turned to sit up and leave his single bed in the house about eight miles from the U.S. border. His aunt lived with him. His mother had moved west when things had started to get bad in Florida and he had not heard from her since. Of course, he hadn't tried too hard to reach her either. Her younger sister was actually much closer to Leonard's age. She managed the household and Leonard provided either money or went out and traded for what they needed. Like most people in the Quarantine Zone they had a garden and raised their own potatoes, squash, corn and tomatoes. He bought the occasional goat or chicken; they lived pretty well.

In the living room of the old Florida house his aunt smiled at him.

"Hello, Lenny. What's on your schedule today?" No wrinkles or other telltale signs of aging, but by Quarantine Zone standards she was ancient.

"Gotta go up into the Lawton District."

"What for?"

"I gotta meet with a cop."

Tom Wilner walked through the main doors of the Eastern hospital and was surprised at how busy the staff looked. The emergency room at the end of the hall actually had patients waiting to be treated. There was even a visitor at the front desk waiting to go up to the recovery ward.

A tall black man in a security guard's uniform barked at him, "Hey, you. Where the hell you think you're going?" He marched up to Wilner in an intimidation move Wilner had seen a thousand times in the service. He didn't say anything, letting the man feel in control.

The guard said, "I asked you a question."

Wilner reached inside his windbreaker, past his heavy-duty pistol on his hip to his rear pocket and pulled out his ID with a bright gold star affixed to one inside flap. "UPF and I don't like your tone."

Instantly the man stepped back and lowered his voice. "Oh, shit, I'm sorry, sir, I didn't know."

Wilner eased up and said, "But you didn't need to address me like that in the first place. What happened to just asking if I was lost?"

"Too many years in the army I guess."

Now it was Wilner who felt like he needed to apologize. "Where'd you serve?"

"South Africa for the duration."

Wilner looked at him. That was a term only used by one kind of soldier. "You were in a penal unit?"

The man nodded. "We bled just like everyone else."

"But you were sentenced to the military for a crime?"

"Yeah. Got into a beef with my wife and ended up busting her up. Judge gave me the South African conflict until it was finished. Lucky for me we were only deployed for two years before the new government stabilized."

"How'd you get a job as a security guard with a record?"

"You kidding? Short as they are on manpower they loved hiring a six-foot-three man. Just had to promise to keep my cool."

Wilner nodded, then held up a photo of the slain nurse. "You know her?"

"Donna, sure. We all did. The whole place is in mourning over her."

"How'd everyone find out?"

"Newscast over our V-coms."

"Know why someone might do something like this to her?"

"That girl never said a harsh word to no one."

"Nothing unusual about her?"

"I didn't say that."

Wilner tilted his head and gave him a stare. "You know I don't have time for games. What's the scoop?"

"She didn't much care for men after her marriage broke up."

"And?"

"She got herself a girlfriend that works up in the terminal ward on the fourth floor."

"That's the only thing unusual about her?"

"That and the girl loved to gamble. Snuck into the Quarantine Zone to play at their casinos whenever she could."

That got Wilner's attention.

Johann Halleck was not prone to loneliness. He had spent long segments of his life separated from his closest family, usually with the thought that soon the world would be different and he wouldn't have to worry about man's cruelty or the designs of the Simolits. He had lived so long—more than five human lifetimes—that he was back to facing some of the same old menaces. Somehow he knew, after the tears and agony of World War II, the world might have to face German aggression again. As news of Hitler's cowardly death spread through the Polish countryside, where he lived at the time, he realized that it was too easy to blame the whole mess on just one man. Now, generations later, he knew he was right.

He sat alone in his living room of the large, empty house in the Western District, watching his gigantic video broadcaster. It seemed as if the top of every hour started with a brief story on the advancing alien ship, the next story was on the cleanup of the decimated Iranian capital and then a story on the German army that had remained stationary inside the Polish borders.

The German advance had halted when the news of the nuclear explosion in Tehran had spread. It was as if the event reminded the new German chancellor that there were still nuclear weapons in the world and someone might use one on the rapidly advancing German troops.

It was only after several days that the world discovered that Iran had been responsible for its own fate. While working on a new type of fusion bomb an accident had caused a reaction that had cost millions their lives. But, in light of the German halt, it may have saved millions more.

In the interceding months, the United States, England and the remnants of old Russia had moved troops to the area, adding to Germany's reasons to forget their new search for *Lebensraum*.

But Johann was concerned with much more immediate things like the safety of his good-hearted but naive friend, Steve Besslia, and the whereabouts of any members of the dangerous Simolit family left in the Lawton District.

Since he had been forced to kill Radko Simolit in order to save both Besslia and Tom Wilner, he knew his name was cursed around Simolit gatherings. Although there was a treaty in place to keep relative peace between the two ancient families, there were always exceptions. The question was if they viewed his actions as one of the exceptions to the treaty.

It was never known what had happened to Tiget Nadovich, a ruthless leader among the Simolits. He had stolen Wilner's wife, planned to take over the Lawton District and was now presumed dead. But it was never wise to ever assume a Simolit was dead unless there was a body. It was the Simolits who inspired the vampire legend. It was even true that a stake through the heart, if it destroyed the muscle sufficiently, would kill them. But so would enough bullets in the brain, an explosion, fire. Anything as long as it was devastating enough.

He had seen the effects of the propane explosion that had destroyed part of the building on the edge of the Everglades. But he had not seen a body. He had searched the Zone River but the rapid current, fed by the constant rainfall, had flushed everything south. He hoped he had seen the last of the intelligent, Serbian-born Nadovich, but much like the Germans, he was afraid he would see him again.

EIGHT

Leonard Hall had made his way into the Lawton District once again by bribing his way through one of his most reliable checkpoints. It was the farthest west, near the Zone River and no one much came through that way. Recently there had been an influx of new residents out west. Not people relocated by the government, but secretive, reclusive people. There was a rumor that they were a religious cult, but Leonard thought they just were the type that valued their privacy. They were in the right place. No one wanted to live out there. Even the government wasn't sending people to the swampy, cold wasteland.

Once in the district he went right to the main headquarters of the UPF, thinking that would be his best chance of seeing the cop he had become so interested in. He planned on visiting one of the libraries in the district to search what was left of the records on the Internet. The dilapidated network of computers had faltered since the mid-2020s. More attention was paid to terror and wars than shopping and information. As the military and government focused on security, the private sector stagnated and much of the effort that went into the Internet was turned elsewhere. Just like the decline of inventions and innovations not related to the military, the Internet slowly suffered and was reduced to an unreliable string of computers and mainframes with little more than out-of-date archives and pornography.

Leonard had seen a lot of things. He'd lived a long life and experienced many places under a number of different names, but he clearly saw a parallel between the declining supercomputer network and the rest of society. He hoped he'd be around to witness the end of it all.

After twenty minutes of waiting in the hybrid Honda that had been converted to run on propane and electricity, but couldn't go faster than twenty-seven miles an hour, Leonard saw his cop leave by a side door. A minute later the hive that the cop had used to chase him left by the rear lot. It was one of the new government models with the engine set in the middle for balance and the chamber to make the hydrogen reduced to a small cylinder. They were fast, efficient cars but lacked any of the comfort of the early Chevys and Fords that had cushioned seats and air-conditioning. Those were relics as forgotten as the Supreme Court.

Seven minutes later he found himself watching the cop pull up in front of the biggest of the district hospitals. He hesitated as he considered when and where would be the best place to surprise the UPF detective.

He noticed the activity at the front as people came and went. Then an odd light spread across the five-story structure and he realized the sun was breaking through the clouds for the first time in weeks. He loved the sun almost as much as he loved necks. The combination of the two drove him wild and he made up his mind instantly.

He pulled the old Honda to the side of the street and hopped out, hustling toward the entrance to the hospital.

Tom Wilner hesitated at the doorway to the break room. He knew the young woman watching the news was Donna's lover. The security guard had been quite specific and maybe a little graphic. He cleared his throat to get her attention. When her red eyes focused on him he knew that she hadn't been watching the video broadcaster as much as staring toward the big screen.

"Terry?"

She sat up, her broad shoulders turning toward him. "Yes?"

He held up his ID. "I'm Tom Wilner with the UPF."

"You're here about Donna."

He nodded.

"You know we were close?"

He nodded again.

"I'm not embarrassed, just a little surprised you found me so fast."

"I came by the hospital to ask a few questions. I don't want to intrude."

She gave him a slight smile. It wasn't until she moved her right hand he realized what was different about her.

She saw his expression and raised the robotically enhanced prosthetic hand with eight fully controllable fingers. "I got the model designed for detailed work. They knew I wanted to go into medicine."

Wilner couldn't take his eyes off the high-end prosthetic as he came closer.

The thirty-five-year-old nurse said, "I lost it in the First Iranian War. Infantry."

Wilner looked her in the eyes and said, "I was a marine during the Second Iranian War."

"I figured you'd seen action. Seems like more and more vets are from the penal regiments. Nice to see a real one."

Wilner eased into the chair next to her. He glanced up at the TV and saw it was a sports show focusing on the new World Football League. The Madrid Raiders were the team to beat and the Toronto Jets were the perennial losers.

Wilner finally got around to saying, "I just wanted to know something about Donna. It might help me in the case."

"I thought the checkpoint weenies shot the killer."

"We didn't find a body. I want to be certain. Did Donna come in contact with a lot of men?"

"You mean because we were together?"

"No, not really. I just wonder how he picked her."

"She swung both ways. We both did. It's just that there are so few decent guys around we sort of gravitated to each other."

"So it wouldn't have been a guy from the hospital. You would know that, right?"

"No one here. But she did . . ."

"What?"

"Well, she liked to gamble. Blackjack especially. Since the government eliminated the Seminole reservations and outlawed casinos she had to look elsewhere."

"Like the Quarantine Zone."

Terry nodded. "I didn't like it but she crossed into the zone a couple of times a month."

"To the big casino right near the border."

"Isn't that where everyone goes?"

"Yeah. I even go sometimes. When I get bored. She ever meet anyone over there?"

"I dunno." Then she paused. Her blond hair swayed as she tilted her head. "Yeah, I guess she did. She introduced me to a guy last week."

"What was his name?"

"I don't remember."

"What'd he look like?"

"Shorter. A little older. It's hard to say. I just remember he looked like he was in pretty good shape."

"Where's he live?"

"I didn't talk to him. But I bet I could come up with his name. I remember Donna saying it."

It was all Wilner had. As he was about to ask for more details his V-com beeped.

Leonard had no trouble getting into the hospital. He always dressed nicely and walked with a certain assurance. He didn't think the cop had seen his face clearly enough to recognize him immediately, but he wanted to be able to make the first move. He didn't want to be surprised, so he kept his eyes open, scanning every face as soon as it came into view.

The tall blond cop would be easy to spot and then Leonard would find the right moment to spring. It was his old urge building. He had to do something to relieve the buildup of anticipation that had started when he felt the cop so close on the canal bank. The danger of the man had made him the perfect target. Also the fact that the cop wasn't just assuming the checkpoint guards had killed him. By acting now he would be cutting off the source of any link to him.

Leonard managed to make it through the lobby and first floor without being noticed or questioned. But he had not seen the cop either. He took the empty stairs in the rear two at a time. The second floor had a nursery and some kind of vast maintenance area. He took a quick look on the third and fourth floors but could see quickly that no one was in the hallway. The fifth floor looked like administrative offices. A receptionist looked up immediately. "Can I help you?"

Leonard smiled and said, "No, I'm going to six." He slid back into the stairwell and shot up the final flight of stairs.

As soon as he opened the door to the top floor he saw the cop on his V-com at the end of the hallway near a wide window that still held a sliver of sunlight. The endless clouds had already started to close formation again. He stepped back into the stairway, realizing this was his moment. The cop hadn't seen him and no one was around. He took a deep breath and reached into his deep pocket on his synthetic all-weather pants. The rubbery feel of the inside of the pocket slowed his right hand as he gripped the handle of the German army surplus combat knife. He didn't use the lever to open the gravity-fed blade, instead he opened the combat spike, his weapon of choice for the past sixteen years. He had found it on a merchant seaman he had killed.

With the spike open he knew he could move fast. With the right movement the cop wouldn't even know Leonard was here.

He peeked out the stairway door and saw the cop still talking on his V-com and now facing out the window to catch a final glimpse of the sun before it was covered by gray formless clouds.

His heart raced, but a smile crossed his face as he prepared to rush the unsuspecting cop. This was going to be sweet.

Steve Besslia had been impatient to find his friend once he arrived at the hospital so he called him on the V-com. It took Wilner a couple of beeps to answer, then Besslia spoke so fast he had to stop, take a breath and calm down.

Wilner said, "What is it, Steve?"

"I didn't just push my bike to get over here in ten minutes from the Quarantine Zone to tell you over video link. Where are you in the hospital?"

"Sixth floor."

Besslia kept him on the line as he found the only operating vertical transport shaft. The VTS was a wide bay that was propelled by the expansion and expulsion of gas that acted as a hydraulic. The VTS passed from the first floor to the top floor and back, pausing briefly on every intermediate floor. The idea had been developed when the push to conserve energy had been tremendous. Now that energy wasn't a concern, no one had the extra cash to convert the slower VTS back to elevators. At least not in the wasteland of Florida.

He was the only one on the big lift system and fidgeted every time it stopped at an empty floor.

NINE

Leonard Hall was ready. He had his weapon and the big cop was still on the video V-com, looking out the window. Just as he started to push open the door, the VTS door opened right next to the stairway door. He instinctively slipped back into the stairs. Through the glass pane on the stairway door he saw a uniformed cop emerge, the two men began to talk. He heard the uniformed cop address his prey. "Wilner."

He smiled. Information could be as important as a weapon. Now he knew something about who this cop was.

It was obvious the two cops were staying together for a while so he started down the stairs to get lost on a lower floor.

Terry started taking down notes of what she remembered of the man she had met with Donna in the zone as soon as the handsome UPF detective had left.

She had been so upset by the news of Donna's death that she never would've come into work today but she was needed in the new nursery. They had three babies for the first time since she had been employed and she didn't want to miss this special time. Talking to the cop had helped by giving her a purpose. Almost like giving her some control over what had happened. She needed to help.

She stood up and straightened her clean white and blue uniform. Her prosthetic fingers functioning like her own except for feel. If she watched what they were doing she could do intricate work, but she never felt what she touched. There was a rumor engineers were very close to new technology that could transfer some sense of touch to the fingertips. She looked at her titanium hand and started down the stairway.

The nursery was on the second floor near the facilities and maintenance area where they stored building supplies, non-medical supplies, fixed equipment and burned anything not recyclable. The huge furnace reduced the size of the hospital's trash output by 80 percent. The filters kept the emissions to a minimum. It bothered her that they used the furnace to cremate patients as well as burn trash, but that was the way things were now. Practicality overtook sentiment.

Near the second-floor stairway door she slowed as she saw someone coming. She paused to let them pass.

She saw the firm shoulders of a compact man, then smiled at him out of good manners and habit.

She froze as she realized who she was smiling at, then heard the man say, "You remember me, huh?"

Tom Wilner said, "You sure of this, Steve?"

The thin uniformed cop nodded his head. "There's a trail of crumpled brush that goes right from the bank. It would explain why there's no body and we didn't even see any blood."

Wilner knew his friend was right. He had a hunch the killer had escaped into the zone the night before. The question was, where had he come from? Was he a zone resident or just hiding there?

Wilner looked out the window and saw the last ray of sunshine disappear into the clouds. He knew this one was going to keep him busy for a while.

TEN

Tom Wilner sat on the floor with his children watching a show designed to explain to kids the current issues going on in the world. It was produced in Toronto, which was now considered the broadcasting and video filming center of Western civilization. With its modern electronics and the layout of the Canadian city it was extremely attractive to the entertainment industry. The city had thought ahead in the early century and had installed efficient, reliable mass transit and had all but outlawed personally owned vehicles. The cost at the time was widely criticized but after ten years when the city started to flourish everyone jumped on the environmental and comfortable bandwagon.

Prices of apartments and houses soared, sending many to live in other cities. Homelessness was dealt with by constructing a permanent lodge and updating laws eliminating panhandling. Now if someone was on the street they were given a choice to leave or be housed in the clean, warm lodge. The big gray building could house four thousand in one of fifty wide dorms.

The show Emma and Tommy were watching had a young girl with light features talking about what the current news issues might mean for young people. The first story was always the approaching Uralians. Since they were estimated to make live contact in just under five years the young people of today might well be the military of tomorrow. But the commentator made sure to point out that there was no reason to think the Uralians were anything but friendly. Their messages, which had been arriving regularly, talked about sharing technology and culture.

Wilner laughed at the idea. He wondered if the aliens had any idea how little technology had been invented in the past twenty years and hoped the whole world wouldn't be in armed conflict when they arrived. He had some reason to believe the United States might be done with several of the current wars it was fighting. It appeared that the Syrians had been pushed farther out of Lebanon and that Damascus in ruins had given them something to think about. The U.S. peacekeepers in Latvia and Estonia were also due to be pulled out soon.

That left Germany. What would happen if they moved forward into Poland? Negotiators worked night and day to resolve the conflict, but if they did continue their advance it would be a war unlike any living person had seen. Except one of the Simolits or Hallecks. He knew both families had a number of members who had fought in World War II. In fact both families fought against the Nazis, although in different ways. That was how he had discovered his wife was a member of the Simolits. A photo from 1945 showing her and Tiget Nadovich cheering the surrender of German troops and the freedom of their beloved Serbia.

The differences between humans and the other humanoid race were so subtle he had not seen it during their marriage.

But later he realized she had not aged. Svala had still looked nineteen even after two kids. She had never been sick; not even a cold. She didn't work out yet looked like a model every day.

Now he looked at the children he had raised as his own and wondered how they would react to the news that they were something other than human. There would come a day when they wondered why they were never sick. Why they aged so slowly. How they recovered from injuries so quickly. And all these questions were only if one of their blood relatives didn't track them down and tell them first.

As he considered all this his V-com beeped. He didn't recognize the caller's ID, but allowed the video and audio to broadcast anyway. On the unit's tiny screen he saw a man in a well-lighted room, then recognized him as a UPF lab technician.

"Detective Wilner?"

"Yeah, what's up in the lab?"

"I have something interesting on the fingerprint you brought in from the homicide in the Lawton District. Can you come by and talk to me tomorrow?"

"Yeah, sure." He didn't mind the ride up to the Northern Enclave. "What's up?"

"I'd rather discuss it in person."

Wilner agreed to the meeting and closed his V-com.

"What is it, Daddy?" asked Emma.

Wilner smiled at his beautiful, dark-haired daughter and said, "Just work, baby. Nothing I need to worry about tonight."

Leonard Hall sat at the long bar of the Quarantine Zone's most popular nightspot, the Chaos Pit. He was thinking about his visit to the district hospital, the cop named Wilner and the nurse's friend he had met at the casino. She had been a complete surprise.

She had no idea why he was there when she saw him on the second-floor stairwell. She had surprised him as much as he surprised her. He had the combat spike already out for the cop so it was an instinct to thrust it without thinking into the nurse's neck. Even though she didn't have much of a neck. Her head sat atop thick, strong shoulders but the blow had done the trick.

She never uttered a sound as he withdrew the spike, then eased her to the ground.

The only trick had been dragging her body to the furnace. He didn't know what he would've done to dispose of her if the furnace hadn't been on the same floor.

He had spent a few minutes admiring her artificial hand before shoving her into the wide steel door of the large furnace. He had noticed when he stuck her with the spike that her hand had splayed out in an odd manner. It was amazing how they got those things so connected to a person's muscles and nerves now.

He took a drink of the homemade vodka with some orange crushed into the glass. He liked most aspects of the gigantic bar except the noise. Between the music for the dancers, the loud conversation of the patrons and the hoots and shouts of the men watching the dancers, the place sometimes gave him a headache.

He found some of the dancers attractive. He didn't much care for the dancers missing legs or with some other unusual feature. He liked the ones that looked like they were happy to be alive and didn't mind showing what they had. Sure, he was always attracted to long, graceful necks but there were other things he found appealing too.

Right now it was the dancer on the little stage closest to him. Her short brown hair stuck out in wild directions and her compact, shapely body swayed to the rhythm of an old rock anthem. She had a wide, bright smile and seemed to look right at him every time she swung around on the brass pole.

The music finally stopped and the beautiful little dancer carefully stepped down the stairs to her stage. She didn't look comfortable in the high heels.

She walked along the bar collecting U.S. suds, UN traders or the new zone currency from each of the rough men who had been watching her up close. She slowed when she came to Leonard. His cleaner appearance obviously made him seem wealthier than the other men.

She held out a tiny hand and said, "What's your name, handsome?"

"Leonard," he answered as he tried not to focus on her neck. She had the most spectacularly sculpted breasts he had ever seen. But a neck that was a little short.

"What are you doing tonight?" Leonard asked.

"You," she said, followed by that great smile.

Leonard didn't know if he could take all this excitement in one day.

Unified Police Force Detective Tom Wilner had dropped his kids off at school, checked in at his office, then started the drive north out of the Lawton District into the Northern Enclave. The enclave was basically the former counties of Palm Beach, Martin and Hendry merged together. When Florida was reorganized into twelve areas, dropping everything from Miami south, the enclave became a nice compromise for coastal and southern living. It had about three times the population of the Lawton District and was one of the three areas, along with the district and Pointe Florida that made up what was now considered South Florida.

He pushed his new hive up over a hundred, knowing that there was no real traffic and that Steve Besslia was one of two traffic cops for both the Northern Enclave and the Lawton District. He pulled onto the old, decrepit Interstate 95 and hugged the inner left lanes. The outer two lanes held the remnants of crashes and broken-down cars that had been just shoved to the side. Practicality had overcome any need to make the highway pretty. With so little traffic two lanes handled the population well and people had gotten used to the mountain of twisted metal and rotting rubber on the side of the road.

The UPF lab was just off the interstate in a one-story building by itself. They had maintained the lab in this spot because the force couldn't find lab people and one of their main lab techs lived nearby and insisted the lab stay where it was.

Wilner pulled into one of the ten open parking spots and entered into a reception area. The last few times he had been inside the building the lone lab tech was the receptionist, forensic specialist and the janitor. He hadn't been shy about expressing his frustration about it either.

Today a young woman sat behind the glass-enclosed reception area.

"May I help you?" she asked, a smile lighting up her eyes.

This was something unusual: a friendly government employee in South Florida.

"I'm Tom Wilner." He was about to go on when she buzzed the door and said, "We've been expecting you, Detective."

Wilner walked through the door into the lab where the lone tech looked up and immediately stood and rushed toward him.

"I'm glad you could make it."

Wilner looked back at the receptionist. "Looks like you got some help finally."

The man shook his head. "New arrivals. We got so many they don't know where to stick them all." He tugged on Wilner's arm, pulling him through the lab to a computer on a table by itself.

The lab tech said, "I know a little of what you and Besslia got involved in a few months ago."

"You do?"

"I have my own theories. I saw some of the DNA work. I know you guys had some rough times down in the district."

"Did you take a sample of the blood on the chair fragment in this case?"

He shook his head. "It had been diluted by the rain by the time we got it. I don't have the equipment to take such a washed-out sample. After your last lab submission, I was interested in what you dug up."

"And how's this related to the new case?"

"Look." The lab tech held up an enlargement of a fingerprint.

"So?"

"This is the print I took off the wood you sent in the other night." He brought up a screen on the computer. "Here's a matching print in our database."

"That's great, who is it?"

"It was never identified."

"Why was it in the database?"

"A murder. Neck injury just like yours. A girl named Mary Harris."

"No kidding." Wilner could see the loop and swirls of the fingerprint and how both prints matched. "Who worked the case?"

"It was the old Pompano police."

"Before UPF?"

"Yep."

Wilner froze. "Wait a minute. How long ago?"

"Forty-nine years ago."

"But that would mean . . ." Wilner trailed off.

"And the same print shows up in a burglary case, two more murders and a car theft every few years until about eleven years ago."

"I wonder what happened to him eleven years ago."

"I have an idea," said the tech.

"What's that?"

"They shut down the Quarantine Zone about eleven years ago. I bet this cat lives down there."

Wilner nodded, knowing that's exactly where his killer lived.

ELEVEN

Tom Wilner kept his voice under a shout as he leaned to-ward Johann Halleck. He knew the big man who was at least three hundred and fifty years old could take any punch Wilner tried to throw, but he was pissed and he wanted Johann to know it.

"It has to be one of you. The fingerprint was at a crime scene almost fifty years ago and at a scene from this week. How do you explain that?"

Johann shook his blond head. "Tom, you must calm your-self. I am not your enemy. I need time to figure this out as well."

"Your fingerprints are the same as humans, right?"

Johann held up a big paw of a hand and shoved it in close to Wilner's face. "Same as you. Whirls and loops, no two are the same."

Wilner took a breath and sat back on a stool. They were in a sports bar in the Eastern District close to Wilner's house. "Could it be a Simolit?"

"Anything is possible." Johann's accent bleeded through every comment. To Wilner it sounded German, but it was really a mix of the many countries Johann had lived in over his long life. Johann continued, "I thought they had all fled the district after our trouble. Certainly we killed several and Tiget Nadovich was blown to bits."

"Was he?" asked Wilner. "We never recovered his body."

"You saw the killer. Was it Nadovich?"

Wilner shook his head. "No, I didn't get a good look at him but it wasn't Nadovich. As far as I can tell, all the Simolit family members fled the district. I think the killer came over from the Quarantine Zone. They could be living in an armed camp over there."

"They could, but I think I would've heard about it. I have many contacts in the zone and travel there frequently. I believe this will take more investigation. I will help in any way I can."

"Will you check with your family and see if they ever experienced anything like this before?"

"I will."

"I'll go into the zone and see what I can find out."

Johann grabbed his forearm. "Either way there is danger. You must be careful. This man is a killer."

Leonard liked that this girl, Darla, sat so close to him as he drove. He'd slipped her into the house he shared with his aunt and for a mere one hundred zone credits, spent the night engaged in adult games. This was a different kind of urge. One he could curb. He could get gratification from sex with women. And this woman in particular excited him. Her wild, uninhibited ability to satisfy him was a new feeling.

When he was younger he thought that only the feeling of

someone's life draining away through their neck could excite him. It was nice to find other means of release.

Darla lived in a house with another dancer from the Chaos Pit on the edge of the Zone River closer to the border.

"How do you get to the club at night?" asked Leonard.

She smiled that wide smile and said, "I can usually find someone willing to drive me."

"You have never driven a car?"

"Nope. They closed the border when I was thirteen and then we couldn't get gas. Men started doing me favors like driving me when I was fifteen so I never got the chance."

"Where were you born?"

"South Dade County."

"You're an American citizen, why didn't you just go into the district?"

"My brothers were all coming up on eighteen and my daddy didn't want them fighting no rag-heads off in some desert so he decided to stay. Then my brothers were listed as fugitives from the draft and couldn't go back. Now we all live down here in the zone except my brother Bobby. He moved to Canada with his wife. She was a Canadian citizen so they took him too."

"You ever hear from him?"

"No, he was caught in the Winnipeg terror attack. He died of anthrax poisoning about a month later."

"They didn't treat him?"

"Canadians were treated first, then they ran out of medicine. Now my daddy hates Canada and the United States."

She pointed to the house as he chugged down the street at fifteen miles an hour.

Leonard said, "You got neighbors on both sides of you."

"Yeah. Lotta people live over here."

Leonard pointed to an elderly black woman standing on

the broken-down porch of an ancient wood house from before the turn of the century. "Who's that?"

"That's Mrs. Lolley. She's crazy. She found some guy washed
up in her backyard from the river. Been caring for him ever
since. I ain't seen him move once. He looks like a mummy, all
bandaged up."

"How's she feed him?"

"I only seen him twice. He gives me the creeps. I don't
know what goes on over there."

As they pulled in front of Darla's house, Leonard noticed a
tall blond woman come out the front door. She had on a robe
and waved to Darla, then climbed down the four stairs to the
front yard and walked toward them.

Leonard took in her long, muscular legs and shapely body.
Darla said, "This is my roommate, Lisa."

Leonard smiled but couldn't speak. He was hypnotized by
one thing. Lisa's long, graceful, lovely neck.

Wilner had taken his own police car into the zone. Why not?
He was on official business even though he was in a different
country. It only took one wrong turn before he found Mari's
school.

He admitted to himself that he was surprised at how nice
the school and grounds looked. He had to get out of the frame
of mind that everything and everyone in the zone was screwed
up. He'd seen it on his last few trips down here. Things were
organized. At least some things. People weren't running wild
in the street like the news would have you believe. They didn't
have warlords that controlled whole sections of the zone.
They did have gangs, but from what Wilner had learned they
were not much worse than some of the U.S. gangs and fo-

cused more on organizing and building than stealing and terrorizing.

He parked his hive on the side of the street. A newer pickup truck and a steam-powered converted Cadillac were parked in front of him on the road. It wasn't unlike visiting his children's school in the district. He stayed on the decorative rock path that led from the street to the front of the small schoolhouse.

He stepped through the wide main doors and was immediately greeted by an older woman.

She assessed him for a moment before asking in English, "May I help you?"

"Mari told me she worked here."

The woman gave him a doubtful glance.

He couldn't keep from smiling at the small woman's stern expression.

"Really, she did. My name is Tom Wilner."

The woman said, "The policeman from the UPF."

"Yes, ma'am."

"She's been expecting you. One moment." She motioned him to a chair in the corner of the greeting room and then hurried down one hallway.

Wilner looked at the well-kept walls and floors, the plaques hung near the hallway looked like any other school's boasts of academic and athletic achievements. Then, less than a minute after the first lady had left, Mari Saltis stepped in through the same hallway door.

She smiled and held out her hand as she approached Wilner.

"Hello, Detective."

"The lady who greeted me didn't look like she liked me."

"Miss Kelbert? No, she's just protective and I don't get many visitors."

Wilner doubted that as he looked at her delicate face and beautiful, dark eyes.

"Any new breaks, Detective?"

He told her about his fear that the killer had escaped. By the time he was done, they had sat together on a small, low couch in the greeting room.

"You knew about murders here. You said you had heard of two."

She nodded. "Not far from here. A woman no one could identify was stabbed in the throat and then about six months ago a waitress at one of the restaurants that has its own farm was found dead in the field behind the diner. She had been stabbed in exactly the same way. The people down here have been referring to him as 'the Vampire.'"

Wilner gave her time in case she wanted to say something else.

She looked up at him and said, "The Miami Quarantine Zone is not like you think it is. I know the United States looks down on us like a bunch of savages, but life is dangerous whether you live in the district, Philadelphia or the Quarantine Zone."

"I agree."

"A killer like this would strike wherever he lived. It just happens that he lives in the Quarantine Zone."

"The difference is that someone would try and catch him in the district."

"People tried here too. It just didn't work out too well."

"How so?"

She hesitated, then told him a story as terrifying as the killings.

TWELVE

Leonard Hall had seen the cop's new hive by accident. Although the new vehicle stuck out in the zone, he wouldn't have even seen it if he didn't need to go to the market near the girls' school. He liked the way a couple of the teachers looked and didn't mind some of the older students either.

As he chugged down the street he saw the car from a block away. He thought it might be someone else, but as he slowed his old Honda he saw Wilner and the head teacher walk out of the front door. Incredible. He couldn't control his wide grin. His heart raced as he felt a wave of excitement, even joy, wash over him. He had admired the teacher's form for months, but hadn't thought about making her one of his prizes. Now, if he could find her and the cop together, she was too tempting a target.

The sight of the two of them had made him completely forget Darla's roommate, Lisa. He could deal with her any time. He knew where she lived and where she worked.

He followed the cop and teacher to see where they were going together and to find out why he was down in the zone. It had to be about the murders. He'd be disappointed if this cop had already given up on him.

He stayed back until the hive pulled from the curb.

Tom Wilner strolled next to her inside the old city hall of a town that used to be known as North Miami Beach. The building was run-down, but it was clear it had been used regularly since the creation of the Miami Quarantine Zone. Mari's trim shoulder occasionally bumped his arm and he felt his heart pick up speed like he was a hormone-plagued teenager. It reminded him of his first girlfriend in tenth grade. He had taken her down to the beach in his hometown of Ocean Grove, New Jersey. She gave him a sense of shelter. Just a few stolen hours away from his father's drunken abuse and his chores that seemed to never end. That day, when Anne Bocock reached down and grasped his hand, was as clearly burned in his memory as the battle of Bandar Abbas or the street fighting in Tehran.

Now, with this beautiful woman telling the tale of the Quarantine Zone's failed attempt at criminal justice, he realized how lonely he had been the past year and a half. Once Svala left him it took a year to reconcile that she was not coming back. Then, after his relationship with Shelby Hahn had developed, he learned the truth about her and her family. It wasn't the fact that she was so different, she still had human emotions and sensibilities; it was the fact that she had lied to him. After the deceptions of Svala it was more than he could take. He missed a woman's company.

Mari let her hand sweep across the large, open chamber. "This is where they brought the suspect they captured after the first murder. He was just twenty and scared. His Jamaican accent making it difficult to understand all his frantic protests."

"Who identified him as the killer?"

"That was the problem. Five members of a gang that used to call themselves the Marvel Men."

"That's a weird name."

"It was after some old comic books. Now they call themselves the Zone Police. After what happened people didn't want anything to do with them. So they changed their name and image. Now they patrol and collect 'taxes' to keep the order from the border to a little past here. They don't even venture into the old city of Miami. Too rough for them down there."

"What happened at the trial?"

"It wasn't a trial. The crowd screamed about the way he killed the first woman and that he was why no one wanted to return to the United States. They thought this place was free of creeps that preyed on women." She turned her dark eyes up to his face. "Which wasn't true. At the time most people did want to go to the United States." She looked out over the chamber again. "He denied any of the accusations. Then a judge, who was really a member of the gang, sentenced him to death. He was dragged out into the street and hung on the front entranceway to the building."

"What happened to convince people it was wrong?"

"The next week another body showed up. Then people learned that the young man had been in an argument with the Marvel Men. It was the first and last trial the Quarantine Zone ever had. People started handling conflict immediately between one another."

"And you really like living here?"

"I like the girls at the school. The residents are here to stay, no matter what the United States thinks. They need people who'll do things like teach or nurse. You know we have a working hospital?"

"I heard there was medical treatment down here."

"We have doctors from all over the Caribbean." She turned toward him and put her hands on his arms. "We need real policemen to make us safe."

He felt the attraction and it wasn't just on his side. It was like a magnet was pulling him. He leaned his face down, ready to feel her lips on his when a shout startled him. He jerked his head up and saw four men standing in the gallery above them.

One man said, "What's this, a visitor from the United States?" His Spanish accent was thick.

Wilner reached for his gun under his jacket but a voice behind him said, "Don't try it."

He turned and saw that a short, muscle-bound man held an old shotgun on him and Mari. There was nothing he could do.

Johann Halleck liked this restaurant in the Northern Enclave. It was quite a ride in the hive he had recently purchased. Manufactured by General-Ford of the United States, it had the body of a larger Ford vehicle with the smoother engine and fuel efficiency of a General Motors product. The partnership had kept the two automakers competitive with the new carmakers from Asia and Africa.

He took the old Interstate 95 past the former town of West Palm Beach into an area he had only traveled to once before. The last visit was for the same thing.

Per the treaty set out between the Simolits and Hallecks he was unarmed and counted on the honor of the man he was meeting to keep him unarmed as well. Bejor Simolit had hesitated to meet with Johann when he called after the talk with

Wilner. He had told Johann that the family was looking into the circumstances of Radko's death and there was a strong suspicion that Johann had played a part in it.

Johann explained that he had a matter of mutual interest to both families and that he felt it was important to meet. Since Johann had never insisted on a meeting like this before, Bejor agreed and they found a mutually acceptable meeting site at a restaurant frequented by the few tourists that made it down this far into the state. It used to be that tourists chased the sunshine. Now the few that came were more interested in seeing what the state had become and how it was rebuilding after all the horror it had seen.

The Northern Enclave had a sense of what Florida once was with some shopping and restaurants open and oceanside hotels operating. But the cool, wet weather and stark vista scared many away. Everyone was used to more of a domestic military presence but in South Florida, with the large contingent of National Guardsmen at the border, there was a constant reminder of how America had changed.

The final and most significant blow to tourism was the breakdown in air travel. As terrorists focused more on airliners and as costs rose, the airlines looked to diversify in other transportation industries. Now Delta Railways was as big as the airline had once been. Except for the government, military and a few outrageously expensive charter airlines, the skies were empty of planes.

Johann saw the restaurant called the Outpost and pulled into the nearly empty parking lot. A light spray of cool rain hit his face as he cut across the small lot into the one-story restaurant with a nautical décor. Nets and pier posts jutted up inside the building and old photos of fishermen and crab ships lined the walls.

He immediately saw the de facto leader of the Simolit family in Florida sitting alone at a table in the corner of one of the dining rooms.

Johann stepped down into the dining room and froze when he saw a second table occupied by three men. All had dark hair and oval eyes. The slightly flared nostrils told him that Bejor had not come alone as he had promised.

Johann had honored the treaty and had not brought a weapon. He was a little bigger than any of the men but four on one wouldn't be fair. It wouldn't even be a fight.

He stood and stared at Bejor, trying to decide if he could kill the one man for his betrayal before the others leaped to their feet.

THIRTEEN

Tom Wilner nearly had his hand on the butt of his 11 millimeter duty weapon and its thick handle, which housed a stacked magazine of twenty rounds. He had a second magazine clipped on the left side of his belt. He clutched Mari and pulled her close to him. It was an instinct and not tactically smart. He needed to be able to move and shoot and wanted to draw fire away from Mari, not pull her into an easier target for these thugs to shoot.

He heard the sound of a rifle action behind him and turned. A dirty, skinny man in his midtwenties smiled, showing off yellow, rotted teeth. In his hands he had an ancient army surplus bolt-action rifle; the kind that were used in one of the world wars of the twentieth century.

"So, Mr. Policeman, what brings you down to the zone?" called a man from the upper level.

"Why do you think I'm a police officer?"

"First thing is that big autopistol under your jacket." The beefy man paused and smiled. "You don't recognize me?"

Wilner thought he might be familiar but couldn't place him. He shook his head.

"I was in a group called the Zone Troopers. Now you remember?"

Wilner knew him now.

"You busted us up pretty good a few months back. Now I'm a policeman myself."

"That what you call yourself?"

"That's what I am and you broke the law by entering the zone illegally. And this is your second offense. You gotta pay."

Wilner saw the men upstairs start to spread out. One of them had a black eye patch with a white cross over the patch. Another man joined the one with nasty teeth on the lower level.

He tensed, knowing that there was no negotiating with creeps like this. The best he could hope for now was to get Mari out of the building safely.

Then one of the men behind him hit the ground with a thud. His old rifle clattered across the scarred marble floor. The other man stood staring at his friend as blood started gushing onto the grimy floor.

Wilner made the next move.

Steve Besslia had discussed the case of the killer with Wilner and thought he might have a way to help identify who or what the killer was. He had veered off his normal patrol route and pulled his Hive-bike into what used to be the Pompano police department's parking lot. The building was east of Interstate 95 in a very sparsely populated section of the Eastern District.

Besslia knew a little of the history of the area and the city of Pompano was one of the first to go to a more cost-effective collective police enforcement. They used the old Broward County sheriff's office until that went belly-up due to lack of tax revenue. The remnants of the county sheriff's department and the state police became what was now the Unified Police Force.

Besslia wasn't sure what he might find but he knew he could contribute and prove what kind of cop he was.

The old three-story building had a drainage ditch around it like a moat. The driveway over the ditch had collapsed years before and now wild plants and weeds sprang up in the middle of the crumbling road. Besslia guided his bike to one side, then cut at an angle across the shallow ditch. The water beaded off his good boots. The engine had been designed to be completely submerged and still worked as long as the exhaust wasn't blocked for more than twenty seconds.

He parked the bike under what used to be the main entrance to the building. A wide synthetic sheet designed to be cut- and tear-resistant was draped across the front. A stenciled message across it read, DO NOT ENTER.

Besslia considered the hanging sheet and message. He jumped up and grabbed two handfuls of the tarp and yanked down hard. As he suspected, whoever had installed the sheet of synthetic fiber had purchased nearly impregnable material, but failed to use anything but nails to hold it in place. After all the years of hanging there, Besslia's weight bent the supporting nails and now he was faced with the next barrier.

Besslia looked at the sheets of rotted plywood secured across the front. He rapped a piece with his knuckles and it crumbled like wet paper. After years of constant rainfall the simple wooden barrier fell away as Besslia pushed it.

Now he was looking at cracked and broken glass panels that at one time made for an ornate and useful entrance to the Pompano police department. He used his expandable stun baton to clear out the sharp edges of glass in one of the small frames, then leaned down to crawl in and realized his gear belt with the big duty weapon and V-com would keep him from slipping inside. He unclasped his belt and stuffed it into one of the weatherproof saddlebags on his Hive-bike. He pulled a smaller, old-style 9 millimeter he kept for emergencies from the bag and tucked it into his belt. He didn't think anyone would be inside, not with all the usable houses around, but he didn't want to take any chances. Now, in just his uniform with the gun tucked into his pants, he felt more agile.

Inside, the musty, damp smell was so strong he tasted it. He flipped over the baton to use the powerful flashlight built into the handle of the weapon. He had a choice of stairs or two doors on opposite sides of the lobby. He figured that an archive or evidence room would be on the first floor of a building. No one wanted to carry things upstairs or try and jam larger pieces of evidence into an elevator.

The heavy wooden door was locked but degraded enough that a kick by Besslia sent it snapping into two pieces. He started checking offices and doors with no luck. Then he found an old map of the building. It was under a glass desk cover and not completely faded. It was designed to show telephone extensions but Besslia saw what he was looking for: a separate building in the back that housed archives, files and stored evidence.

He found the rear door and kicked it hard enough that it opened, tearing out the plywood and bringing down the fiber tarp all in one motion.

Besslia stood and smiled, feeling like a kick-ass cop with legs of steel. Looking up at the rusting old radio tower he wondered why no one had really moved into this neighborhood. He didn't hear much about the area on patrol. People used to claim that wild dogs roamed around but he hadn't heard that in at least a year. Besides, who'd be scared of a few dogs after everything that had happened?

Crossing the lot that had a few inches of standing water, he was glad of his good boots. The small one-story building had metal poles sunk in the concrete all around it. The metal fence had long since rusted and broken away from the poles. Remnants of the barrier sat in piles between the standing poles.

As he stepped over one pile of fencing he thought he heard a sound. He turned quickly but the lot was empty. He moved forward under the overhang and rapped the door with his knuckles. This one was solid. He tried the handle. Locked.

He looked to each side, then heard the sound again. This time clearer. It was a growl. A light, steady, unsettling growl.

This time he spun and reached for his duty pistol. He froze as he realized the stories about wild dogs were true. But no one was going to believe what he was seeing now.

Johann Halleck decided to sit down at the table with Bejor Simolit like everything was all right and there wasn't a pack of Simolit men ready to spring at him.

Bejor didn't rise or acknowledge Johann other than with a flick of his black eyes.

"You are alone, Johann?"

"I am. I see you decided to bring friends."

"You are still viewed with suspicion by my family."

Johann looked at him until their eyes met. "I will not speak of the incident. I was within treaty guidelines and reported the incident as required."

"This is something still to be determined. That is why I brought my sons. None of us is armed and we will not harm you, if you have come with peaceful intentions."

Johann just glared at the old man's arrogance. He was insinuating that Johann could not be trusted when, as a Simolit, he was by definition untrustworthy. Although he knew Bejor was at least three hundred years older than him—somewhere between six hundred and fifty and eight hundred years old—he looked only slightly more worn. He had a few gray streaks of hair and a wrinkle on the side of his face like about a thirty-five-year-old human. He was known as a warrior and had fought for a number of different nations in wars. He didn't seem to have a cause or creed he fought for. He just liked to fight. He had even been in the first and second Iraqi wars; the ones that started the entire Middle East conflict. The Simolits often crowed about their contribution to their adopted countries but Johann knew most joined the military because they liked the thrill of battle.

Finally, Bejor became weary of the staring match and said, "What is so important we must meet face-to-face?"

"A killer," was all Johann said.

"Of humans?"

Johann nodded.

"Why should I care what happens to a few humans?"

Johann knew the question was coming and was ready. "Because part of our treaty says we will not exploit or prey upon humans. None of us."

"That was your family's demand."

"Which your family agreed to."

"Why do you think it's one of us?"

"The first murder occurred almost fifty years ago. The killer outran a UPF detective and fled into the Quarantine Zone."

Bejor rubbed his chin as he considered the information. He looked across the room out a wide bay window as the rain picked up intensity and started falling hard.

Johann said, "Fifty years is a long time to be killing for a human."

"But I can't imagine why one of our people would do it."

"We didn't know why some have done things in the past but they did things too dark for us to record. There've been murderers, rapists, all the faults that afflict humans we have also seen over the years."

Bejor nodded slowly. "I will never understand your family's concern for the humans but I respect your concern for our honor. I will see if a Simolit family member is responsible."

"I will ensure that a Halleck is not responsible as well. Whoever the killer, we must find a way to deal with them. The transplant of humans here will help us all."

"How so?"

"More commerce, more choices, more restaurants, I don't know. But we must live among them."

"My cousin, Tiget, had his own ideas."

"And where did those lead him?"

"I wondered about your role in his death too."

"I will answer you honestly. I was involved in Tiget's death. And frankly, he got what he deserved."

Bejor smiled. "I appreciate the Halleck honesty. I will be in touch soon."

Tom Wilner darted toward the man, frozen with indecision. He knew his only chance was to act while the others were in confusion. Before he could even strike the man, he realized something was wrong. Then the man toppled over, his body thumping onto the hard floor without the slightest hint of life left in it.

He motioned for Mari as he stared down at the two dead

men. Blood filled the floor from unseen wounds. He knew to worry about it later. His combat experience told him that now was the time to figure out how to escape.

He dragged Mari into the main entry as he scanned the area with his pistol out. She stared at the dead men but didn't ask any questions. He shoved her into a tiny closet with no door but with thick walls all around it as the heavy footsteps rumbled down the stairs.

The first man in view said, "Chingala, how'd you—"

But Wilner's bullets silenced him as he scrambled back up the stairs. Wilner charged the stairwell and fired up a couple of more times. One round answered, striking wide on the front wall.

"Mari," he called out. He took her hand as she scurried out to meet him and then both fled toward the front door.

They raced down the front pathway to his waiting car.

"How'd you kill those men? Is it a new kind of weapon?"

"I didn't do anything." He ducked low by the car and opened the passenger door for Mari to dive in.

The front door of the old city hall burst open and the three surviving men raced out with their old long rifles. Two of them fired at the car. Wilner opened up, this time aiming for the men. He couldn't risk them hitting Mari.

One man toppled from the top of the stairs and the man with the eye patch grabbed his leg and fell straight forward. The last man, the one from the old Zone Troopers, retreated back inside, firing a round as he abandoned his friends.

As Wilner screeched away from the curb one of the wild rounds struck the back of the car.

FOURTEEN

Steve Besslia eased his finger off the trigger of his little backup weapon and said quietly, "Nice doggies." He felt his breath return and fought a smile that crept across his face. The seven wild dogs in front of him stood in the shallow water of the old parking lot, snarling and showing their teeth. The biggest one had his belly out of the water but the rest were half submerged.

"C'mon, fellas, who are you tryin' to fool," he said as he looked at the pack. As best he could tell there were two Chihuahuas, three dachshunds and two that looked like some kind of small but long dog mix.

Had these dogs really terrorized the neighborhood? This was the legendary Pompano pack?

They all advanced quickly, barking and snarling, so Besslia retreated into the building, not wanting to hurt any of them. He weaved between desks and filing cabinets, narrowly avoiding the snap of one dachshund.

He tumbled over a stack of fallen roof tiles and then felt concern, as his face was level with the tiny pissed-off dogs.

As a light-colored Chihuahua raced toward him, he struggled to work his pistol past the debris to fire. He had no choice.

The dog was faster than he thought and closed the distance instantly. A dachshund was right behind the Chihuahua.

This would be an embarrassing way to die, he thought briefly, but a noise froze the dogs in their tracks. The Chihuahua skidded to a stop and turned just inches from Besslia's face.

The UPF patrolman sprang to a sitting position and by the time he stood up the little dogs had all scurried out of sight.

Then he saw why.

Leonard Hall heard the gunfire from outside. He had been admiring his work on the two men inside the North Miami Beach city hall. He particularly liked how one of the men had managed to stay upright so long. It had diverted the cop's attention enough for him to fade back into the maze of narrow hallways. He hadn't meant to strike both men but it was too much of a challenge and too exciting.

He had also enjoyed seeing this cop in action. The man was smooth and fast. He had to have some kind of military training. There was no indecision in him. He also managed to protect the woman during the entire fight. Leonard admired that.

He had heard Wilner and the woman race out of the building and the curses of the three men following them.

Now only one man had returned. He faced the front door with his rifle aimed like the cop might come busting back inside.

Leonard smiled as the man backed directly into him without ever looking behind him. The gang member thought he knew the old building was empty. This was his turf.

Leonard had the spike on his German combat knife extended and the weapon solidly in his grasp. He waited until the muscular young man had moved almost close enough to hear his heartbeat, then he struck first on the right side, slipping the spike quickly out, and flipping it to the man's left side, he struck again.

The man collapsed flat on the ground, his nervous system shutting down due to shock.

Another gang member, clutching his leg, hobbled in through the front door. He used an old rifle as a crutch. Leonard met his single visible eye. The other eye was under a black patch with a white cross on it. The man stared at him, frozen for a second.

Leonard stood over the corpse holding the bloody combat spike.

The man struggled to pull the rifle he was using as a makeshift crutch up at Leonard.

Leonard decided he'd had enough fun. His urge, for now, was satisfied.

The man struggled with the rifle, trying to raise it before Leonard could act.

Leonard simply slipped away. He wanted someone to spread the rumors of what had happened.

It had been an exciting and interesting day.

Wilner felt like he was dropping off a date. Mari stood in front of him with her hand wrapped around his arm. He knew that kind of excitement could traumatize some people. He'd seen it in the military. But she appeared to be taking it well.

"Thank you," she said in a quiet voice.

He smiled. "For what?"

"For taking the time to look into something that affects the zone. People here feel abandoned. But they still wish they had policemen and firemen to depend on. They shout about how great no government is but most people would welcome back the United States if they wanted us."

"What about you? Would you welcome the United States?"

"I never hated the United States. Like many, I used to blame them for all the problems of the world. Now I see the truth. Every nation must take responsibility. The United States and your presidents have only been trying to secure the country." She looked up and smiled. "I'd get to see you again too."

"I promise I'll be back. I'm going to find this killer. What I need is someone who can identify him. A living witness."

Mari nodded. "I'll ask around and see if anyone knows anything more than just gossip."

"Do you have access to a V-com or old-time phone?"

"I have ways to pass messages. Sometimes one of our computers can connect with another that could send a message. The United States blocks most satellite transmissions from south of the border."

Wilner handed her his access number written on the back of a UPF general report page.

"You won't forget us?"

"Not a chance."

She reached up on her tiptoes and kissed him on the lips.

Steve Besslia now understood the wild dogs' fear. The smaller dogs had fled and he now faced what he thought was a pair of large Doberman pinchers with unclipped tails and ears, but they could have been some kind of Great Dane mix. They were gigantic. The darker one stood four feet high on all four legs. The lighter one behind him was taller. Neither looked underfed. But both looked hungry. Or, at least, threatening.

"All right, good dogs," he crooned softly. He was up now, backed against a wall with his small pistol up. Compared to his duty weapon this felt like a toy.

One dog stepped to the left. Then the other moved to the right to make sure Besslia had no escape. Was that intentional? Were they really that smart?

As much as he didn't want to, Besslia aimed at the darker dog. He had enough rounds to shoot one, then spray the whole room on the other side. He'd prefer to get out of this without having to kill one of the dogs, but he didn't see a choice.

Then he noticed several of the small dogs had returned to the room and were now bunching up close to the large light dog. All of them turned their heads at the same time toward the exit.

Besslia let his eyes track to the door as well. He instantly knew he was in deep shit.

Three more of the big dogs had crowded around the doorway. Two had slipped in and moved to each side.

He eased to his right. Another thick door with the knob still intact was recessed into the wall a foot from his left hand. He eased up his empty hand and tried the knob. It turned but wouldn't open.

If they all rushed him he'd have a hard time hitting each one with his backup pistol.

They were all growling and grunting. Another moved in toward the big light dog and that's when Besslia realized what was happening. They were communicating. These feral dogs had developed a language.

FIFTEEN

Wilner sat inside the UPF commander's office and briefed him on all aspects of the case except the old fingerprint. He couldn't risk official interest in the other hominid species without risking his own children.

Wilner finished by saying, "I can't get a hold of the other nurse to see what details she remembers. I'm going to go by the district hospital tomorrow."

The commander shook his head. "If you really did scare him back into the Quarantine Zone then this is done."

"What?"

"With the new arrivals I'm going to need everyone in the district. Hell, I won't even address the fact that the Quarantine Zone is another country and you have no jurisdiction. Or that we have no way of helping you if something happened to you down there. No, Willie, I want you to stay in the district."

"What if he kills more people in the zone?"

"That is not the concern of the UPF."

"C'mon, boss, you know that's not right."

"No, but it's what we have to do. I don't think you know the importance of bringing in new residents."

"Even if they don't want to be here?"

"That's why we have to keep things quiet. No one wants them to have an excuse to start screaming to go back to Ohio or Pennsylvania. We have to keep them happy and feeling safe."

"So now politics is more important than saving lives?"

"Politics has always been more important. Why else would we have fought in all those distant lands?"

Wilner let out a sigh and looked down at the floor.

"I don't think I ever saw a marine pout before."

Wilner looked him in the eye but said nothing.

"Go home and see your kids. Get some rest. You'll see things clearly in the morning."

Wilner didn't answer but knew this wasn't over.

One of the big dogs grunted again and all the little ones charged Besslia. He twisted to one side and yanked the door handle at the same time. It was locked but he pulled the lock out of the frame and the door opened. He slipped inside the dark, windowless room and pulled the door shut amid the yelps and snarls of the approaching dogs.

The thick wooden door slammed solidly but there was no way to lock it. He held the handle with one hand and snatched his stun baton with a light built into it from his belt line. He found a length of twine right next to the door and fashioned a makeshift lock in a few seconds. Then he backed away, still dazed by the idea of dogs communicating with one another. Then he shined the light up and down the long, dusty room. He needed help and immediately reached for his V-com, then remembered he had locked it away in his saddlebag along with his duty pistol. Now he was trapped in a building, out of sight of any road with only nine shots from an ancient conventional pistol and big, mean, smart dogs had him cornered. This was a little embarrassing.

He took a deep breath and started to calm himself. He decided to make use of his time and started his search of the old evidence and archive room for the Pompano Beach police department.

Besslia rummaged through a few random boxes just to see what kind of stuff was in the room. In one sealed plastic container, he discovered a stack of newspaper front pages. He pulled them out and started to browse. They were in chronological order and he realized they told the story of the region and how it turned into this place since the early twenty-first century. He laid out a couple.

The first headline on the old, brittle paper announced President Clinton winning reelection in 1996. Besslia was just a baby. He had no recollection of Clinton other than in history books. The next headline was from September 12, 2001, detailing the first of the 9/11 attacks. It wasn't that big compared to the later September 11 attacks but since it was the first one it took everyone by surprise. The next few headlines all covered subsequent attacks. Most, like the dirty bomb that closed down New York, occurred exactly on the eleventh day of September, but others occurred around the national Day of Remembrance. The feds attributed it to faulty planning. Besslia shook his head at the idea that an attack that kills people isn't that well planned because a bomb went off a day early or a day late.

The final headline he found covered the ban on immigration

and the new Miami Quarantine Zone. He figured that this old building was just about done by that time. People were either dying or fleeing Florida by then. The climate had slowly started to shift. Real estate had collapsed and government was about to downsize in a big way.

He slowly looked away from the newspaper clippings that didn't apply to this case or his life in any way. He skipped past the crimes-property filing cabinets and finally found the death investigations. There were a dozen cabinets just on deaths in the city limits of Pompano Beach, when it was still a separate city.

The last three cabinets were marked "cold case." He searched for the name Wilner had given him, Mary Harris. He blinked hard when he found a file in that name. He pulled it out and re-alized it was one of three thick files. The files were crammed with newspaper clippings that had faded, reports, lab analysis and handwritten notes. He pulled out the three files and started reading through them. Most of it was useless details, especially for the current date. The death of eighteen-year-old Mary had occurred almost fifty years ago. Besslia's parents had not even gotten married yet.

After more than an hour of careful reading, Steve Besslia saw a sheet that might help Wilner in his investigation. He stuffed all the files into an old, nasty, nylon book bag sitting on the table. He hesitated, then grabbed a few of the old newspaper clippings.

He slung the pack and stepped back toward the door, then paused and listened to the low growls and grunts of one of the big dogs. He'd been off the air for more than seven hours. Someone had to notice he wasn't around. They'd send help. Even if he didn't really need it. He decided to rest a few minutes before trying to run the gauntlet of smart dogs.

Mari Saltis sat in her open, sparse office and smiled as she thought about the detective who had ridden into the zone like a knight from one of the Camelot tales. She had always found an escape in books about brave knights or soldiers. She loved stories where the damsel in distress could also be counted on to do her share.

She also liked the company of decent men. They seemed to be in short supply south of the border. There were things that kept her in the zone; the girls at the school, her elderly neighbor, who depended on her for help, the lack of a military or need to fight foreign wars.

But there were trade-offs and one of them was missing the chance to meet a man like Tom Wilner.

Now she daydreamed of how her life would be different if she had met Wilner before the new border and ban on immigration. She knew by how he talked what kind of father he was. She wasn't sure how he ended up raising two young children alone but hoped to learn more about him in the near future.

There was a knock on her door that shook her out of her pleasant thoughts.

"Yes," she called out.

The door cracked open and an older, tall black woman poked her head in. "Miss Mari," she started in a thick Jamaican accent. "There is a man who says he is interested in the handyman job we have open."

Mari was back to all business. "That's great, Lucille, send him in."

The door opened wider and a small man with graying hair entered. His smile showed clean, healthy teeth. She couldn't tell how old he was. He was so firm and fit he could have been anywhere from forty-five to seventy. It was hard now with poor nutrition and the wide range of diseases to judge anyone's age.

She offered him a seat and said, "What's your name?"

He continued to smile, his clear green eyes on her. "Leonard. Leonard Hall."

SIXTEEN

Leonard Hall knew he needed to do something to release the building pressure and that's what had led him to this noisy, smelly, obnoxious place.

The Chaos Pit employed his two new favorite dancers and was as good a place as any to celebrate his new job at the school for girls. He had come to the club shortly after agreeing to work at the school. The pretty head teacher, Mari, had no idea who he was or what he was really interested in finding out.

This job, like any in the zone, required no fingerprint and other tests to know who people really were and if they had been implicated in any unlawful activities. Leonard wasn't certain but had surmised from news coverage of some of his earlier crimes that the police had a record of him; either from fingerprints or DNA. He didn't want them to be able to put a name with the prints. He had always kept a very low profile. His whole family had not mixed with others around them. That was one of the reasons he had such problems dealing with people until he got out from under his father and moved in with his aunt.

Leonard had always thought that his father's accent and status as a resident alien had kept him from interacting with the neighbors. Now he knew the truth. The secret his father didn't want to get out. If they had lived in a place like the zone, no one would have noticed or cared. But in a place like Pompano Beach, when the state of Florida was still crowded, it would have been difficult to keep secrets.

Now, leaning on the old wooden bar of the gigantic strip club near the U.S. border, Leonard took a gulp of the locally brewed beer as a new song blared over the scratchy sound system. In front of him, the shapely, but diminutive Darla, climbed onto the small round stage with the help of several eager patrons. On the similar stage across from her, Lisa stepped onto the elevated platform, her long legs lifting her without assistance. She looked in his direction and gave him a little wave and she started swaying to the Latin beat of the music.

She dropped off her loose top to the cheers of the drunken men nearest her but all Leonard could see was that long, beautiful neck. He lost himself in her movement and the muscles that occasionally twisted and flexed in her neck. He lost himself so completely that it wasn't until he felt a tug on his arm and looked down he realized that several minutes had passed and Lisa was finishing her dance.

In front of him was Darla, still topless and ignoring the men nearby offering cash for her dance.

"Hey," the small dancer barked. "You never even looked up at me."

"Yes, I did."

"No, you didn't. You stared at Lisa the whole song. Have you lost interest in me already?"

"No, no, it's not that."

"What is it then? I think because I let you sleep with me you're ready to move on."

"Let me? You charged me a hundred zone credits to sleep with you." Leonard looked up and saw Lisa strolling toward them, accepting cash from each man she passed.

She eased to a stop and slipped her top over her head and shoulders. "Hey, Lenny, what's happening?"

Darla cut in. "I'll tell you what's happening. This guy thinks he can treat us like old trash and dump us anytime he wants."

Leonard felt the uncomfortable stares of other patrons. This was not keeping a low profile. He started thinking how to end this quickly.

Lisa remained quiet but turned her full attention to Leonard, waiting for a response.

He looked from one girl to the other. "What if I said I had three hundred zone credits to work everything out?"

He liked the smiles he got.

Tom Wilner lay in his bed, watching the video projection of an old movie on his ceiling. He felt relaxed with each of his children on either side of him. Emma snored soundly with an arm draped over his chest and Tommy was crammed into the nook under his shoulder. Their standard positions. They had both been asleep more than an hour but Wilner had no plans to move them. These were the moments he lived for. These were the moments he never thought he'd see as a combat marine in Iran. Those long days and nights of constant vigilance had taught him nothing is forever. He saw the results of violence against children and families as well as brutality between combatants. He had even seen a penal unit that had revolted and killed the three, noncriminally charged officers.

Now, in a comfortable home, with healthy kids, he felt like he had conquered the world. But even as he watched the old movie about a postapocalyptic Australia, his mind went over the facts he had in his case. He was upset that his boss wouldn't allow him back into the zone but he had to admit the commander had a point. The transplanting of people to Florida was vital to the continued viability of the state. There were already a number of places that had been retaken by the wilderness. The west coast of Florida south of Sarasota was one gigantic forest and swamp again. Old, crumbling houses lurked beneath the thick foliage but no one lived there. At least no one who paid taxes or was recognized by the government.

His mind also lingered on Mari Saltis. Her dark hair and eyes, beautiful face and gentle nature, had taken root inside Wilner. The fact that she didn't freak out under the pressure of the gunfight at the old city hall made her that much more attractive to him. In his head he worked on ways to get back into the zone to see her.

On the table next to his bed his V-com beeped. He reached across Emma, knocking her off his side but still not waking her up. He pressed the receive button and immediately recognized a dispatcher from the UPF headquarters. She was in her uniform shirt, her light brown hair hanging to one side of her face.

"Sorry if I woke you, Tom, but we got a problem."

"What's that?"

"We haven't heard from Steve Besslia since early this afternoon."

"Where'd the GPS put him?"

"That's just it, with the cloud cover and interference our

last fix on him was on Interstate 95 in the district about seven miles south of the Northern Enclave."

Wilner considered the location. There wasn't much in that area. Not even people. "What was his last transmission?"

"That he was back on the road after stopping at headquarters. Then we had him north on the interstate. About six, Sergeant Chapman asked about his status. We started checking, couldn't raise him, sent out patrolmen to search and now we're worried. Really worried."

Wilner sat up and said, "Let me get a babysitter and I'll help." As he got dressed, he considered the location the dispatcher had given then checked his map pinned up in his garage. It was an area known as "old Pompano." He remembered someone saying something about Pompano Beach recently. Then he froze. The lab tech said the fingerprint of his killer came from an old Pompano Beach case file. He thought he knew where his friend might have gone and why.

Leonard Hall lay awake in the dead, dark silence of the Miami Quarantine Zone. Without streetlights or any serious traffic, life got very quiet after dark. Now, near two in the morning, nothing moved and no sound was made except the rhythmic breathing of the two naked women on each side of him.

They had jumped at the chance to bring him back to their house for three hundred zone credits. He had spent the evening having fun but there was another reason he had stayed. Lisa's lovely neck haunted him. He rolled onto his side to stare at the curves in the soft moonlight that trickled between the clouds. It was just enough for him to fantasize about her neck and what he could do with it.

He sat up carefully and scooted off the end of the bed.

Neither woman stirred. He had worn them out properly. Finding his pants in the darkness without making a sound was a challenge. The combat knife was stuffed in the cargo pocket of his favorite khakis. He pulled it out and opened the combat spike. It looked like his old barbeque skewer with an even finish. Six inches of solid death.

A smile crept across his face as he carefully considered who had seen him leave the bar with the women. No one should have because he picked them up a block away; closer to where he had parked.

He was free to act as he saw fit. He knew the closest neighbor was an older woman who was nursing a silent burn victim she had pulled from the Zone River. Even if one of them woke up it wouldn't be a problem.

He crouched down to the left side of the bed where the sleeping Darla lay flat on her back, her large breasts flattening out to each side. The moonlight landed directly on her pretty face and he could see each line of her peaceful expression. He took a moment to savor the feeling as he looked at her short neck. It wasn't the kind of prize he dreamed about but it would do. The real reward was on the other side of the bed.

He carefully lined up the spike and leaned in, inches from her face. Then he thrust the spike cleanly into her neck. He felt it snag on her vertebrae and bounce into her esophagus. Her eyes snapped open for a second but closed. He removed the spike and watched her small body twitch slightly, then settle into her final resting position. The best part was that she had not disturbed Lisa.

He crossed around to the other side of the bed. The taller, less shapely Lisa spread out like a long pretty tree branch in bed. She lay on her side facing away from her dead companion.

Leonard took a moment to light one of the gas lamps in the

house that had no electricity. The soft glow gave him much better visibility but still didn't awaken Lisa.

He couldn't stop himself from caressing her magnificent neck. She smiled and purred without opening her eyes. He did it again and saw her nipples harden and goose bumps appear on her neck. Perfect.

He placed the spike on her neck, slowly pressing against her skin. When her eyes opened in surprise he pushed the weapon hard enough to break the skin, then slowly worked it into her neck. She remained still for a second as her eyes focused on his face. Then she realized what he was doing but it was too late. He withdrew the spike quickly. She sat up and automatically placed her hand over the wound. She saw the blood around Darla's head and neck then looked back at Leonard. She tried to speak but no sound came out. Instead she toppled over onto the bare, wooden floor. Blood spit out of her wound and made a wide, sticky puddle on the floor.

Leonard stood, then got dressed. This had been some kind of exciting day. Tomorrow he started at the school as their handyman. Tomorrow could be as exciting as today if he allowed it to be.

SEVENTEEN

Steve Besslia was tired, hungry, and although he'd never admit it to others, scared. He was not a combat veteran like so many other members of the UPF, both male and female. Although he had done his required time in the service, he was in administrative services in the army. The worst he had seen was a bomb planted by insurgents near the end of the South African conflict and one air raid in Syria. Now, having not eaten in twenty hours, sleeping only a few minutes during the night on a hard floor and knowing he still had to get back to his bike, he felt the stress affect his judgment.

But he knew he had to run for it. If for no other reason than to get Wilner the information he had found out on the Mary Harris murder case.

He had found a list of five suspects. That might help. He had done some real police work. Not just pulled over the errant speeder or reckless driver. Investigative police work. It felt good and he didn't want it to go to waste.

He was ready. The sun should be up, giving him some

light. The patter of rain had continued the entire night. He hoped the dogs were as uncomfortable in the cold rain as most humans were. He secured the backpack holding all that he had found on his back and held the stun baton in one hand and his small conventional pistol with nine rounds of ammunition in it in the other hand. This was it.

He untied his makeshift lock and pushed open the door. Nothing.

He eased through the first room to the open doorway he had kicked in the day before. The parking lot water was undisturbed except for the drops of rain.

He started across the lot to the main building at a steady pace, his head swiveling to avoid any furry surprises. Less than halfway between the two buildings he saw the big brown dog that seemed like the leader of the pack step from behind a pile of rubble. It was a calculated move to conceal himself and surprise Besslia. These dogs were much more than they appeared.

The dog let out a howl and one loud grunt, but didn't move.

Besslia stopped but felt some safety in the weight of his pistol and baton.

From behind him he heard a splash and turned. Another large dog rushed at him, its gigantic paws slapping the water.

Besslia didn't panic. He raised his pistol and fired.

The dog yelped and slowed but didn't stop.

Besslia fired again and again.

The dog started to lope like one leg was injured.

Another round went wide, kicking up a splash in the parking lot.

Besslia continued to fire. Five, six, seven times. Finally the eighth shot caused the dog to fall in a heap into the water, its snout below the surface and blood spreading into the brown water.

Besslia turned quickly but the lead dog still stood motionless. Then three more large dogs joined him.

Besslia had one shot left and had seen how ineffective the little 9-millimeter rounds were on the dogs.

He realized he wasn't going to get the evidence to Wilner.

Mari Saltis usually walked to work as the sun came up. She knew most of the people who lived between her small clean house and the school. Many were up with the sun. Since video was difficult to receive down here and many houses had no electricity other than generators, the sun directed bedtimes and wake-up calls much like it had in the earlier centuries before the widespread use of electricity.

At this time of the morning, people would be tending their small gardens or feeding the livestock. She had grown used to the smell of goat pens and pigs. The two hardiest kinds of animals were now the world's largest source of nonsynthetic meat. Cows were still used but the spread of mad cow disease and other contaminants had curtailed beef consumption.

She walked up the path to the front of the school and through the unlocked courtyard door. As she reached for the key to the building she stopped.

Her new maintenance man, Leonard, was already working on the hinges of an old outdoor storage locker.

He turned and smiled. "Hello, ma'am."

"Leonard, you surprised me."

"I'm sorry, but without keys I had to start out here."

She looked down at his waist. He had a tool belt with a hammer, screwdrivers and pliers hanging from it.

Mari said, "You're early and prepared."

"Try to be."

"I'm very impressed." She stepped closer and saw that he had already organized the few rakes and shovels inside the locker.

"Your family doesn't miss you this early?"

"No, ma'am, I live with my aunt. She doesn't notice when I'm around or not. What about you, does anyone miss you when you're gone?"

Mari looked at him and said, "I don't know. Maybe. I just met a man." She smiled at the thought of Tom Wilner.

Leonard said, "Really? Tell me about him."

She liked the handyman's friendly manner and interest in her. She found him easy to talk to.

It was an hour after dawn when Wilner finally found Steve Besslia's Hive-bike. There had been several old buildings that had housed police departments in the area over the years and this one was the oldest and least marked on old maps and city plans. Wilner had checked two other buildings with his flashlight, hoping to see the bike or some sign of Besslia. The sun had made the search much easier.

He pulled his police hive up to the point where the old entrance to the building had crumbled into the drainage ditch, then called in his location to the dispatcher. He was too worried about his friend to wait for anyone else to show up.

He hustled through the shallow drainage ditch, the chilly water soaking through his shoes and pants. His legs went numb as he trotted toward the bike parked near the entrance to the old building. The Kevlar drape on the ground and hole in the front directed him where to go. He used his powerful duty pistol to blow off one of the supports to fit into the building easily. Inside he slowed to let his eyes adjust to the low light. He looked up the stairs and at each of the doors to see if there was a clue as to which direction Besslia had gone. One door was slightly ajar. As Wilner started to walk toward it, he heard the gunfire from the back of the building.

He broke out in a run toward the rear exit.

Mari looked up from her desk as one of the third-grade teachers, Mrs. Poolex, tapped at her door. Mari was used to the Haitian woman's bright smile, which contrasted against her dark, beautiful skin, but now she had a different look on her face.

"What is it, Anne?"

"I heard someone found two dead women a few miles from here."

"How did they die?"

"Stabbed in the neck."

Mari took a quick breath. "Where were they?"

"In their own house. One of the men from that Chaos Pit had to drop off something to them and found them. They had just been killed."

Mari knew this was the Vampire. She worried for her girls and the other teachers. They were defenseless here.

She looked out the window and saw the new handyman Leonard working in the courtyard. She wondered if he would be any help if there was trouble.

Steve Besslia braced for the two dogs that were now charging him to hit. He had one bullet and his stun baton. He was going to fight but had little hope of surviving this encounter.

He took aim at the dog in the lead as it cut through the puddles, splashing water in every direction.

He raised his pistol, then heard the head dog bark three times.

Both the attacking dogs froze and looked over their shoulders at the leader.

Besslia couldn't figure out what had caused the attack to be stopped. Then he saw a man step out from the main building with a pistol in his hand. It was Wilner.

He hadn't fired, but the lead dog knew the threat and was now backing away with the other dogs falling in behind him.

Wilner called out.

"Steve, you okay?"

"Watch the dogs, Willie, they're smart."

"They're big too. C'mon, hustle over this way."

Besslia didn't waste any time to reach his friend and get out of this place. He had a lot to tell him and the dogs that communicated with one another weren't even first on his list.

EIGHTEEN

After finding Steve Besslia, Tom Wilner had cleaned up at home and seen his kids off to school. Besslia was on fire from the experience but Wilner didn't have that luxury. He had kids that depended on him and a lot on his mind. He'd promised to meet his friend later and go over things with him after the patrolman had been checked out by a doctor and rested for a few hours.

Now Wilner arrived at the district hospital to talk to the nurse, Terry, again to see if she remembered anything about her friend Donna's man from the zone. She had never called him but he needed to tie up the loose end anyway.

After checking in the nursery, where she worked, he learned that she had not been to the hospital in a couple of days. Wilner found the large security guard and tried to get any details he had about the missing nurse.

"I ain't seen her and the hospital sent me by her apartment and no one there has seen her either."

"You call the UPF?"

"No, man. You know how it is. Sometimes people want to get away. We were gonna give her a little time. She was grieving."

Wilner considered the comment. "Has she ever skipped work before or been unreliable?"

"Terry, no way. This is about all she has. She always felt like we accepted her. Because of her fake hand, she didn't mix with many outside the hospital much. Like I said, we thought she just needed some time."

"No one has seen her since I was here?"

"That's right."

Wilner wondered if that made her a suspect.

"I'll see if we have any report of her at my office and I'll get back to you."

The security guard said, "You do that. We're startin' to get worried about her."

Late in the afternoon, Wilner stopped at Steve Besslia's condo in the Northern Enclave. He was surprised to find Johann Halleck visiting too.

"You feeling better?"

"Thanks to you."

"You woulda gotten out of it, besides you found the suspect list."

Johann said, "Are there any names that match current residents of the district?"

Wilner said, "We checked the five that were on the list. One guy, John Mckeague, was killed in the fourth Iraqi war. One suspect still lives in the district. Two are missing and no one has any idea if they're dead or alive. And one has had several names." He looked at Johann. "One of the names was Janos Dadicek."

"The name is not familiar."

"But it is Eastern European."

"That doesn't make him a Simolit."

"Doesn't mean he's not either."

Besslia spoke up from his chair. "What now?"

"The commander says no more trips into the zone, he wants us here."

"Here in the district?"

"Here in the United States."

"I'm gonna see if there are any names matched to other crimes where they found a fingerprint?"

"That's good," said Wilner. "I'm trying to get a photo of the suspects if one is available to see if we can match it to the guy I saw."

Besslia said, "The old city of Naples had one of the cases."

"That's nothing but underbrush and wilderness now."

Johann said, "I could go with Steve. Maybe we would turn something up."

Wilner nodded. It was as good as any other suggestion.

Leonard Hall had nervous energy stored in him like a canister of expanding gas. He knew word would spread quickly about his activities at Lisa and Darla's house. He never cared too much about the aftermath of his actions, as long as no one suspected him. It was the instant of seeing something plunge into a neck that excited him.

Although it was early in the morning and he was new to the job, he liked working around the school. It was just that the excitement of his evening was still coursing through him. At least he wasn't thinking about the cop anymore.

Leonard had dealt with a few cops before the Quarantine

Zone was established. The first time was a Pompano cop who talked to everyone near the place where he had killed his first victim, Mary. The tall detective had come to the house first, then asked him to come down to the old police station. Leonard had spoken to three detectives before they released him. He had seen one of them following him once, but no one ever arrested him. That's when he knew he could go on doing this forever. That was his first time and he learned more each time. He knew it would be harder and harder to catch him.

Down here in the Quarantine Zone, without a court system, people tended to take a vigilante view of justice. A crowd might go on a rampage if he did too many killings. They could grab him by chance and wouldn't need to make a case. The question was whether once they had him could they keep him contained? He doubted it.

The sun popped out from a cloud as Leonard trimmed a bush outside the head teacher's office window. He looked over his shoulder and wondered if he was seeing the sun more often lately. Then, as he turned back to the bush, he caught a glimpse of Mari Saltis speaking with one of her teachers. She was a beautiful woman who had been nice to him.

She confused Leonard.

On the second floor of the district's largest hospital, Kern Green, the hospital's security guard, and Toby Reed, the facilities manager, enjoyed a couple of mouthfuls of Baht. The African drug had soared in popularity as veterans of various African campaigns returned to the United States. The police did little to stop it. With so many other problems, especially the repeated terrorist attacks, drug enforcement had been severely curtailed. Very few businesses could afford drug tests and didn't care anyway.

Toby said, "What do you think happened to Terry?"

The big black guard said, "No idea. But if anyone's gonna find her, I think it's that cop Wilner. He seems like he's got his shit together."

"I didn't talk to him but I seen him around. He's been in here a couple of times. He was in a big shoot-out at that bar on the Zone River. Caused some kind of explosion."

"How you know that?"

"He was in here for treatment and I was working."

Kern shrugged, chewing some more root as he watched Toby clean up near the furnace, then open the door to the unlit chamber.

Toby leaned in and looked up. He shouted back, "I'm gonna have to climb up and change them filters soon. We been burning a lot more stuff since the new arrivals came. People been bringing in stuff from home to burn too."

"Like what?"

Toby pulled out his head from the cool furnace. "All kinds of stuff. Financial records, old immigration records. Nobody wants to risk someone taking their information. Burning the stuff up is smart and free if you work here."

Toby looked back into the metal chamber and wiped down the window inside the door. The heavy fireproof polymer had dirt and grime on it kicked up by the intense heat. "Hey, look at this."

Kern eased up off the stool he was resting on and ambled over to his friend at the furnace. He looked inside where Toby was pointing.

"What is it?"

"I don't know, but it didn't burn."

"What wouldn't burn?"

"Some of the new alloys with titanium. I see it every once in a while." Toby leaned in the furnace and plucked at the shiny item on the floor under a sheet of ash. It was larger than he first thought as he clutched it and lifted it free of the ash.

Kern watched him blow off the soot and ash and hold up a prosthetic hand with eight fingers and synthetic tendons that reached below the hand for seven inches.

Toby said, "I can tell by the weight that this thing is titanium. It's awful high-end. Look at the eight fingers."

Kern frowned. "I only saw one like it."

"Where?"

"Here at the hospital. That was Terry's fake hand."

Leonard had offered to escort Mari to the site where the two bodies had been found. Of course he knew precisely where the house was and he knew why she was so interested but it was a lot of fun to play along. He loved being ahead of the game.

His steam-powered car rumbled and hissed to a stop down the street from the house. He smiled at the crowd that had gathered around. They had no idea.

Mari said, "If this kind of stuff upsets you, I'll go on alone. I just want a little information."

"No, ma'am. No telling if the killer is hanging around. I'll come with you."

They walked slowly as Mari told him how she had never been in this neighborhood by the Zone River.

He noticed the old woman who lived next to Darla and Lisa on her porch. In the lounger next to her lay the heavily bandaged figure that Darla had talked about. The man who had been pulled from the river had hardly moved since.

Mari said, "Wonder what happened to him?"

"Burns."

"How'd you know that?" She looked at him. Her big brown eyes fixing on his own.

"I can tell by the bandages."

"Poor man," she said as she turned toward the house with the bandaged man.

Leonard wondered where the hell she was going. He turned and followed her.

As she approached the older woman, Mari said, "Excuse me."

"Yes, dear." The woman had an odd Spanish-Jamaican accent

"Are you here alone?"

"Just me and my patient."

"Does he need to see a doctor? I could help."

"No, dear, he has refused all attention other than my bandaging. I think that's more vanity. He's getting better. A few weeks ago he wouldn't have made it out on the porch to see all the excitement."

"Is he a relative?"

"No, just a refugee, like all of us. Except I think he came from the district here instead of the other way around."

Mari smiled and backed away. On the way out of the yard she said in a low voice, "There's something odd about that injured man."

"Tell me about it. He gives me the creeps."

They walked to the edge of the crowd where several men and a woman pulled out the sheet-covered bodies from the house.

"Does anyone know what happened?" asked Mari.

"Someone stuck them in the throats. Looks like it's the Vampire."

Mari gasped, unable to answer such a blunt and accurate statement.

Leonard hid his little smile.

They waited as Mari listened to all kinds of rumors. Someone said it was a killer from the district. Another man said it was Jack the Ripper who was now two hundred years old and someone else said it was a double suicide. Of course no one was right.

Leonard knew the truth but he wasn't going to say anything. He liked the nickname "the Vampire."

Mari turned to him and said, "I need to get into the district to talk to someone."

Leonard nodded his head and said, "I can get you into the district."

NINETEEN

Tom Wilner had listened to the lab tech bitch about how he was tricked into coming all the way down into the district for the last ten minutes.

Finally Wilner said, "Look, I'm sorry, but this is important. I needed you."

"Then why didn't you ask? Pretending to be the commander and saying you needed to meet me at the hospital is stupid."

"It worked."

The tech looked at him, concealing any emotion.

"I told you, this is important."

"If I ask the commander will he agree?"

Wilner thought about it. At least this lead was in the United States. Maybe his boss would go along with the use of a lab person on this.

The lab tech stood to his full, gawky six feet. "Would he agree how important this is?"

Wilner glared at him and said, "If you want to make it

back to your office in the Northern Enclave you better believe it's important. I've wasted too much time being pleasant. There's no one here who can tip you or offer you any incentive other than the knowledge that could help catch a serial killer. Isn't that enough?"

The tech's eyes lingered on Wilner for a moment and looked down. He mumbled, "I guess so." Then he went back to work. He held a blown-up copy of the print Wilner had found a few nights earlier that matched the old, unsolved homicide. The tech sprayed a mist onto different areas around the furnace to see if he could match it. He wore a small lens that quickly evaluated all the prints that weren't involved in the case.

Wilner said, "All I need is one print that matches to show he was here. Then I'll work the leads we might find from that."

As the tech continued his search in an expanding arc, a young doctor walked in.

"Wilner, I thought you'd be here."

"Hey, Doc."

The young man stepped over to the table where the prosthetic hand was laid out, its titanium frame intact but the electronics and crystals had been shattered by the heat. He held up the hand and examined it. "Yeah, this was Terry's." He shook his head, then looked up at Wilner. "Any idea what happened?"

Wilner took him away from the tech and the security guard who watched the hunt for a fingerprint. He trusted the doctor because he had been trained in the two-year medical program for military doctors in Kansas and then served in several combat zones.

Wilner said, "My guess is that the killer knew I'd try and talk to her. He might have lured her down here to make disposing the body easier."

"Could it be someone here in the hospital?"

"Maybe. It was someone who knew Terry and Donna and, unless he was just lucky, knew where the furnace here was located."

The doctor held up the prosthetic hand. "What're you gonna do with this?"

"I'll hold it as evidence until we catch the guy."

"Then what will happen to it?"

"Discard it I guess. Is there anything you can do with a used prosthetic arm?"

"This isn't like the days when we had the resources to make more prosthetics. Despite all the advances in prosthetics, money for rehab and the operations to attach them had dried up. Many vets are being fitted with the old-style hook. A hand like this could be of use to someone and see a second life after it got new electronics. Don't toss it."

"I promise, Doc. When the case is over you'll get the whole thing."

The young doctor nodded. "Thanks."

Then Wilner heard the lab tech shout, "Yes."

Wilner rushed to him as he lay a white strip across one print on the side of the furnace front. "A perfect match."

Now he had one more piece of the puzzle.

Tom Wilner sat at his desk for the first time in days. He knew he didn't have to gather too much evidence anymore because the judges were so likely to convict and send someone off to a penal military unit. Absolute guilt was no longer an element of the criminal justice system. It was rare a court case went more than one hearing. Usually the evidence and testimony was presented to a judge on the day the defendant first appeared in court. The sentence followed within minutes and it usually involved service in some foreign war.

He had spent a whole day eliminating every male staff member from the hospital by checking their prints against the killer's. Now Wilner was using what few effective databases were left to track the names that were on the list Besslia found in the old police files. The problem was that no database was up-to-date. At least here in Florida.

He couldn't help it, but he focused on the one eastern European name, Janos Dadicek. He decided that if he cleared each name it would take too long. Someone else might die that he could save. Instead he went with his instinct. The killer couldn't be human. Not if he left prints at different crime scenes fifty years apart. The Simolits were from Eastern Europe so it made sense that if he found Janos Dadicek he might find the killer.

The other problem he had was that the killer could've changed his name a hundred times in the past fifty years. He could be called John Smith now. No, this was an investigation that would require him to start fifty years earlier and work his way into the current century.

Besslia had checked out one of the UPF all-terrain trucks with solid, wide wheels by saying he didn't feel up to riding the Hive-bike but would still work. The UPF was so short-handed that they'd take him anyway he could come. The state government simply had no money to hire more cops. That was why the relocation program was so vital.

Besslia also told his boss he intended to check on the extreme western roads that rarely got patrolled. His boss saw a double win there because, although they were supposed to cover the entire southern tip of the state, they really stayed on the east coast.

Besslia smiled from behind the wheel of the giant, hydrogen-powered truck that felt like it could rumble over anything that got in its way. He had his friend, Johann Halleck, in the passenger seat. The big man gave Besslia more confidence, although he made the occasional joke too. Like now.

Johann chuckled and said, "So these smart dogs figured out how to wait for you?"

"I'm tellin' you they talked to each other."

"In English or another language?"

"In grunts and barks."

"How would they write that?"

"Funny, but people said the same things about dolphins once. Now humans can interact with them through translation machines."

"On a limited basis."

"But that's just it. People used to think they were just fish and couldn't talk at all."

Johann nodded in agreement. "I still don't know why you had to risk your life going down there anyway."

"I had to do something useful. I'm tired of the other cops laughing at me behind my back."

"And did you accomplish this goal?"

"Sort of, but Wilner had to bail me out again. If it wasn't for him I'd be dog food."

"But you did, in a way, save him as well."

"How's that?"

"You found a list of suspects for his case. He might be able to stop this killer because of you."

Besslia paused and turned to look at his friend. "Do you think it's one of your people?"

Johann shook his head. "I don't know. The time span seems to point toward a member of my family or the Simolits but I don't know if it rings true."

"What other explanation could it be?"

"Perhaps we finally found someone with identical prints. It is only one finger. It's not like the whole hand has been printed."

"That would sure screw up a number of cases where someone was convicted based only on prints."

"DNA exonerated a lot of people when they still used it regularly."

Besslia nodded as they turned onto the remnant of the old Alligator Alley or Interstate 75. There were still long stretches of usable road, but years of neglect and the lack of demand sent the highway through the Everglades into a spiral of disrepair.

The Tamiami Trail, old Highway 41, was hardly visible where it cut through the Everglades to the south. The giant swamp had reclaimed it as completely as India had reclaimed Pakistan. All it was now was a hard trail under a few inches of water in some places. No one had used it for travel in years. At least no one from the United States.

This could become a dangerous trip as they exited off the old road. No one talked much about how the southwest corner of Florida had crept back to nature. First the hurricane had turned most buildings into ruin, the residents left in the thousands and all government offices shut down. They tried to clean up a few areas but then everyone abandoned the area.

Ecoterrorists claimed huge victories and went back to demolish the remaining buildings so nature could return more easily. Now, without government monitoring, there were only sporadic reports of people in the area. Most of the reports were of missing persons who had told someone they were on their way over there to salvage buildings or explore.

The UPF had little patience with people who ventured into places like Naples. The force didn't have the resources to spread patrols all across the state when every taxpayer lived on the east side of the state.

After more than twenty miles of smooth driving, the road disappeared into a low snarl of brush and swampy water.

"Shit," called out Besslia as he fought to maintain control and slow the massive vehicle down. He felt it float for a moment and thought they were in real trouble if the truck sank. But the front tires touched solid land again and brought it up on a bumpy stretch of muddy soil. A gigantic alligator, unused to any human presence, skittered out from in front of the truck. It slipped into the water and Besslia got a good look at a twenty-foot alligator swimming away, its long, muscular tail propelling it slowly away from the truck.

Johann said, "Perhaps we should return to the road when it appears again."

Besslia looked at him. "Thanks for that tip."

In a minute he could see the interstate resume and look like it was in good shape for a mile more. He wondered what had caused this particular section to fold in on itself.

Once they were on the smooth highway, Johann said, "Do you think that was a smart alligator?"

Besslia mumbled, "I think I'm riding with a smart-ass."

They were still miles from what once was the city of Naples.

TWENTY

Mari Saltis was nervous as she looked down the street in the Miami Quarantine Zone at the bridge that led to the southernmost point in the continental United States, The Lawton District. She sat in the passenger seat of Leonard's steam-powered Honda. They had reached the car's maximum speed of twenty-four miles an hour.

Mari said, "I don't know about this, Leonard."

"C'mon, you want to talk to the cop. I can get you into the district easy enough. I do it all the time."

"I haven't gone into the district in eight years. Last time I risked it was when one of my students had a bad infection and had to go to the district hospital. There was no choice then. But the whole idea of sneaking into the United States scares me."

"We're not really sneaking so much as bribing our way in. These guardsmen know me. There won't be any problem."

At the bridge a tall black sergeant walked up to the idling car. He smiled as he got closer. "Hey, haven't seen you in a while."

"Been busy. Got a new job."

"Look," started the sergeant. "They're cracking down on crossings right now."

"Why?" asked Leonard.

"They have a whole bunch of new people moving down and they want them feeling safe. There was a murder up here last week too. The killer tried to make it to the zone before our boys knocked him down with heavy fire."

Mari knew that the killer had escaped. She had seen what he could do.

Leonard said, "That a fact. If you killed him, he can't be a problem, right?"

The big sergeant scratched his chin.

"And I been through here before and always came back like I said, right?"

"Yeah, I guess."

"So if you were to make an extra fifty in U.S. cash, I could go over for a few hours, couldn't I?"

The sergeant thought about it, then leaned into the car. "But who's this?"

"That's my boss. She runs the school in the zone. I'll make sure she gets back with me."

The sergeant eyed her.

Mari smiled, not wanting to show her nervousness.

The sergeant snatched the bill from Leonard's hand and said, "Okay, but be back before midnight when my shift ends."

"You got it, Sarge."

They crossed the bridge and Mari found herself in the United States for the first time in many years.

Wilner got the message on his V-com. Mari had managed to send a text message to some errant Internet connection through a site in Tokyo to him, saying she intended to come into the district this evening and would like to meet him at a new chain restaurant near the border. Wilner knew the monstrosity of neon and cement. He had even eaten there once since it had opened. It was the talk of the district and apparently the zone too. No chain had ventured this far down in almost fifteen years, but with the arrival of the newcomers and the promise of growth, the chain decided to risk a location near the end of the known United States.

Wilner raced home to see his children before he met her. They charged him like Libyans rushing the Russians at the battle of Surt. Wilner snatched them up and stood to his full six-foot-one-inch height. He noticed the babysitter smile from the corner of his eye. The girl lived with her parents on the next street and was studying small engine repair with her father a couple of days a week. She was one of the few younger people who didn't profess a desire to leave this wasteland as soon as she could. That explained the practical trade like engine repair.

Wilner turned to her and said, "Ali, could you stay a few extra hours tonight?"

The tall, pretty girl scrunched her nose and thought about it, finally saying, "Sure, Mr. Wilner. It'll be fun."

Even the kids cheered until they learned that it meant their father had to leave.

Overall it was easier than he had thought as he piled into his hive and headed off to meet Mari Saltis.

It was much later than Besslia had hoped it would be when they came to the end of the road. The interstate literally seemed to disappear into a thatch of wild underbrush and flowing water. He knew by the GPS coordinates that they were near where the old city of Naples had once been.

Without waiting for any questions from Johann, Besslia turned to one side, avoiding a leaning banyan tree, and let the truck's large tires roll over stumps and other brush. He felt the truck buck from one side to the other, then level off as it rolled over thick brush. He couldn't see anything in front of him but branches. It still beat trying to walk through this mess of limbs, leaves and vegetation.

Somewhere close by, he heard the croak of a large alligator and a flock of white egrets took off. Besslia knew there was water at the base of all the brush, he could smell it and hear an occasional splash as the truck thumped hard on top of the trees.

Johann braced himself with both hands and managed to say, "How far do we go like this before we turn back?"

"The jungle scare you?"

"No, your driving does. And I no longer think there is anything left of the city."

"We have to look. This could be a big lead if we find something in the old burglary report that identifies a suspect. We might be able to narrow down the list of suspects in the murder. C'mon, where's your adventurous spirit?"

"I left it on my journeys with T. E. Lawrence."

"Lawrence of Arabia?"

Johann smiled. "You know your history."

"Yeah, but he's huge. You were in World War I?"

"I fought the Ottomans."

"Why?"

"They were propped up by the Simolit family. At the time, I fought with anyone against the Simolits."

"When did that philosophy change?"

"When the Simolits stood up to the Nazis."

Besslia was always amazed at the things Johann had done.

Before he could ask any questions the truck rolled out of the brush and into a wide, clear-cut field. Besslia had to take his foot off the gas to slow the truck down enough.

He took a moment to make use of the fading light and look at the astounding sight in front of him.

Johann said, "This is not what I expected."

Besslia, still staring straight ahead, said, "No one expected this."

Tom Wilner stood in front of the entrance to the new restaurant. The giant yellow arches were the brightest light for fifty miles in any direction. The bored staff chatted with one another and aimlessly swept clean rags over any surface within reach. There just weren't enough residents to support a place like this yet.

Wilner had heard about some of the negotiations involved in luring the restaurant down here and how it was tied to the transplants as well. Wilner had heard that the restaurant chain didn't want to build a store in the district unless there was a cop stationed there twenty-four hours a day. That was ridiculous considering the strain the UPF was under already. It wasn't like this was the Miami Quarantine Zone.

Then he caught himself. He had held that stereotype and he had *seen* that the zone was not the lawless Wild West he had once thought it was. There were schools and businesses and people who liked living there. That made him realize that the rest of the country, at least the parts not affected by terror attacks or quarantine zones, viewed the southern tip of Florida as some kind of lawless area itself. The west coast had reverted to nature. The bottom tip of the state was now another country. Didn't people realize that they worked hard to make the Lawton District livable?

The other thing that Wilner had heard was that the restaurant agreed to open if the property and business didn't have to pay taxes for five years and they were assured that at least twenty thousand people would be relocated to the district in that time period.

Now Wilner leaned on a bench and watched the sun slowly set through a late-afternoon break in the clouds. There was still more than an hour of daylight left as he felt his heart rate speed up at the thought of seeing Mari again.

He wished verbal communication over the V-com was more reliable but the decades-long embargo of Cuba had extended to a block of satellite signals after the United States had developed the technology to keep orbiting satellite transmissions from hitting specific areas of the globe.

Once the Miami Quarantine Zone was created the United States extended the satellite blockade to include most of the zone.

The Cuba blockade had started with some old leader named Castro who thumbed his nose at the United States. Wilner had learned about him in his elementary school history class. He had turned to an old confederation of countries called the Soviet Union. The only real nation left from that union was Russia. Many of the others had turned to the spreading Islamic practice of tribes without real national borders. It had cut down on violence and strife in the region but made many of the bordering countries, like Turkey, nervous.

Decades after Castro had died the U.S. blockade of the island nation endured through a brutal communist takeover of Castro's Cuba, a short-lived fascist government and now the

Islamic fundamentalists who had been invited onto the island by other anti-U.S. regimes. Now the joke was on the former Cuban leaders who found themselves on the outside looking in as most of the native Cubans had fled to other countries.

Wilner watched different cars pass by. He realized there was an increase in traffic and saw more and more factory-built hives and fewer converted cars. He recognized a lot of the steam-powered cars where the owners had painted their names or slogans on the boiler. The district wasn't so big that a resident didn't notice the same unusual vehicle over and over again.

Then he saw the older Honda and Mari's smiling face as the car passed by. He couldn't see who was driving her, but hustled down the street to greet her as the car came to a stop.

Leonard Hall liked playing Mari's security guard and guide. He had no doubt he'd kill anyone who threatened her on this trip. This pretty, soft-spoken, kind woman had taken a chance on him and offered him a job at the school. She made him feel more welcome than he did in his own home. She stopped to chat or comfort anyone she encountered in the street. She didn't seem to have any downside.

As he pulled down the street near the new monstrosity of a restaurant, he wondered which was the stronger need; to kill the cop or be near Mari? He also wondered if the cop had gotten a good enough look at him to recognize him when they met.

He hated the idea of killing the cop in front of Mari, then having to kill her to keep from being identified. He didn't even like the idea of exposing Mari to the killing of a man she clearly had feelings for. So he decided, with his combat knife opened next to him by the door, he'd see what happened.

If he had to act quickly he could. If the cop didn't recognize him, then maybe he'd let this game play out a little longer.

He saw the tall cop straighten in front of the restaurant as he recognized Mari.

She smiled at him but Leonard didn't stop.

"That's him." Mari pointed at Wilner.

"I don't want to stop in the street like that. Habit leftover from when things were busy down here. Let me pull to the side street." He increased speed slightly to stay ahead of the cop who was now walking quickly down the street toward them.

For the first time in a long time, Leonard Hall didn't know what to do.

TWENTY-ONE

Steve Besslia and Johann Halleck sat in the cab of the truck, staring at the men approaching them. Besslia let his hand slip to his holster, hidden under an untucked camouflage shirt, but Johann stopped him from drawing the weapon with a quick hand gesture.

"Not yet, Steve."

"This doesn't look good."

"They're as surprised as we are."

Besslia looked out over the structures built off the ground, into the tree trunks, and at the passing canoes. The six men approached them on a path that led from the sprawling village to the edge of the brush. Swampy water flowed into pools around the field.

Johann surprised Besslia by opening his door and swinging from a handle onto the soggy ground.

Besslia followed out of reflex, not out of desire. The men had knives in their belts and one had an old-style gunpowder rifle. It wasn't automatic. The lead man was stocky with long light hair and thick glasses. Another was big with close-cropped hair and the look of a pissed-off soldier. They all had darker skin and hair.

As Besslia tried to think of some hand signals, the man in the front of the group said, "Who the hell are you guys?"

Besslia blinked and said, "Steve Besslia, UPF."

The man looked back and forth between Johann and Besslia then said, "No one called the cops."

"I know. We just extended our patrol zone and thought we'd see what was back here."

"Why? Did you hear rumors about a lost tribe like us?" The shorter man looked to make sure his friends were still right next to him.

"No, actually, we don't hear anything about this area. I had something I was interested in looking up in the old city of Naples."

"Well, you're standing in the middle of it right now."

Besslia looked around. "This is Naples?"

"Used to be. The rivers overflowed and pushed tons of sand over any roads and buildings left here. The other parts of the town are still fading but there's some concrete and buildings to show they were here."

"Who're you guys?"

"Refugees."

"From what?"

"You and all the bullshit that caused us to move here."

"You mean you moved here *after* things had changed."

"About four years ago."

"From where?"

The tall man shrugged. "All over. Philly, Nebraska, Texas and right here in Florida."

"So you're not all Seminoles?"

"Indians? No, we're just people living quietly away from you. That a problem?"

"No, I don't care where you live."

The man smiled. "Then we'll get along. My name is Victor. We don't use last names here."

"My name is Steve and this is Johann."

"You guys hungry?"

Besslia nodded.

"We got real meat, cow meat. We have potatoes and asparagus we grew ourselves."

"I don't think I ever had asparagus before. At least *real* asparagus."

"You eat that rubbery synthetic crap?"

"Sometimes."

"You're our first visitors who haven't come to hurt us. We might benefit from a little police protection. You boys follow me and we'll show you what you're missing in that world you think is real."

As Wilner hustled to the car, Mari stood up, turned around and waved to the driver. Before Wilner was at the old Honda it drove off down the street.

Mari surprised him by embracing him and kissing him on the lips.

Wilner couldn't let his curiosity wait. "Who was that?"

"The school handyman, Leonard. I think he's shy and didn't want to meet you."

Wilner shrugged, lost in Mari's dark clear eyes. "I'm really glad you came into the district."

She smiled and hugged him softly.

Wilner said, "I was told not to go back into the zone on this case."

"Why?"

"Political and manpower reasons. All anyone cares about is repopulating the state. They want places like this restaurant to flourish and forget about anything south of the border.

"But that's why I came up. I had to tell you."

"Tell me what?"

"They found two more dead women in the zone. Both had been stabbed in the neck."

Wilner felt like he had been hit with a punch in the stomach. Dammit, the killer was still active and he was stuck on the wrong side of the border. What could he do now?

TWENTY-TWO

Steve Besslia and Johann Halleck had decided to stay overnight in the western wilderness. It made sense to have a few extra hours to try and find the old Naples police department. The only problem was that Besslia woke up stiff. The unevenly padded mats that he and Johann Halleck had slept on had reminded him of camping as a kid. Except he wasn't eight and he didn't like the way his blood had been cut off to different parts of his body. He lay still and listened to the light rain patter off the top of the "guest" house for the small settlement. The raised houses were a combination of lumber, waterproof material like tents and sheets of old roofs or synthetic building material salvaged from the surrounding area. The floor was a simple wooden base about six feet off the ground. He had seen a couple of the houses had cots and one had a full-size bed on the floor.

The men of the village had promised to take him and Johann on a hunt for the old city hall and police station later. They had said that much of Naples was intact under a thick layer of brush that had grown over the top of some of the smaller buildings or the ruins of the ones that had been knocked down.

Next to him, Johann stirred, then sat up with a groan.

Besslia said, "I thought you were immune to aches and pains."

"I can heal quickly. I grow old like you only much slower." He rubbed his blond hair and added, "If you were my age you'd be dust."

They dressed and armed themselves, then found a communal building with no walls where breakfast was being served.

Besslia sat next to the nominal leader of the group, Victor. He had been a college professor before the country had changed so drastically. Now he managed to keep the settlement safe and running. It was an enviable accomplishment.

Besslia sampled the wheat cake and strip of meat. "This is good."

"Bacon," said Victor.

"Real bacon?"

"From a pig."

"Wow, and I thought last night's meal was the best I ever had." He wolfed down everything on his plate and noticed that no one left any food. They had learned a lesson from the rest of society.

After an hour of preparation, Besslia, Johann and five men from the settlement set out on foot along a path that inched up out of the water and led west. After an hour they came to a wide section that asphalt and sidewalk had kept clear of much overgrowth. It was several blocks long with buildings and even a few cars rotting on the side of a weed-filled street.

Besslia said, "Why wouldn't you make use of the buildings and live here?"

Before Victor could answer Besslia saw a movement on the far side of the clearing and then all the men with him ducked down. Besslia joined them as Victor said, "They're the reason we don't live here."

Wilner sat at his desk, allowing the commander to see him in the office. He wanted the boss to know he wasn't disobeying orders and running down to the Quarantine Zone. His heart had sunk when he watched Mari slip into the steam-powered Honda to cross back into the zone. They had talked for hours. She had asked about his children and hinted about her curiosity about his wife. All Wilner could manage was to say that she was no longer here. He couldn't bring himself to explain that she had been killed saving him. He knew he could never talk about what she really was. The origin of his children's DNA would be his most closely guarded secret.

Now he stared down at the open, moldy files that Steve Besslia had risked his life to retrieve. The lab reports and photos had all faded but remained readable. He kept wondering, if the cops had a fingerprint and suspects, why didn't they just fingerprint the suspects? He knew the laws governing police conduct were radically different back then, but that only seemed like common sense to him.

He could prove the current crimes if he only knew who the killer was. It had to be someone who could cross the border between the zone and the U.S. easily. The dead nurses seemed to be proof of that. He thought of Terry's vacant, motionless prosthetic hand that had been fished out of the furnace. What he needed was an eyewitness. To his knowledge anyone who had seen the killer was dead.

He flipped through the files, occasionally glancing at the

list of names. The two cops on the case had both died of natural causes years earlier. There was no one to talk to. He had to focus on what he had.

And find a way to get back into the zone.

Mari Saltis sat at her desk, thinking of Tom Wilner. She could not get the image of the tall, handsome police officer out of her head. He reminded her of her husband. In the course of their long conversation she had meant to mention Guillermo, but after he was so evasive about his wife she felt funny about talking about her own situation.

Her mother had told her she was too young to get married at eighteen when she and the twenty-six-year-old engineer walked down the aisle in Cartagena. He had a fire in him. A burning desire to confront authority that she had found irresistible. That was why, only a month after their marriage he had dragged her to Miami to protest the way the United States was treating immigrants. He had no personal experience with the treatment, but used a work visa to fly into the city. He walked with protestors and played to the CNN cameras. Then the next September eleventh attack occurred in Los Angeles. The footage of rejoicing Mexican immigrants tied with the news that the terrorists were Mexican nationals pushed the government into action.

Flights were canceled too quickly for them to leave. Then rumors of bioplague victims spread through the city, and before she realized it U.S. Army troops stood at the new border and she was a scared teaching assistant at a small private school.

Miami had been declared a Quarantine Zone. Lost to the country. It joined the other two zones before New York and the South Dakota zones were established.

Then the news of Hugo Chavez marching the Venezuelan army into Colombia as part of his campaign to invade all of South America had unnerved her more. The United States had its own troubles and couldn't stop the South American Hitler.

The final blow was short and simple: Guillermo caught an infection. It spread to his lungs but without antibiotics he died. Quietly at their home. Only five months after they were married.

She had seen the evolution of the Quarantine Zone. Now there were doctors and medicine. Perhaps not as much as before under U.S. control but things had stabilized. And now she was excited about a man again. A good man.

She smiled to herself as she gazed out the window. Then she noticed Leonard working on a sticky window across the courtyard. He saw her and waved.

Maybe men were coming to her rescue.

"Who are they?" asked Johann Halleck as he peered over the low brush at the armed men. There were seven of them, each carrying a long rifle and moving in military formation.

Victor said, "They're Zoners."

"What is a Zoner?"

"They come out of the Miami Quarantine Zone."

"Do they cause trouble?"

"That's why we stay hidden. They raid the settlements, kidnapping and killing."

"There are more settlements?"

"Sure, dozens, maybe a hundred."

"Have they ever found your settlement?"

"Once. At our last location about eight miles south on the banks of a river."

"What happened?"

"They killed three men and took four women and two children. We moved the next day to where we are now."

"Why'd they take women and children?"

"Don't ask. There are places in the zone that have uses for them."

Johann considered this disturbing information then said, "How can you let that happen?"

"What can we do? We're not fighters. I was a college creative writing professor, Sean was an IT guy, Duane ran a small newspaper in Philadelphia. We're not prepared to fight."

"But you're prepared to let your women be sold into slavery?"

"Do you have any ideas?"

Johann nodded. "I do."

Wilner kept looking down at the second name on the list, Janos Dadicek. The one report listed him as a twenty-eight-year-old plumber from another, now forgotten town named Deerfield Beach. Wilner searched every database and found only a few references to him. He had paid into Social Security until the program was eliminated and all records sealed. He had been listed on a watch list for his travels to Europe but was never arrested and there were no specific charges against him. He could find no photos and his last address was in the district thirteen years ago. That was the sum total of the man's life: a few cryptic references in questionable government databases.

To Wilner it sounded like a man trying to keep a low profile. It could also be a man who had changed his name. Maybe more than once.

On one report, in a hand-scrawled note in thick blue ink next to a paragraph about talking to Dadicek, someone had written: *This guy is a crooked freak.*

That was enough for Wilner.

Leonard Hall smiled at Mrs. Martinez, the science teacher, as she moved her giant mass of flesh and bones down the outside hallway. She always had a wide smile for him. He wondered if she thought, since she was only in her thirties, Leonard found her attractive. He did not. It was not her size but her shape. He had liked many large women over the years but Mrs. Martinez's girth gave her too many chins, which in turn covered anything that might be considered a neck.

He nodded politely and went back to his newest undertaking at the school: replacing the outdated and dangerous wiring system that ran through all the exposed hallways. He wondered if they wouldn't be better off with gaslights instead of the cumbersome, ambient light panels that had been on the roof since before this was a Quarantine Zone.

He really did like it here in the first few days. It was a new adventure and the young women all impressed him with their manners and attitude. He knew that Mari was responsible for most of that. Some of the girls even called him Mr. Hall. He was glad that was the name he had chosen all those years ago when he moved south from what was then Broward County. He always liked the name Leonard and Hall was easy to remember. It had taken him much longer than he had thought to get used to answering when people called him Leonard or Mr. Hall. Perhaps the hardest part was getting his mother and aunt to go with it. They didn't see why name changes were necessary. He didn't want to go into detail but they agreed regardless. Now he felt like he had a complete identity. Leonard Hall, maintenance man.

He liked the free meals at the school. It didn't occur to him that they would make enough for him to join them at lunch. This was the most interaction with people he had experienced in his whole life. He also liked the little smiles and waves the headmistress threw his way during the day. Why not? He had proven helpful and he liked his little trip into the district with her. Especially because he didn't have to meet her cop friend face-to-face. Now if something happened to Detective Wilner he'd never be suspected. At least not by Mari.

He was surprised how much his little romp with Darla and Lisa had done to satisfy his desire to use his combat spike. He still relived the actions in Darla's house. Just the startled last second look on Darla's pretty face, or Lisa's surprise at what their "date" was capable of, gave him shudders of excitement.

As he focused on the rat's nest of wires while standing halfway up on a folding ladder he heard a shout then a scream come from Mari's office. He didn't hesitate to rush to the front of the building and barge through her door.

He skidded to a stop as all the men turned to him at once. They started to laugh as the man in the middle, their leader, said, "And what do you want, old man?"

Then Leonard noticed the pistol in one man's hand.

TWENTY-THREE

Tom Wilner started with a worker's hall, which was as close to a union as existed now. He wondered if there could be any clues as to the origins and current whereabouts of Janos Dadicek. As a plumber in the twentieth century he probably belonged to a union of some kind. Wilner remembered his father belonged to some kind of welder's union in New Jersey. Once many of the union's strong-arm tactics and wage inflation had been blamed for several recessions, and then the all-out meltdown of the economy during the first Iranian war, unions had fallen out of favor. It was really just public perception, but they started losing political clout and then membership dried up as the unions endorsed candidates that were union friendly but stood against the values of most union members. The result was one state after another moving to a "right to work" status and any reliable way to find skilled laborers faded.

Wilner had nothing else to work with so he now found himself inside the small administrative offices of the New

Florida Hall of Labor in the former city of Boca Raton, now just the southern end of the Northern Enclave.

The attitude of the man behind the counter was imported from New York. Many of the transplants had mellowed and adapted since they were forced to flee the shattered city, which was now a Quarantine Zone of its own. But this fifty-five-year-old man clearly had not wanted to lose the attitude it took him a lifetime to build in the former northern big city.

The heavy man said, "What do you want?"

Wilner was surprised and said, "Is that how you address people in your job?"

"That's not a question I have to answer. You a carpenter? You look like a carpenter. Kinda big and strong but not too bright."

Wilner shook his head.

"You ain't no steelworker because there's no work for you down here. I doubt you're an electrician because you look too damn stupid." The man leveled a tough stare at him. "So unless you want me to dump your ass out on the street you better tell me why you're here."

Wilner casually flipped open his identification. "UPF. What's your name, sir?"

The man swallowed hard. "Sorry, Officer, I didn't realize—"

Wilner cut him off. "I don't care what you realized or not. I asked you your name and the next words out of your mouth better be your first and last name." He gave the man his own stare.

"Anthony Perelli."

"Now, Mr. Perelli, first, I don't like rude people. There was no reason for you to be rude. You're not in New York now. Second, I need to look at some records."

"What kind?"

"Old union records. I was told you guys incorporated most of the individual unions."

"Is this for a case?"

"Mr. Perelli, normally I'd be friendly and chat and tell you. But you were a dick so what I'll do now is tell you. Take me to the room where you store records and do it right now. Understand?"

As they trudged back through a maze of halls that didn't seem possible by the size of the outer walls, Wilner felt guilty for being tough on the man but he was sick of seeing civility disappear because people accepted rudeness.

With a little effort Wilner found himself in front of a row of file cabinets that covered all the union records back to the 1960s. That was some impressive record-keeping.

He settled in and started in the first cabinet. His mind wandered as he flipped though files of records on carpenters and refrigerator repairmen.

Leonard hadn't hesitated to burst through the door. He had no intention of being subtle or using stealth. He wanted these punks' attention on him, not Mari.

He stopped in the doorway with a hammer in one hand and a long, straight screwdriver in the other. This was also a ploy. His blood was up and he wanted to release the animal in him. But not with a rusty claw hammer and screwdriver. Where was the fun in that? Mostly he didn't want Mari to have to see any of the things he wanted to do with these men.

Mari shrieked, "Leonard, no. Run."

Leonard didn't yell, he didn't have the voice for it. He growled instead. "What is your business here?"

The man with the gun in his hand turned to Leonard but didn't raise the pistol. "The school is way behind in its taxes."

"This is the zone. There are no taxes."

The man smiled. "That's what we're working out here, old man. Miss Mari can pay cash or trade. Since you guys seem short on cash we're taking it in trade."

Leonard felt an anger rise in him. A fury he had not felt in years. He smiled at all the things he intended to do to these men. Leonard took a moment to look at each face in the group. He recognized most of them. Then the man in the corner stepped from behind a tall black man. It took a second but Leonard knew him. The eye patch and limp. It was the man he left alive from the old North Miami city hall.

Johann Halleck had tried to obtain as much information as possible about the raiders these settlers called "Zoners." They came in groups of up to eight, were heavily armed men and showed no regard for life. Usually they trashed camps and took women. The last time they had entered Victor's camp they took a sixteen-year-old girl and killed her parents.

Johann had no problem with the idea of killing men like that. He listened as he started to formulate a plan.

Tom Wilner sat at his desk with the moldy, smelly files that Besslia had recovered piled all around him. He knew things were different fifty years ago when there were cops in every city. He had seen movies and read history books about the painstaking detail detectives went through to arrest the right person in serious crimes. He couldn't imagine having resources like that. The files related to the murder of this one girl, Mary

Harris, were almost equal to the whole department's reports for a year now. He knew that oversight was different. That people wanted to know how things were investigated and how the police came to the conclusions they had reached. That was before the world had spiraled out of control. Even before the big terror attacks the public had grown weary of street crime and violence. The movement to find and punish offenders had its own head of steam by the time jihadists came into the picture and started stirring things up.

Now Wilner's problem was using his common sense to see how the detectives back then approached the problem. His first question was still why, if they had a fingerprint and suspects, didn't they just fingerprint the suspects?

His next question was why they released someone like Dadicek who they clearly thought was involved in the crime. That question probably had a lot more to do with the climate at the time.

His next concern was that with the collapse of unified databases, how would he find a man who might have changed his name ten times since the crime? He tried to thumb through one file of reports on a separate subject but the years and moisture had fused the pages together. All he could see was a brief question-and-answer sheet and something about a school. He tried but couldn't find any more readable text.

He also had a single sheet of paper from the worker's hall. It showed that a Janos Dadicek was in the plumber's main union as late as fourteen years ago. His listed address was in the northern section of then Dade County. What was now part of the Miami Quarantine Zone. Wilner thought he might be on the right track. He leaned back in his chair and thought about Mari. He wondered what she was doing at that moment in the Miami Quarantine Zone.

His boss said he couldn't go there on official business but Wilner didn't think that prohibition applied to his personal time. He could go over as a civilian. He had to if for no other reason than to see Mari.

Leonard focused his attention on the man with the gun. The other three showed no weapons. But the man with the eye patch stepped closer for a better look.

Then, without hesitation, Leonard heaved the hammer at the man with the pistol, then turned and darted down the hallway, slowing enough for the men following him to see where he was going. He galloped through the main hallway and out the side door. Cutting across the rear courtyard he paused to make sure all the men had joined the chase. The man with the pistol barreled out of the door followed closely by the others. Leonard noticed the man with the eye patch limped at his own pace, giving the men a chance to catch and subdue Leonard first.

The leader raised the pistol and fired one shot while on the run. A bullet thumped off the vine-covered rear wall a few feet from Leonard.

He concealed his smile as he slammed the handle of the rear gate and ran out into the empty side street toward the vacant apartment buildings that had lost their roofs and windows in the last hurricane nearly fourteen years earlier.

He waited near the first building until his pursuers clearly saw him.

The leader took another wild shot. This one pinged off a lifeless metal streetlight pole.

Leonard knew this building and the catwalk between this one and the one next door. There were also several rear exits.

He couldn't risk letting the man with the pistol getting too close. Even an idiot like that could get lucky.

He bounded up the stairs on the inside of the dreary cement building.

The gang piled in and then spotted him at the top of the stair.

He stepped through the doorway to the hall and waited. He felt the heft of the screwdriver and decided that it would do.

TWENTY-FOUR

Steve Besslia could tell where pavement remained even though he couldn't see any. The grass, weeds and vines had covered anything that was left of the old city floor except a few places where the blacktop bulged in the center of the street.

Victor said, "I think this is where the old police department used to be."

Besslia stared at the two-story cement structure but saw no indication that it had ever served any purpose.

They had made sure no Zoners were around and the settlers had been smart enough to post pickets at strategic points to see if they headed back in this direction.

As they slowly walked through the deserted streets, Victor said, "Are the aliens still coming?"

"Yep."

"They don't know what they're in for."

Besslia looked at the shorter man. "How long have you guys been out of touch?"

Victor shrugged. "I started thinking about finding a new

empty frontier before the ban on immigration. The problem was that there weren't any. Once Florida started to empty out like a milk jug with a hole in the bottom, we knew this was the spot to be. It was after the Quarantine Zone was set up. Maybe six years."

"Long time."

"We still at war?"

"Yeah, but not with the same countries as we were when you went underground."

"Where are we fighting now?"

"Syria, Somalia and closing down operations in Nicaragua."

"What did Nicaragua do?"

"Jihadists took them over and used the country as a place to launch attacks into Mexico."

"Central America has Muslims now?"

"Not too many. That's why we stepped in." Besslia added, "Oh, yeah, Germany invaded Poland a few months back."

"Where are they now?"

"Still there."

"The Poles put up that much resistance?"

"No, not really. A nuke went off in Tehran and it spooked the Germans. By the time everyone figured out it was an Iranian nuclear test gone bad too many Allied troops had been moved up to block the Germans. Now it's all negotiations."

"Any more 9/11 attacks?"

"Every year."

Victor shook his head. "That's why we came here. Same old shit every year."

"I'm not questioning your logic."

Now they were next to the building looking for a way in. Several of the windows were exposed but an empty doorway would be better. Finally they found a way in. Johann stepped up to go inside with Victor and Besslia. The others stood guard outside.

Johann said, "Victor, you really need to find a way to stand up to the Zoners."

"That's easy for you to say. We're not fighters. That's one of the reasons we came all the way out here."

Besslia listened to their conversation as they used radiant tube lights, a form of depleted nuclear waste that kept the small lights running for more than a year of continuous use. The building looked completely cleared out until a stairway into the lower levels revealed a storage room.

Besslia could hear the rustling of rats and other animals that had made a home in the dark, dank room. Some wire mesh ran along part of the room but time and possibly vandals had taken their toll on the building. Besslia wiped off a sign with the palm of his hand. The square wooden placard apparently hooked into the screen and he could only make out the first few letters: EVIDE.

Johann said, "Evidence."

They were on the right track.

Leonard took several deep breaths as he waited for the first man to come through the door. He tried to get in the mood for this so he could derive some form of pleasure, but it had happened too quickly for the buildup to really kick in.

He knew that he could take his time with the others and hunt them down. That would give him something to occupy his mind until he went back to deal with the cop. Leonard also knew he shouldn't let the man with the eye patch get away on the chance he might tell someone what he saw and who killed the men in North Miami city hall.

He heard some shouts and footsteps and could tell they were running down the wrong hallway and hadn't even come up the stairs yet. Leonard rolled his eyes at the incompetence of these thugs. He remembered gangs in the early days of the Quarantine Zone that terrified people. Now all they could field were mopes like these.

He stepped out of the doorway to get someone's attention and was surprised by a bullet striking the solid wall next to his head. He ducked and scrambled behind cover and instantly heard heavy footfalls on the stairs. He stood, took another breath and swung his hand with the screwdriver just as the man appeared in the doorway.

The blow drove the screwdriver completely through the man's muscular neck. The impact of the handle striking as the shaft exited on the opposite side threw the man down the stairs.

Leonard looked down and saw the pistol on the floor at his feet. He had struck the right target by luck. He now stepped from behind the doorway in a new light. No longer the hunted.

The remaining three men gathered around their fallen leader, staring at the thick screwdriver securely wedged in his neck.

Then all three men gazed up at Leonard and stared. Their eyes gave it all away. Without a tough guy with a gun they were just scared residents of the Quarantine Zone.

The two taller men darted in opposite directions. Only the man with the eye patch remained, frozen in fear.

Leonard smiled, feeling his buildup begin.

"That's right, son. You bothered the wrong schoolteacher."

TWENTY-FIVE

Steve Besslia peered beyond the fence that used to separate the evidence room from the other office space. A few rats scurried from the radiant light but nothing unusual appeared in the beam. Johann Halleck stepped up behind him.

"You really think we can find anything in that mess?"

"I want to try."

Then Besslia paused. Something didn't look right in relation to the rest of the cluttered, moldy room.

"What is it?" asked Johann.

"This looks like a façade. See." He shined the light on a set of file cabinets and boxes.

"No, I don't."

"Nothing is disturbed. The boxes are all lined up and evenly coated with grime. Except for over here." He moved the light. "There is a path where the floor is clean and the front of that row of cabinets have no dust."

Johann considered the scene, then said, "Like someone uses that aisle as a path."

"Exactly."

Victor moved up next to them and raised his round face to them. "Isn't this what you were looking for?"

Besslia nodded.

"Then why don't we go in?"

"We want to make sure there are no surprises."

"Surprises here, like what?"

Just then a shotgun blast boomed in the enclosed room like an artillery piece. The plaster on the ceiling above the three men crumbled as the buckshot ate into it.

They ducked and scrambled behind a stack of crates.

Besslia looked at Victor and said, "A surprise like that."

Tom Wilner hesitated at the bridge that crossed over to the Quarantine Zone. If he really was going on his own time he didn't want to show his official ID. He needed to cross like anyone else.

He looked at the two young bored National Guardsmen leaning on the rail of the old cement bridge.

He didn't want to make them suspicious but wasn't sure how to proceed.

Then he saw a group of nine younger people walk onto the bridge like they had done it everyday. They looked like newcomers, hair cut in straight fashionable lines, clothes from mainstream stores. One girl had a Jersey accent.

He fell in behind the group as they stopped next to the guardsmen. The private flirted with a blond girl next to him while the sergeant counted and then said to a hunched-over young man, "Twenty-seven bucks."

"C'mon, man, don't we get a frequent-traveler discount?"

The sergeant stared at him.

"What about a group discount?"

The sergeant said, "It's about to go to four bucks a head."

The young man gathered money from everyone and paid the sergeant.

Wilner stepped up and reached in his front pocket.

"Five bucks," said the sergeant with his hand out.

"You just charged them three."

"And I'm charging you five."

"Why?"

"Because I can. If you want to cross you'll pay it."

Wilner resisted the urge to badge or threaten him. He needed to get across and see Mari. He pulled out a five dollar silver coin, a Carter humanitarian coin, and slapped it into the sergeant's hand.

He crossed the bridge, knowing he had less than a mile's walk to the school. He didn't want to risk a UPF car over here on personal time. He still carried his UPF-issued pistol. He wasn't crazy, just trying to stick to his orders that his commander had given him.

As soon as he started on the street an old pickup truck with potatoes in the back slowed. An elderly man with graying hair said, "You want a ride?" in a thick Spanish accent.

Wilner smiled and found himself at the front of the school a few minutes later. The older man wouldn't accept any money for his trouble. "That's just how things are done here. Tell the people up in the district that things aren't that bad here."

Wilner smiled. "I will." He watched the old converted steam truck chug away.

He walked up the path to the school and froze when he found Mari in the front lobby with two other teachers.

Mari was sobbing when she looked at Wilner with red, puffy eyes.

Leonard loped after the fleeing man with the eye patch, enjoying the feeling as it rose inside him. The man hobbled from the wound in his upper leg he had received at the last fight in the city hall. A rough bandage was wrapped around his thigh. Leonard had his compact, German paratroop knife in his hand but the blade was still concealed in the handle. He had ignored the other two men. He recognized them as regulars at the Chaos Pit and would be able to track them down easily enough. But this man could identify him. He needed to be silenced.

Although the man was only in his thirties he had no endurance. Leonard could tell he was struggling with each step, especially when he cut across soggy grass or through brush-covered lots. If anyone noticed the two-man race they didn't acknowledge it. People in the zone preferred to mind their own business.

Now they were on a busier street. Leonard knew there was a shop that repaired steam-powered cars and two decent food markets. He slowed his pace, not wanting to draw any attention.

He watched the man duck into the fruit market. Leonard calmly slowed to a walk and made his way around to the back of the market that featured fresh tomatoes and pears. He pulled out the combat spike on his knife and gazed at the extended steel. There was still some of Lisa's blood on the base of it. He never cleaned it after using it on a person. It added to the thrill.

He leaned against a dead, rotting black olive tree behind

the market and contained his smile as the younger man with the eye patch blundered out of the back door. He froze as he looked at the casual way Leonard leaned on the tree. Then his eyes tracked down to the open combat spike in Leonard's right hand.

"End of the line, son."

Leonard took a step forward when he heard a noise. He froze midstep when he realized it was a cry from children. A cry of terror.

Besslia drew his pistol while they crouched behind the boxes.

Johann placed a gentle hand on his arm and said, "Wait a second. Let me try." He stood and moved toward the opening in the fence where the path started. He called out to the unknown and unseen person with the gun. "We're not here to hurt you."

He heard the racking of the shotgun's action. He stepped onto the path and raised his hands. From his peripheral vision he saw Steve Besslia aim his pistol.

"At least say something before you blast me."

A man's voice came from the end of the path. "This area is restricted." The voice wasn't strong but it had a certain official tone to it.

Johann stopped just inside the fence.

"Who are you trying to keep out?"

"Anyone not authorized to enter."

"What if we're authorized?"

Johann could hear someone moving and then saw a light from another room. A rail-thin figure with a shotgun in his hands moved across the light from the room. Now the voice came from the new position.

"Are you from the government?"

"Yes."

The guardian was ready with a quick question. "What agency?"

Johann hesitated, then heard Besslia shout, "Unified Police Force."

There was a pause, then the guardian said, "You mean the state police?"

"Yes."

"Step forward and let me see you. All of you."

Johann waited for Victor and Besslia to join him, then they all slowly advanced.

A beam of light fell across them and a voice said, "Let me see some ID."

Besslia fumbled with his wallet, then held up his badge.

There was another pause then the guardian said, "Christ, finally some help. Come ahead."

The three men slowly advanced until they saw the boney man in a tattered blue uniform shirt step from the rear room.

"Jim Sewell, Naples PD." He held out a skeletal hand.

Johann took it carefully. "I'm Johann Halleck, this is Steve Besslia and that guy is Victor. He's our guide."

The man slumped back against the wall. "I've been waiting for relief since we suspended operations."

Besslia said, "Suspended operations? How long ago?"

Sewell shook his head. "Must be close to a year now."

Johann realized the poor former cop had lost it in the chaos of the past ten years. He knew they had to state their mission quickly and clearly. "We're here for some reports on a case."

Sewell brightened. "Got a case number?"

Besslia read off the reference number from the fingerprint database.

Sewell said, "No problem, just follow me back here."

The man shuffled his toothpick legs into the lighted room and Johann followed. He already was thinking of how to save this poor, crazy man.

TWENTY-SIX

Wilner sat with his arm around Mari as she recounted what had happened. Not only was she unnerved by the threats from the street gang but now she was concerned about the safety of Leonard who had risked his life to lure the men away from the school.

"I'll go look for him."

"I'm afraid what you might find." She started crying again.

Wilner couldn't convince Mari to wait as she fell in next to him. He trotted down the street behind the school and ducked into several empty buildings to see if he could find any sign of the missing Leonard.

Mari said, "Maybe he did outrun them."

"How old is he?"

"I don't know. At least fifty, but he looks very fit."

They cut across a vacant lot onto the busier market street and stopped at one store to ask if there had been anything unusual. No one had seen anyone being chased.

Then they saw a gathering of people at the far end of the street. Wilner had to speed up to catch the panicked Mari as she raced toward the disturbance.

Fifteen people had gathered around the pond that fed into the border canal. Mari pushed through the crowd with Wilner right behind her.

He took in the scene and waited for Mari to say if she recognized anyone involved. Either living or dead.

Leonard could have finished the cowering cornered man but the scream from the child hit him deeply. It immediately took him back to his own childhood where his screams for help were consistently ignored. Weeks at a time locked in the shuttered "hurricane safe room" his father had constructed.

He turned toward the scream and saw a woman bent over at the retaining pond that linked to the border canal. He looked back at the man with the eye patch, then grunted as he knew he'd have to help the woman and child.

His muscular legs carried him across the muddy field faster than he even thought they could. Before he had reached the edge of the water he saw the woman futilely reaching for the outstretched hand of a young girl with blond hair that fanned out in the water. Another body floated facedown in the water behind the girl.

Leonard dove into the murky water and in a second had covered the fifteen feet to the girl. He felt the vines and weeds catch his booted feet and realized how the floating person had probably drowned.

He wrapped his arms around the girl and felt her tiny arms around his shoulders. He kicked hard and then felt the muddy bottom. The mud was so thick he ended up tossing the girl to her mother, then turning back to the body. As soon as he grabbed the loose shirt by the shoulder he knew it was a man. He tugged the lifeless figure closer to shore, then took a second to catch his breath. He noticed other people rushing over from the market.

By the time he felt hands pull him from the water, someone was already giving CPR to the man he had pulled from the water.

He looked past the crowd to see the man with the eye patch take one more peek at the scene, then disappear around the other side of the market.

Steve Besslia was amazed that anyone could live in the rear of this building for so long. Naples was abandoned not long after the big storm. It was just so isolated that no one worried about making it into a forbidden area.

He had sat and listened to Officer Jim Sewell but he really wanted to view the data disk in the old format that looked like a one-inch coin. The disk held all the information related to the case that was referenced in the fingerprint database. He held the disk tightly in one hand and waited to tell the officer they had to be going.

The wild man in a police uniform explained that he had been a patrolman for about a year when things went bad.

He said, "My captain said, 'Sewell, keep an eye on the evidence locker and don't let any assholes get in there.'"

Besslia had so many questions that he just stared at the man, trying to figure out his age and what the hell could be going on in that confused mind. He had a thick matted beard and eyebrows that looked like the underbrush surrounding the city. His skin was white with deep flecks of embedded dirt.

Johann used his soothing voice. "What have you been eating?"

"I had military nutrition packs for a while. Then I found a cache of canned food down the street. The rats here are fat and lazy so they make up most of my meals."

Besslia was speechless.

Victor turned away and held his hand to his mouth to forestall vomiting.

"Is there anyone else? Do you have anyone to talk to?"

"Sometimes I talk to the dogs."

Besslia perked up at that, thinking about the smart dogs at the old Pompano police station. "Wait . . . so you can understand them?"

"No, but they wag their tails when I pet them and talk to them."

Besslia sagged. He scanned the well-kept room they were in now. The file cabinets were arranged in tight formation and little dust had made its way into this room. In the corner was a little cot and a stack of paperback books.

Besslia pointed to the corner. "Is that where you live?"

He nodded. "I take one day off a week."

"What do you do?"

"Visit the rest of the city."

"Then you know what's happened. There's no reason to stay here."

"I have no reason to go anywhere else."

"You just guard the forgotten evidence of the police department?"

"I guard the whole station but this is the most important part."

He seemed rational for a guy who had essentially lived in a cave.

Finally Besslia stood up. "We need to be going, Officer. Why don't you come with us?"

The walking stick stood up, the shotgun still in his hands. "My duty is here."

"Your duty is done. No one could ask any more of you."

"I'll visit the settlers and Victor now that I know where they are, but this is my primary assignment."

Besslia was going to say something else, but Johann leaned in and said, "Give him time, Steve. This is a big shock to him."

Besslia nodded and looked up at Sewell. "Thanks for the disk. We'll be back to check on you soon."

"Wait a minute." Sewell raised his weapon slightly.

"What?"

"That's evidence. You can't take it out of here." Now he had the barrel of the old shotgun pointed right at Besslia.

Tom Wilner stood at the edge of the crowd and watched the woman wail over the body of the dead man. They were both young, in their twenties. Mari had stooped down to an older man with gray hair that now hung into his face, dripping water onto the little girl he held in his arms.

Mari hugged the older man and called him Leonard.

Wilner knew now that this was the handyman who had been helping Mari and had just saved her life. It looked like he had taken time out to save the little girl as well.

Wilner kneeled down and checked the pulse of the prone man. He was dead and his body temperature had already dropped. He looked at the girl, checking her eyes and pulse. She was in shock, but someone had already retrieved a blanket to wrap around her. There were others who knew what they were doing as well.

Mari helped Leonard to his feet and guided him toward Wilner. The older man kept his face down and coughed. Then mumbled something to Mari and turned to head back toward the market.

Mari turned toward Wilner and said, "He thought he might vomit and didn't want anyone to see." She looked toward him, then back to Wilner. "Would you check on him, please? I think he'd be all right with another man."

Wilner nodded and jogged after Leonard.

Besslia froze as the crazy former cop pointed the shotgun and said, "That is evidence. It stays here."

"You have a computer or power?"

Sewell shook his head.

"Then how am I supposed to see what's on the disk?"

He hesitated and seemed to get more agitated with the questions.

Besslia started to move toward the distraught man when he heard him suck in a breath and he knew that meant he was going to fire.

Suddenly Johann leaped in front of Besslia just as the shotgun erupted, spewing gases and a blinding muzzle flash in the dimly lit room.

Besslia felt Johann's body weight as the pellets from the blast knocked him back. Then he slid onto the ground, blood already showing on his chin, neck and chest.

Besslia reached for his pistol while Sewell was still in shock that he fired.

From the floor, Johann coughed, "Steve, don't."

That was enough to freeze everything.

The look on Sewell's face said it all as he dropped the

weapon then jumped forward, landing on his knees to render aid to the fallen Johann.

From behind him, Besslia heard Victor mumble, "What is he?"

Besslia stepped past the men on the ground and picked up the shotgun. He turned to see Johann sitting up.

Sewell was still speechless.

Victor said, "You're a cyborg, right?"

Johann shook his head. "Nothing so fancy. Just an old round with weak powder. The pellets just skimmed me."

Sewell started to cry. "Man, I'm sorry, I'm sorry, it just went off."

Johann patted him on the back and said, "It is okay, but now you have to help yourself. Victor's group might be able to use a man like you."

Besslia looked down at the calm Johann knowing he had jumped in front of him to save his life.

TWENTY-SEVEN

Leonard Hall didn't think the cop would recognize him but he was nervous about him getting too good of a look. He had also hoped to catch the man with the eye patch but so far none of that had worked out. He had stopped inside the small fruit market just to step out of the drizzle for a moment. Not that it made much difference now that he was soaked with the noxious water of the retention pond. He could tell that the man was dead. But he couldn't let the woman and little girl see him just floating there.

He was about to dispose of the gang leader's body and retrieve his favorite screwdriver when he saw the cop, Wilner, jogging up the slight incline to the market. He didn't want to make it seem like he was running away or avoiding him. He saw no alternative but to confront the man. Then he remembered his combat knife still in his pants. He could just finish the job right now.

The problem was that right at this moment he didn't feel the buildup, the urge. The detective was still working on the case and Leonard had heard that they had found the prosthetic hand of the girl he had dropped into the furnace at the hospital, but he didn't think this cop was close to figuring out who had done it.

He gripped his knife as the cop came closer. He held it behind his back and let the gravity feed open the blade. He saw no other alternative.

Then he noticed the outhouse behind the market. The current state of plumbing in the zone had made outhouses with portable buckets the safest and cleanest form of sanitation. Before they started using them the waste problem had started to get out of control fast. An engineer from Romania had explained the need to dispose of human waste properly. Now the little structure offered him a chance of hiding.

He had to make a choice and do it now.

Mari Saltis decided to take control of the drowning scene. She went to the mother and little girl and took her jacket off, wrapping them as best she could. She looked up at several men standing there silently. "We need blankets and someone to find a dry place to move them to right away."

Two of the men jumped at the orders.

She checked the girl's eyes again and patted her blond hair.

The woman sniffled. "She just slid off the bank and then the weeds tangled around her feet. Barry thought he could just snatch her out. Instead he slid deeper and deeper."

"It'll be all right."

"That man. Where'd he go?"

"He went to dry off and clean up. I'm sure you'll see him."

"I recognized him."

"He's lived here a long time."

"He went out with my neighbor."

"I didn't know Leonard had a girlfriend."

"She was a prostitute. They found her dead last year."

Mari just stared at the young woman.

Tom Wilner could see Leonard standing inside the market as he approached. Then the older man shot across the rear lot into the wooden outhouse and pulled the door tight.

Wilner slowed as he reached the outhouse and called out, "Leonard, you all right?"

He got no response. He was a little worried and started to pull on the handle.

Then he heard, "I need some time."

"That was some pretty brave stuff back there. These canals and ponds are deadly." He rattled the handle but it was locked.

From inside he heard a groan and retching. "Look, I'd rather not see anyone right now. I'm fine."

Wilner hesitated then said, "Okay, I'll see if I can help Mari."

He walked away, a little disquieted. The voice didn't match the behavior or retching.

TWENTY-EIGHT

It had taken nearly four hours to get back to the settlement outside of Naples. Besslia was happy with what he had accomplished. Not only had he made a makeshift stretcher from a strip of canvas and two metal poles that had supported shelves inside the old evidence room, but he had convinced Officer Jim Sewell to come with the group. The wild man who had snapped in the line of duty realized he had gone too far and didn't want to leave Johann's side.

For his part, Johann had convinced both Sewell and Victor that the pellets had not pierced his skin drastically. Besslia knew that was just a lie and that his odd and superior physiology was what had kept him from dying on the cold, damp floor of the old police station.

The trek through the underbrush and along the paths, which only the men from the settlement knew how to find, made Besslia think about his life. On the east coast he was just a patrolman who had served in the army but had never seen combat. He was comfortable in his state-assigned condo and simple job of patrolling nearly empty streets. But here, just a hundred and twenty miles west, he could make a difference. They needed someone to maintain order. They needed an armed man to help deal with the Zoners raiding into the wilderness. No one in the state government cared. This area all the way north to Sarasota was officially designated as not habitable and was not provided with any services.

They entered the camp just as the sun was setting, casting a weak glow into the endless cloud cover. Several campfires and a few hanging oil lamps, which were fueled by the remains of abandoned cars or forgotten oil drums, lit the camp.

The evening meal was about to begin in the community shelter, which sat in the center of the settlement. Four long tables could hold the thirty or so children and forty adults.

Victor led Sewell toward the group. As he ducked into the big tent he said in a loud voice, "This is Jim. He's going to be staying with us."

Besslia could tell a few of the women were skeptical looking at the wild hair and dark furtive eyes of the new arrival.

Besslia sat with Johann, Sewell, Victor and Victor's wife and young son as they ate a stew with fresh vegetables and a meat he couldn't identify. He held a piece at the end of a fork and stared at it for a moment.

Victor whispered, "Opossum."

Besslia looked at him.

"Tastes like cat."

Besslia's eyes widened and Victor smiled.

"Just kidding, can't tell it from chicken."

"Why not use the chickens here in the camp?"

"Because they give us eggs whereas the opossums are plentiful and if we don't thin them out they get into camp and steal the eggs. Trust me, people have been eating opossum for hundreds of years."

Besslia took a leap of faith and continued to eat, deciding he liked the stew. In fact, he liked the whole idea of the camp.

He looked across at Johann, who had started on his second bowl of stew, and said, "The pellet marks on your face are already healing up. They're just red marks now."

Johann nodded, checking to make sure no one was listening to them. "By tomorrow I will be fine. I need time to concentrate on healing and stopping the bleeding. The wounds on my chest are much more severe."

"What's it feel like to heal yourself like that?"

"I'm not sure, I never thought of it like that before. I just think about the injury and, if I can avoid physical exertion, I can heal it. I guess it tingles somewhat."

"What's the worst you were ever hurt?"

Again Johann looked from side to side. "A German artillery shell not only blew shrapnel through me but the concussion injured my internal organs. Then I had to retreat with the rest of my unit of Norwegian partisans. I had to lay still for nearly a week. The partisans thought I was dead and left me in an abandoned building. I think I was found by a German patrol, which also mistook me for a corpse. It was more than a month before I felt normal again."

Besslia shook his head as he did at many of the stories that his friend told him.

Johann said, "I still have a couple of scars from that one."

"I didn't think you guys scarred."

"Oh, yes, if the injury is severe enough or if we can't concentrate for some reason. Of course, if it's that important to someone they can always find a time and place to concentrate and heal the scar. But I don't mind the ones from the artillery shell. They're like a keepsake. I also have one from a knife fight. Just a personal decision."

Now Victor leaned away from his conversation with his wife and said to Besslia. "I'm glad you visited and hope you return but you must keep our location a secret."

"You don't want to see if I can get you some form of aid?"

"Like what? Food? We eat better than you. We have all we need."

"Except security. What if the Zoners find you again?"

Victor frowned. "We're working on an early warning system where we can hide if they come back."

"I've been thinking that if I stayed, I might provide enough firepower to scare them off for good."

Victor and Johann stared at him.

"I'm serious. I could help."

Johann reached across the table and placed his hand on Besslia's arm. "I know you are. I also know you could be of great help here but you have a calling and a task right now. The UPF is more important everyday. Especially with the newcomers."

"But what about the Zoners?"

"I intend to stay."

"You."

"God did not give me the abilities I have and not expect me to use them to help others. This has been my family's mandate for centuries. You know this. Besides, Wilner needs the information on that disk and you have to help him find the killer."

"Me, I'm no help to a guy like that."

"You don't give yourself enough credit. You're the only one he counts on. Without you, Tom Wilner would be lost."

"What will I do without you?"

Johann smiled. "I'll be back soon. As soon as these people are safe again."

Johann's smile made Besslia feel like he did have a reason to go back. He finished his meal and prepared to leave first thing in the morning.

TWENTY-NINE

Tom Wilner sat next to Mari Saltis at a large, round table where she and some of the teachers from the school shared barbequed chicken from one of the nearby shops. The shop-keeper's daughters attended the school and he provided food for the school as well as the occasional dinner for the teachers.

Some of the teachers' husbands sat with them and it felt like a party back in the District. In fact, the fresh chicken reminded him of barbeques from when he was a child back in New Jersey before the great changes that had occurred in the country that started slowly with the first Islamic attacks in September of 2001. He was too young then to know how profoundly life on Earth would change. But throughout his years in the marines and as a cop he was surprised that life continued to evolve no matter what seemed to spring up in front of him.

Just a few months ago he would've bet he'd be in Europe fighting to contain Germany and he never would've thought that he would discover that humans were not alone as the only hominid species on the planet. Now he sat in a foreign country just twenty miles from his home, eating a meal as ordinary and pleasant as any he had experienced as a child.

Mari said, "I wish Leonard had felt well enough to eat. He certainly earned it today."

Wilner nodded.

The woman next to Wilner said, "Mari told us you're trying to find the Vampire."

"I can't believe you guys named him. Does anyone know how many killings have occurred all together?"

The woman shook her head. "No one really knows because of the way rumors start. I heard about them as far back as seven years ago. The last one I know of was the two dancers from the Chaos Pit."

Mari added, "I saw the house and the people moving the bodies."

Someone down the table said, "I heard four gang members were found down at the old North Miami city hall with neck wounds last week."

Wilner looked up.

Then Mari said, "I heard about a prostitute that was killed. Leonard might have known her."

Wilner looked at Mari's perfect face. "Have any of you ever heard of a man named Janos Dadicek?"

An older Jamaican woman sitting across the wide table looked up and spoke for the first time. "There's a family named Dadicek that lives somewhere over by the Zone River."

"Do you know them?"

"I know what they are. A bunch of criminals is what they are."

"Is one named Janos?"

"Heard that name but don't know which one it is. They're traders. They go into the district and out into the Everglades and bring back things people need."

"What makes them criminals?"

"Sometimes they bring back women."

Wilner had his first good lead on Janos Dadicek.

Tom Wilner agreed to meet Steve Besslia at the UPF district office just after lunch. He was shocked by his friend's condition. He had dozens of scratches and cuts and his uniform was spotted with mud, blood and green stains Wilner couldn't identify.

"What the hell happened to you?"

Besslia held up the data disk. "I found the case file on the burglary in Naples that listed your killer's fingerprint."

"How did you ever find it?"

"It's a long story but this is why I rushed back to you."

Wilner took the small disk and placed it in the slot that read info. The computer screen showed an index of material in the old format of police files before the UPF took over all enforcement and investigative functions.

Wilner said, "There was no violence, just a burglary."

Besslia, looking over his shoulder, said, "Looks like the woman in the apartment heard the intruder and got to the cops."

"Look here, a cop questioned a man on the next street for suspicious activity."

"Suspicious activity? What's that?"

"Not sure, but I don't think they could arrest people for that kind of stuff back then."

"No shit, they just let people wander around even if they were suspicious?"

Wilner shrugged. "The man produced a Broward Community College student identification card in the name of Leonard Dawson."

"The district used to be called Broward County."

"I didn't know there were ever any colleges here."

"That's a long time ago. Look, more than forty years. We weren't even born yet."

"So this is our man. I think I might know where he is."

Besslia said, "Janos Dadicek?"

"Has to be. Look at the dates."

"Would a Simolit go to a community college? Are you sure?"

Wilner said, "There is a family named Dadicek that lives in the zone. They're some kind of traders. They trade women into prostitution sometimes."

"Zoners."

"What?"

"Janos Dadicek is a Zoner; a raider into the western wilderness."

"What are you talking about, Steve?"

Besslia took his time and told him the whole story of his trip.

Leonard Hall was exhausted. He had expended a lot of energy saving the little girl then, after avoiding the cop, retrieved his favorite screwdriver from the neck of the gang leader. He had dragged the body to the top of the empty building and counted on the rats and birds coming in the empty windows to do their job. Even if he was found forensics were so poor down here that no one would be able to tell when he died.

Now he sat in the Chaos Pit hoping to catch a glimpse of the other gang members. Especially the guy with the missing eye. He sat at a table by himself and ate a sandwich made of synthetic beef and synthetic lettuce. Basically a way to eat a few calories and nutrients with some texture but no real taste.

He looked up at the dancers but one of them caught his eye. Sally, a regular with only one arm, smiled at him but she did nothing for him. He missed Darla and Lisa. They made a real connection with him. For the first time in his life he regretted letting his drive overwhelm him. Right now he wished either girl was here to sit with him and hear about his day.

Before he got too wound up in dreaming about some imaginary life he saw two familiar faces. The two gang members had just entered the front door.

Leonard made sure they didn't look his way. He had time. He needed to do this at the right time and the right place. Not only to keep suspicions to a minimum but to let the build-up go on as long as possible.

It was late for anyone to be in the district commander's office. Tom Wilner and Steve Besslia sat across the wide desk and listened as the commander barked out his opinions while wiping down his bald crown.

The commander said, "You think raiders from the zone are grabbing women from the wilderness and selling them?"

Besslia nodded as he said, "Yes, sir."

"Why were you over in that wasteland again?"

"The Naples area is part of our jurisdiction. I was over

there looking for some evidence that might relate to Willie's killer."

"In Naples? What's over there?"

"A report that references a fingerprint that's the same as the killer."

"Jesus, Naples has been abandoned for years. When was the report entered into the database?"

Besslia hesitated.

The commander said, "What?"

Wilner stepped in. "That's the confusing part, boss. The report is forty years old."

"And it has a fingerprint that matches the killer from last week?"

"Yes, sir."

"Is that the only reference?"

"No, there's one from a murder in Pompano forty-nine years ago. And a few since then."

"So your killer is like ninety. I woulda thought you'd notice that when you saw him the first night."

"I just saw he had gray hair. But he wasn't old. He moved like a cat. I never saw his face clearly."

"So you two knuckleheads want permission to go into the zone and find these raiders?"

"Yes, sir."

"And you'll look into your killer over there at the same time?"

"They may be connected."

"Willie, you think I'm a moron? I told you we need you guys here. The newcomers are our main concern. We gotta keep things quiet here."

Besslia said, "The people over on the west coast are residents of Florida. The UPF is supposed to protect them too."

"But from what you say they're not paying any taxes. We're already short-staffed. Give me one reason why we should get involved in something like that?"

Wilner looked him in the eye and said, "Because it's the right thing to do."

THIRTY

Johann Halleck had to admit to himself that he missed doing things like this. He had twelve men from the settlement in a clearing showing them how to operate the guns that they recovered from the old Naples police station and the ones that Steve Besslia had left him. They weren't wasting ammunition, just learning the actions and sighting.

Johann called out to them as Jim Sewell walked between them, correcting positions and techniques.

Johann said, "This is not like a war. One good ambush and we should be done with these raiders. I won't worry about how you clean the weapons, just fire and reload"

The moonlight peeked through some clouds. The gas lights surrounding the clearing provided a good low-light environment.

Victor stood up with a shotgun and walked over to Johann. "Where should we try and ambush them?"

"Since we don't know their schedule or where they go after

leaving the zone, I would say we get as close to their departure point as possible. Maybe even go into the Quarantine Zone and hit them at their base where they won't expect it."

"Is that safe?"

"Victor, none of this is safe. If you do nothing, it's not safe. Don't worry, I'll be there with you."

Victor nodded and leaned in closer. "That shotgun shell didn't have faulty powder, how did you survive? I'm trusting you with our settlement's safety. Trust me a little bit."

Johann looked at him and considered the request.

"It's complicated."

"You're not really part machine are you? I said you were a cyborg because I was excited."

"No."

"Alien?"

"No, I was born right here on Earth. In Norway, to be precise."

"Then what?"

"I'm sort of another direction in the evolution of apes. Human took one route and my people took another."

Victor stared at him. "I've heard rumors of immortals that live among us. I always associated them with Eastern Europeans."

"That's another family in my race."

"How old are you?"

"Three hundred and fifty-seven."

Victor looked unfazed.

"Any special powers other than healing?"

Johann leveled a stare at him and said, "I'm really good at crossword puzzles."

———

Leonard Hall waited patiently while the two men drank the home-brewed beer served at the bar. They were subdued, talking between themselves. Leonard smiled because he knew what they were talking about.

After an hour they both stood and headed toward the front door.

Leonard was careful not to rush out behind them. He didn't want anyone to connect him to whatever might happen to them. He eased up and turned toward the door, nodding to the one-armed dancer and laying down a ten-zone credit note on the stage.

She smiled and winked.

He slipped out the door without drawing any attention. Immediately he saw the two men walking west on the dusty empty street. He fell in at a slightly faster pace and pulled his combat knife. He worked the spike into an open position and used the shadows to creep ever closer to the two men.

They talked in low tones as the plan formed in his head.

He stayed in the shadows and came up on their right side, striking hard and fast into the first man's neck. The blow was perfect. The release inside him intense. The man dropped so quickly and quietly that his friend thought he had stumbled.

He turned to his fallen comrade and said, "Too much beer?"

Then Leonard stepped from the shadows. Before the man could react Leonard plunged the spike into the man's leg, just above his knee. Yanking it out fast he stuck the man's other leg making him topple back, his hands reaching for the pain and trying to stop the spurt of blood that came from each side.

Leonard squatted down and put the sharpened tip of the spike to the man's throat.

"Where's your buddy with the eye patch?"

"Sammy? I don't know. We all ran in different directions."

"Where's he live?"

The man started to cry. He pointed west. "Right up this street. That's where we were headed. He usually goes to the club with us."

"Where you buy beer with other people's money; your taxes."

"No, man. No more. You showed us we weren't cut out for it."

"Which house does Sammy live in?"

He kept pointing. "Four or five houses up on the right."

Leonard put a little pressure on the spike, breaking the skin and causing a tiny stream of blood to run down the man's neck. The sight of it excited Leonard.

The man swallowed hard and said, "I swear to God that's the truth."

"How can I be sure?"

"You can kill me if I'm lying."

Leonard thrust the spike all the way through his thick neck and held it there as the man slowly turned his eyes toward him then went still.

When Leonard looked up from his bloody work he knew the man had been telling the truth. Sammy with the eye patch was staring at him from across the street.

THIRTY-ONE

Sammy Cyclops, a name he had been called for so long he now accepted it, gaped at the scene in front of him. His friend, Raul, seemed to stare at him even though the long spike was all the way in his neck. The handyman from the school looked up and their eyes met. He had seen the man at work. First in the old North Miami city hall, then at the school and now with the last witnesses; all except for him.

He managed to screw up enough courage to turn and run toward the busier area of the northern part of the zone. He ran without looking back because he knew it didn't matter. If the handyman was gaining on him he couldn't run any faster and he didn't want to know what was coming.

He was younger than the killer but the older man was in good shape. He had stabbed half-a-dozen younger men to death and outrun them at the school. He had acted like anything but an old man. He hardly acted like a man. The way he moved and stayed so calm. He was more like a superman.

Sammy gulped air as he turned one corner after another,

knowing that if he slowed down his life was over. His life may not be much but he didn't want to lose it.

His single eye searched for some safe harbor. He had lost the other eye to a simple infection before there were any working doctors or medicine down in the zone. That's when he had acquired the obvious nickname. But down here, with no legal documents or courts, your name was what people called you. No one had called him Sammy Guilla in years.

Finally, several blocks away from where he had seen the demonic handyman, he slowed. There were a few lights on this street that everyone now called Market Row because of the shops. A few of the beverage and food stores were still open and a series of weak, gas-powered streetlights marked the sidewalk. A few people wandered around but no one paid attention to an out-of-breath, one-eyed bully like Sammy. He and his gang had exacted a tax from several of these store owners over the years but now he was a solo act.

He started to catch his breath and his mind returned to rational thought. But he wasn't sure how rational it was to think of a man as a superman. There were rumors of immortal beings living among them. Some people said that they were just waiting for humans to kill themselves off so that they could live peacefully and forever. Sammy never paid much attention to the rumors until now. How else could the handyman do everything that he had?

He shivered, between the sweat and light drizzle he was now soaked through his light shirt.

He ducked into a doorway to escape the rain and relaxed slightly. Directly across the street was a group of young people under a small café's awning. They laughed at someone's joke and several looked across the street at Sammy. He didn't care that he was the butt of someone's joke as long as they noticed him. He leaned on the door frame and sucked in the cool night air. It burned his lungs but at least he was still breathing. Then he felt a cough rise up in his chest and the power of his raspy cough forced him to lean forward.

He felt a swish of air and heard a thump. Glancing over his shoulder he saw that the handyman had come in through the empty building and swung his spiked weapon at Sammy's neck. It was now lodged in the door frame.

Sammy stumbled forward into the street and spun. The older handyman smiled as he yanked the spike out of the old wooden frame. He stepped toward Sammy, forcing him to trip backward and then catch himself.

He felt a hand on his back as he careened into the table where the young people were sitting.

"Get off me, you smelly drunk," said a male's voice.

Sammy straightened and looked back toward the handyman. He had no choice, he had to take his best shot and stand his ground. Maybe someone would help him from the table. His single eye searched for a weapon to use. Anything—a stick or butter knife.

Then he looked toward the street.

It was empty.

He turned his head to get a good look up both sides of the street. There was no sign of the killer handyman.

Sammy's hands trembled and his legs felt weak. He was safe for now. It was times like this he wished there were cops in the zone so he could tell someone who might help him.

Tom Wilner and Steve Besslia had taken one of the nice government hives down to the zone. It was a rare official visit, sanctioned by their commander. The guy was an administrative bureaucrat but he knew the right thing to do when he saw it.

Besslia said, "I like how the boss said we could look for this guy after our regular duties were handled. We used to call that overtime."

"What d'ya mean 'we'? You and I never saw overtime. That was before the reorganization when we still had tax revenue."

Besslia shrugged.

They had a few leads on the whereabouts of Janos Dadicek and his followers. There was no real address system left in the old Dade County, so directions were always a questionable commodity.

Besslia had indulged Wilner and they had made a quick visit to Mari at the school.

Besslia explained Johann Halleck's desire to stay and help the settlers over there. He hoped to solve both the problems at once by finding Dadicek, arresting him for the murders and ending his raids on the defenseless settlers on the western side of Florida.

They spent the morning talking to any resident of the Miami Quarantine Zone they could about leads they could develop on the shadowy Janos Dadicek.

Finally Besslia said, "We need something to eat."

Wilner looked up the quiet street and saw an open-air restaurant with grills on each side of a small open lot. A variety of tarps hung precariously from different-sized poles. It was the kind of place that wouldn't be allowed to operate back in the district for health reasons.

Wilner just nodded his head toward it.

Besslia said, "I don't care what we eat. Just need some food."

They sat at an old, metal, folding table. A young Hispanic waitress said, "You're visiting from the district, no?"

Besslia smiled. "Sure are. How'd you know?"

"I never seen you before. Sooner or later everyone eats here at Hugo's."

"How long you been in business?"

"My papa owned the building and restaurant that used to be here when it was still part of the United States. All together we been here thirty-four years."

"Wow. What happened to the building?"

"Fire just after they closed the border. No firemen, no building. We been like this ever since."

"Good food?"

"The best around. No synthetics. Everything fresh."

"Got a menu?"

She smiled, her brown eyes lively. "We have a different special everyday and chicken sandwiches."

Besslia gazed at her. "What's the special?"

She swept some of her long, brown hair from her pretty face. "Today we have chicken of the tree, rice and beans."

Wilner knew to ask, "Where's the iguana from?"

"Local. My brothers catch them by the Zone River."

Besslia made a face. "I never got used to eating iguana."

"You eat reptile all the time at home."

"But it's in chunks and squares. I hate seeing legs and feet."

Wilner looked up at the waitress and said, "Two specials."

After ordering and allowing Besslia time to watch the cute waitress dart around the small restaurant, Wilner said, "I'd like to find someone who can ID Dadicek. Maybe someone who saw him near one of the murder scenes down here."

"Why? It has to be him. And he has to be a Simolit."

"We gotta be certain or more people could die. We need someone who's been here for a long time and might know the man personally." Then Wilner snapped his head up.

"What is it?"

"Hugo the owner. He's been here a long time. He might know something." He looked over to the grills. There were two young, wiry men grilling, and an older, heavy man barking orders in Spanish at them. That had to be Hugo.

THIRTY-TWO

Johann Halleck had not wasted any time putting Jim Sewell, the half crazy but dedicated Naples cop, to work. First he had used him to help train the settlers in basic combat skills and marksmanship, now they were on a recon to find out how the Zoners traveled back and forth between the zone and this wilderness so easily.

Johann was armed with an old M-20 U.S. Army surplus rifle. The M-20 had been the U.S. Army weapon that had evolved from the M-16 and M-18. Sewell carried his shotgun he had wielded for years since he was sent down into the bowels of the Naples police department to guard the evidence. He had spent many nights foraging for extra food and had proven comfortable in the wilderness that had consumed the city and surrounding area. There were a number of trails with corners of broken asphalt and cement popping up. The wilderness may have returned, but there was still plenty of evidence of man's time in the area.

Four settlers had come with them. If something happened

to him or Sewell he wanted to at least give the men of the settlement a chance to defend themselves. The first step was understanding how the raiders entered the area.

Victor, the de facto leader of the settlement, had been quiet about Johann's admission to being more than human. His interest laid more in the stars.

As they tromped along a wide path with their mismatched weapons slung over their shoulders or draped in their arms, Victor slid up close to the much taller Johann.

"You know what I have missed all these years in the wild?"

Johann looked down at the man's short legs taking two strides for each of his. "What have you missed, Victor?"

"Outer space."

"You can see the stars more clearly than most from your village."

"But not the details about meteors and eclipses and the aliens. I spent most of my life dreaming about the stars. I watched old sci-fi movies, Discovery Channel specials and read every magazine about science I could lay my hands on. Then when the aliens were detected it was like my whole life had a point. I was so excited about what the Urailians would be like. How we would first meet. Everything."

"Then why run away when things were getting so interesting?"

"I told you, it was everything else. But when I think about it, everything else was all man-made. The wars, terror attacks, even the worst plague was produced in a lab. I let men chase me away from what was so interesting."

"You can get radio reception over in your settlement, maybe even some video broadcasts."

Victor shook his head. "No, most of that is shielded. We get a few Spanish-language stations and one wild neo-Christian, anti-Islam station but they never have news."

"Maybe a trip into civilization would do you some good once in a while."

"If stealing women is civilization to you, I don't want any part of it."

Johann laughed. "I see your point." He was about to say something else when he heard a noise up ahead and motioned for everyone to take cover.

He had the others stay in place as he crept forward with his assault rifle off his shoulders and in his hands. It was a gas-powered motor. Like a motorcycle or other small engine. He took a few turns in the trail and then ducked into the high brush on one side.

Looking out over a clearing he saw a man riding a light-weight, tracked, all-terrain "Hyena" past a parked four-wheel-drive Ford that had the telltale sign of steam conversion: a huge water tank on the back. Johann had seen a few Hyenas near his house in the district. The large motorcyclelike vehicle used a heavy, single polymer track across both wheel hubs to roll over any obstacle. They cost a small fortune.

Three men sat on stools around a commercial fire pack under a tarp.

This was the Zoners advance party. Now the only question was how to deal with them.

The big owner of Hugo's plopped into the chair across from Wilner and pulled off his dirty white cap.

He had a deep voice with an educated Spanish accent. "I have been here a long time. I've seen much change."

"What's your last name, Hugo?"

"Chavez." He saw the look on the UPF cops' faces. "I know, I know. I got the same name as the Hitler of South America. Believe me, it was just coincidence. I was born in Cuba. That's one of the reasons I'm glad no one worries much about last names down here in the zone."

Wilner leaned in and said, "Hugo, we're looking for someone."

"He must be a bad, bad man for the UPF to come into the Quarantine Zone."

"He's the worst. He's a killer."

"The one who stabs people in the neck?"

"Exactly."

"Who is it?"

"We think he might be a guy named Janos Dadicek. You know who he is?"

"I know of the family. They been down here since the zone was established. There's a whole pack of them."

"Where?"

"Over by the Zone River somewhere. I wouldn't serve one of them. They deal in people. Women get sold to different pimps and clubs. It's men like that who caused the zone in the first place."

Wilner nodded as he made a few notes. "Would you know him if you saw him?"

"I don't know of anyone who's actually seen Janos. We hear about him sometimes. Supposed to be tough. Heard he was in a bar fight a long time ago and took a knife in the chest and still killed a man."

The more Wilner heard the more he realized that this had to be the man. And that he had to be a Simolit.

Wilner leaned back in the chair and glanced across the street. A man with an eye patch was staring at him.

Besslia said, "That a friend of yours?"

Wilner remembered him from the gang at North Miami city hall. "We had a run-in once."

When Wilner stood up to walk toward the man he fled quickly around a corner. He wasn't worth chasing right now. He'd see him again soon enough. Still Wilner was on guard knowing the man had some friends.

Mari Saltis sat at her desk and absently thumbed through some textbooks that had been proposed by a science teacher. They had been found at one of the closed public high schools but had never been used. They were at least twelve years old but still had the basic information right. She smiled at a chapter on global warming that had to be out-of-date by the time the book came out. Florida had already turned cooler by the time the book had been issued. If only the author could see the former Sunshine State now with its constant drizzle and midsixties year-around. It felt more like the older descriptions of Seattle. At least Seattle had not suffered much change. No terror attacks, no flood of refugees, the climate still lousy but at least normal.

Miami still had a livable atmosphere and a small population. There had been a bioplague camp in the heart of the city but the entire population of the camp had disappeared a few months earlier. No one had any clue where everyone had gone. It took local residents several months to build up the courage to check the camp and confirm their suspicions.

Now it was just another odd story from the Miami Quarantine Zone.

She looked up at a soft knock on her door. A smiling Tom Wilner made her heart race and her own smile spread across her face.

The tall policeman said, "Thought I'd surprise you."

"This is a nice surprise." She was across the room and embracing him before he could continue.

"Steve and I are looking for this guy Dadicek."

"Any luck?"

"Not too much. We think he lives by the river. We're gonna keep looking tomorrow. I thought I'd get to meet Leonard face-to-face."

She shrugged. "I think he's around somewhere." She led him out by the hand and continued holding it as they checked the courtyard, his storage shack and then a few hallways.

Finally she said, "He must be out on some errands." She stood on her toes and kissed him again. "Can you stay a while?"

"No, I have to get home to the kids. I'm gonna drop Steve at the UPF station then head home."

She could see the disappointment on his face. She liked that he was sorry he had to leave. Even if he wanted to stay.

Leonard Hall slipped out from behind the storage cabinet he had placed in the main courtyard. It held the things he needed to tend to the plants in the open-air middle of the school. It also provided him with a handy hiding place. He often slipped into the indentation in the building's wall and slid the cabinet back so he could have some peace and hear what people were really thinking.

Today he had used the secret room to avoid meeting the UPF detective face-to-face. He had turned the corner when he caught a glimpse of Mari and the tall cop walking hand in hand. He knew they'd end up back near her office when they didn't find him. He slipped behind the cabinet and made himself comfortable. The main reason was to avoid the cop. But after a few minutes he realized they were talking as they walked down the hall. This little hole gave Leonard the ability to hear most everything said in the hallway. Like the famous whisper channels in the Capitol or New York's Grand Central Station underground.

He heard the cop say he was going to the UPF station, then home.

After they had moved on Leonard popped back out into the hallway. If he hustled he could beat the cop back to the station, then follow him home. If things worked out he wouldn't have to worry about the cop anymore.

The thought of his open neck excited Leonard and he allowed the buildup to begin.

THIRTY-THREE

Johann Halleck had made it clear to the other men that he wanted to go into the camp alone. No one else was to move from the safety of the brush. Victor knew his reasoning and used his influence to overcome the halfhearted protests. Only the Naples cop, Jim Sewell, really wanted to come with Johann.

"No, Jim. If something happens to me you'll need to get them back and protect the settlement."

Sewell understood and nodded, his bushy hair and mustache waving as he did.

Johann nodded, pulled his M-20 in close and slipped away into the thicker brush. He took his time working all the way around to the other side of the camp. If they did notice where he had come from, he didn't want them to find his friends easily.

This sort of activity wasn't new to Johann. Over his long life he had engaged in many human conflicts. He may not have been in quite as thick foliage, but he had engaged in ambushes and attacks against the Nazis. It was one of the few times the Hallecks and Simolits had ever worked together. It fostered in an era of more understanding and eventually led to the treaty that kept the families in relative peace even today.

These men he spied on now were no battle-tested Nazi veterans. These were bullies who had no regard for other people's suffering and without the ability or courage to fight.

Now Johann edged closer until he was at the rear of the big truck. Three men stood unaware of his presence, watching the fourth man do simple stunts on the Hyena.

He waited until the motorcycle was at the far end of the clearing then made his move. He struck one man with the butt of his rifle, sending him to the ground unconscious. The other two men reacted quickly but not so fast that Johann couldn't kick one man off his feet.

The third man fumbled for a weapon and ducked behind the hood of the truck.

Johann held up his rifle when he heard a shot from behind him and a searing pain in his back.

He turned to see the man he had kicked to the ground had somehow pulled a hidden revolver and fired twice before Johann could hit him with a burst of heavy caliber bullets.

The man's chest erupted in blood and his arms went still at his side almost instantly.

As Johann turned to look for the other man, he realized the motorcycle was bearing down on him incredibly fast. He raised the rifle and got off a few rounds. The rider tumbled off onto the soggy grass but the bike kept rolling, striking Johann hard and knocking him into the truck with a loud thump.

As he lay, dazed on the ground, he saw his compatriots start to emerge from the brush across the clearing. He had told them to stay put but appreciated their concern for him.

A Zoner appeared at the rear of the truck with his pistol raised and pointed at Johann.

Johann stood to face the man, unconcerned about the small-caliber automatic.

Victor raced across the field, yelling, "Stop."

His hair fanned out behind him and his own rifle raised at the assailant.

The rifle cracked and Johann felt a stab of pain in his arm. Victor had missed by four feet.

The next round struck the truck, a pinging sound that moved the man with the pistol back. The Zoner saw the advancing force and Johann standing with no apparent injuries, then dropped his pistol.

Panting and wheezing, the men from the settlement came to a stop near Johann.

Sewell came right to him and grabbed his arm, lifting it for inspection. Then he checked the bullet in Johann's back.

"How are you still standing?" asked Sewell.

"They just grazed me."

The man who they had captured said, "Bullshit."

Tom Wilner held each of his children as he read a report from the interview with Janos Dadicek nearly fifty years ago. A Pompano detective named Kevin Butler had written the report after talking to Dadicek about the unsolved murder of Mary Harris. Even after all of the generations of cops that had come and gone Wilner could tell that Butler was one hell of a cop. He had already investigated a number of leads so he could push Dadicek in one direction or another if he had to.

The detective also had asked for a set of fingerprints and a

DNA sample from Dadicek who was at the time a plumber for the horse track in the city.

Wilner set down the report and tried to picture where the Pompano harness track would have been located. He knew it had shut down long before he moved down here and thought it was part of the clearing project just west of the interstate. In an effort to cut down on vacant buildings and allow a good chance for native vegetation to return the state had bulldozed dozens of square miles in the district and the Northern Enclave. That was back when they thought people would start moving back to the state. It was little enticement. Then, after the New York blast that produced millions of refugees, the state realized that even people displaced by radiation wanted to move anywhere but Florida.

Many of the clearing projects had been abandoned halfway through. The Pompano project had been completed, which was why Wilner couldn't even imagine where the track used to lay.

He read the report trying to get a feel for Dadicek. He knew that there was a lot that went on in the interview that wasn't in print. That was probably the reason the interview wasn't recorded.

It still made him wonder. Butler was obviously a sharp detective, his reports were thorough, he was dedicated. Why didn't he ever arrest Dadicek? Had the shadowy man fled? Did he use his vast network of Simolit connections to hide? Or use them to have Detective Butler taken off the case? Wilner was starting to learn how conspiracies played into everyday life as he discovered more about the other species. The two separate families had multiplied over the years and spread to every nation.

Wilner set down the report. Tommy's gentle snoring calmed him as did Emma's arm flopped over his chest.

He looked up at the video screen on the wall across from his bed. He made a hand motion at the sensor and the screen came to life. Another hand motion lowered the volume to not disturb the kids.

The newscast reran every twenty minutes. This was the second or third story.

Footage showed the transplants settling in their new neighborhoods in the district. Wilner could see a few of the cops he knew sitting behind the scenes keeping an eye on everything. One woman was interviewed.

"I liked my house in Philadelphia but since I had only moved there in the last seven years they said I had to leave. My parents came to Florida years ago but left when it got crazy. I don't see why we have to move somewhere we don't want to go."

Wilner nodded his agreement and mumbled, "You tell 'em, sister."

He watched a few more minutes. One story told of a man planning to manufacture items for the approaching aliens to buy when they arrived. Although, like everyone else, he had never seen them, he said he had had a vision of what they looked like. He held up a sketch he had made of humanoid beings ten feet tall with long, seven-fingered hands.

Wilner was glad that guy lived in Texas where most of the nuts seemed to move nowadays.

He motioned the screen to shut down and let his mind wander as he felt his two most precious treasures snuggle in next to him.

Soon he started to drift off, then he heard a faint sound outside. It seemed to creep into his subconscious. It was a sixth sense he had picked up during his tour in the Second Iranian War. Once it had saved him from an infiltrator's bomb. He had sensed someone nearby in a supposedly secure camp near

Bandar Abbas. He investigated his feeling and surprised a young man planting a charge that would've killed him and his whole squad. He had managed to kick the man away from the bomb and later was congratulated when the man was executed by a firing squad nearby.

Despite the pats on the back, Wilner didn't feel like a hero and wasn't happy the man was dead. Even then he had started to think that they were really the intruders on the Iranian's lands. He knew Iran had deserved some form of punishment for the way it had attacked neighboring Iraq and Israel. But the war had gone on three years with more than four million casualties.

The one Wilner had caught still weighed on his mind.

Now he sat up in his bed, the children slipping off to each side. He scrambled off the bed, glad he had fallen asleep with shorts and T-shirt on. He crouched, perfectly still and confirmed that he had heard someone outside. He thought about going for a gun he had secured high in his closet away from the children but wanted to keep track of the sound.

His heart raced as he slipped into the family room and determined that someone was out front, near his front door. He sidetracked into the kitchen and pulled a heavy utility knife from a drawer with other household tools.

He crept closer to the door, forming a quick plan in his head. He was a combat marine. He was trained to take action.

THIRTY-FOUR

Leonard Hall waited more than an hour before he parked his Honda and started on foot toward the cop's house. He was very pleased with himself for how he had slipped out of the zone before Wilner and waited for him at the UPF station. Had he been alone instead of with the smaller cop, Leonard might have tried to take action there. But this way his anticipation had grown twofold in the ensuing hour.

He had followed the cop discreetly to this neighborhood and waited. He knew that few of the houses were occupied and he'd be able to figure out which one Detective Tom Wilner lived in. It turned out to be easier than he thought when, on his first slow pass through the neighborhood in his steam-converted Honda, he saw Wilner's nice government-made hive sitting in the driveway.

He had driven back to this little park near a pond filled to overflowing with the constant cool drizzle. Leonard played with the gravity-fed German army surplus combat knife, turning it upside down, listening to the click of the blade falling in place. Then he pulled out the combat spike that had proven so effective in shutting down the human nervous system.

Finally, after allowing his mind to consider what was about to happen, he left the old car in the park and cut through bushes, sneaked behind houses and ended up across from Wilner's house.

One thing he had not considered until that moment was what he would do if the children in the house saw him. Mari Saltis had not shut up about Wilner raising his children alone. Leonard would never hurt a child but he didn't want to be identified either.

Then he had a thought. What if he brought them down to the zone to raise himself? His aunt might be of some help and she certainly wouldn't turn away children.

Then he shook his head clear of thoughts like that.

First things first. Wilner had to die. Then he'd worry about anything that popped up.

Leonard crouched down when he heard a sound. It was his turn to be surprised.

Wilner stood to one side of the door with a kitchen knife in his right hand. The security system allowed a thumbprint to open the door from either side. He had to face the door to place his thumb in the small scanner and then wait as he heard the locks unclick inside the solid door. He knew that gave whoever was on the other side a warning but he was prepared too.

He yanked the door back and immediately saw a man's shape. He paused a fraction of a second to assess who it was and saw a distinguished man in a nice all-weather coat that reached to his knees. The man didn't move.

Wilner backed up a pace and stood straight. He looked down on the man by a few inches.

"Mr. Wilner?" asked the man.

Wilner nodded.

"I am Bejor Simolit and we need to talk."

Wilner nodded as he tried to compose himself.

Leonard ducked at the sound and then saw new headlights as a car eased down the street toward the house. A Mercedes hive slowed and turned into Wilner's driveway. Leonard watched as a man stepped from the car and slipped on a long all-weather coat then carefully walked out the door.

He milled around the front for several minutes as if he were deciding whether to knock. Then the door swung open and Leonard saw Wilner allow the man into the house.

It looked like his brilliant plan would have to wait, but at least he knew where Wilner lived now.

THIRTY-FIVE

Bejor Simolit sat on the other end of the long couch with his hands folded in his lap. Wilner noticed how the man's dignified bearing, erect spine and intense gaze made him look like someone out of the nineteenth century. Which might be where he was from.

Wilner had allowed him into his home with a degree of wariness. His experience with the Simolit family had not been positive recently. But the way he had asked and his assurance that he meant no harm made the risk seem a little more manageable.

"I don't often meet with humans," said the man in a calm, quiet tone. "But you know most of our secrets." His eyes flicked to a photo of Tommy and Emma.

"And you know mine."

"This is not why I have made the trip all the way down here."

"What did bring you to my house? An address I didn't realize was public."

Bejor smiled. "You know by now the reach of our family. We knew your late wife's address, which was the same as yours. She was, after all, a Simolit." He looked at the photo again. "As are your children."

Wilner felt a stab at the comment.

Bejor held up his hand. "That is another matter. The family has conferred most recently on Johann Halleck's inquiry as to a certain Janos Dadicek. Unfortunately we are unable to find Johann at the moment."

"Johann is over in the western wilderness."

"May I ask why?"

"Helping some settlers who are being terrorized by bandits."

Bejor smiled. "The Hallecks and their human causes."

"It's better than slaughtering us." Wilner focused a look on the older man and said, "I'm sure you're not here to talk about Johann."

"No, of course not. I was going to tell you that there is no Janos Dadicek among us. That doesn't mean he's not using a different name but based on all we have heard, this man is not a Simolit."

"I'll know more tomorrow."

"You know where this man is?"

"I'm narrowing it down."

"Then I will send my sons to help."

"Why, if he's not a Simolit?"

"Because I want to be sure. If he is, we will deal with him. He is not subject to your laws."

"What's that mean? You'll turn him loose somewhere else?"

Now the man's icy brown eyes seemed to bore into Wilner. "I give you my word, Detective Wilner, that if this man is a

Simolit and has the predilections you have mentioned, he will be dealt with properly. You may even find it harsh."

Wilner assessed the man.

Bejor held out his hand. "You have my word."

Wilner felt the honor in him and took his hand.

It was after midnight when Johann Halleck decided he had pushed the men too far. They had traveled most of the night in the big truck they had captured from the Zoners. The two surviving raiders were tied up and tossed in the bed of the truck. Johann, Jim Sewell, Victor and Sean were crammed inside the truck's oversized cab. Of the settlers, Victor and Sean seemed the best prepared to kill someone for their safety.

Johann had explained that his plan was to use information from the two captured men to follow the trail back across the state, through the Everglades and to the house the Zoners used as a base of operations. The men had said their leader was named Janos and that made him first on Johann's hit list. If he severed the head of the serpent it was less likely the serpent would ever fight back. He intended to make an example for these men so that no one from the zone would think to threaten the peaceful settlers in the wilderness of southwestern Florida.

Now they had three fire packs broken and burning in a pile next to the truck. The two settlers were asleep in the cab of the truck.

The former Naples cop, Jim Sewell, sat back against one of the truck's giant tires. He stared into the fire and said, "You know I never shot anyone."

"Except me."

Sewell's eyes moved to Johann. "And that didn't even do anything."

"I can handle this. You stay back with the prisoners. I don't want to waste your talents."

"I'm still trying to figure out why I wasted years protecting evidence no one would ever use."

"We used it."

Sewell smiled. "You're a good guy to have around to cheer someone up. I guess the long and the short of it is that I'm scared."

"If you weren't, you'd be stupid. Tomorrow we'll recon the place and make a plan. You'll do your share if it means shooting or watching. You need to go easier on yourself."

"I think I'd like living in the settlement. I couldn't go back to regular civilization."

"It's hardly civilized anymore. But you're right, the settlers could use a man like you."

"You think we can stop them?"

Johann smiled. "I've faced a lot worse. This'll be easy."

Leonard Hall had given up on the cop after the man in the Mercedes had stayed more than an hour. He had watched the house hoping to follow through on his plan even after the man had arrived. But when he stayed with no signs of leaving soon, Leonard had decided he needed to get back to the zone and make a new plan.

He had no trouble getting across the same bridge he had used to come into the district. The same guardsmen were on duty.

His little Honda chugged along on the steam power at a decent eighteen miles an hour through the damp and empty streets of the Miami Quarantine Zone. He cut over to the river road and then went south toward his house. Along the way he saw several houses with lights from stored solar power or from their own generators.

As he walked in the front door, shaking off the droplets of rain, he was surprised by his aunt moving suddenly on the couch in the living room.

As Leonard stepped into the small room his aunt said, "What are you doing here?"

"I live here."

"But I hardly see you."

He stared at her, huddled under a real wool blanket. An impulse made him reach down and yank the blanket. He stood back, shocked to see his aunt nude underneath. He realized what he had interrupted, but didn't move to cover her.

For his aunt's part, she didn't seem embarrassed. She stood and faced him, her body still in good shape with large, if saggy, boobs. She was only slightly older than him, which in his family was not unusual. Many uncles and aunts were younger than their nephews and nieces.

Leonard took a second to stare at his aunt whom he had lived with for all these years but had never looked at this way before.

Despite her attractive body and ageless face he noticed one thing more than the rest. Her lovely neck.

THIRTY-SIX

Steve Besslia pulled Tom Wilner over to the side away from the others.

"Willie, are you kidding me? We're gonna take these two into the zone with us?" His eyes cut over to the tall young men standing patiently near the car.

"Why not?"

"For one thing, they're Simolits. For another, this is a police investigation and they're not cops."

"Calm down, Steve."

Besslia realized he might have sounded a little panicked but he didn't like the idea of potential enemies riding with them into an area without laws.

Wilner said, "Bejor Simolit seemed troubled by the idea that a Simolit could be doing the killings. He volunteered his sons. I think they might be a help and it avoids other problems later."

"Like what?"

"Like explaining how we killed a Simolit family member,

if that's what Dadicek is. I'm not worried about them and neither should you."

Besslia wished his friend Johann Halleck was with them instead. Johann had proven to be reliable and trustworthy. He
wondered what his friend was doing out in the wilderness right
now. Besslia thought he could help out there but knew Johann
was right when he said Besslia's destiny lay over here with
the UPF.

Then Besslia realized what bothered him almost as much
as the Simolits being shady. He was worried they might steal
his chance to prove himself.

Johann stirred from a restless sleep, with ants gnawing into
his ankle. The sun was up enough to disperse light into the
low, gray clouds. Now he could see ahead on the trail. He
knew they were on part of the old Tamiami Trail, which had
been flooded after the rains had started in earnest. The water
had receded a little but no one used the road, which was constructed to connect Tampa and Miami. Now it formed the
solid ground for weeds and grass and fungus to cover it; a
perfect back way for raiders out of the zone to sneak into the
wilderness.

He stood and stretched, then checked on the two tied and
gagged men in the rear of the truck. One man had given up
waiting for someone to untie them and urinated in his pants. Johann hopped up into the bed of the truck and roughly yanked
down the gags. "We'll be close to the zone in a couple of hours.
Then you better lead us to the right house or pissing in your
pants will be the most pleasant thing to happen to you."

The man who had shot Johann kept a defiant glare and
said, "You have no idea who you're pissing off."

Johann smiled.

"And you do?"

Leonard Hall felt the buildup in his nervous system. The urge. The usual pleasant feeling that was fueled by anticipation and sometimes built to a fever if he fixated on someone for too long. It was a feeling that could pass if he didn't see his potential victim for a while but once it started it was hard to stop.

This buildup started with the cop. If Leonard could have plunged his combat spike into the big UPF detective's neck then he'd be in a calm, quiet state now. A satisfaction that could last for up to a month. Instead he had seen his aunt in a new light and now was concerned he had transferred the buildup to her.

To make matters worse he thought that she had derived more than a little excitement from Leonard's increased attention. Just the way she sauntered into the kitchen in an open robe and let her fingers dance across his back as she passed. That was unlike anything she had ever done.

Perhaps it was all the years living apart from most other people. Just she and Leonard. He had hardly paid any attention to her at all. Now, as she scrambled two mismatched eggs— one chicken, the other some sort of reptile—all he could do was stare at her neck with her hair tied to one side.

Without turning her head she said, "Are you going to work at that school today?"

"Yeah."

"Will you be back tonight?"

"Why?"

She turned and Leonard focused on her lovely neck. An odd mix of emotions hit him as his buildup increased as well as his uneasiness.

———

Wilner was surprised how diligent the border guardsmen were. Even after he and Besslia had shown them their official UPF IDs they had wanted to see the two Simolit men's IDs too.

"They're with us."

"So?" said a fat sergeant.

"So, it's official business."

"In a foreign country?"

"That's right, it's an invasion, now open the gate unless you guys want to be stopped every thirty feet once you get off duty."

Wilner stared the sergeant down and was a little ashamed at the satisfaction he felt as they roared across the bridge in the flashy hive.

Now they were well into the zone and headed south along the Zone River. Their best information was that Dadicek and his group lived in a series of houses along the river. Wilner had studied maps of the area as well as satellite photographs and saw several areas where it looked like some kind of trail started on the far side of the river. There were even a few houses with little homemade bridges that crossed the small flowing river.

He slowed the car near where he was told two women had been stabbed in the necks. At a house farther south, a man whose face was wrapped with bandages sat on a covered porch. The white wrapped head turned slowly, tracking the car as it went past. Wilner got a creepy feeling from the man.

Soon they were at the first house on his map. He decided they would hit the house hard once they were sure. He'd use regular police procedures down here just like he did in the district.

He parked down the street, leaving Besslia with the two Simolits who had not bothered to introduce themselves. One was tall with a tangle of dark curly hair and the other was beefy with a shaved head. Like with any of their species, Wilner couldn't tell how old they were. Anywhere from thirty to three hundred.

He stopped at a house a block away and knocked on the door. A young woman with long black hair and a beautiful face answered the door. Her appearance was so startling that it took Wilner by surprise.

Wilner smiled and said, "I'm sorry, I was looking for the Dadicek house. Do you know where it is?"

She shook her head then mumbled, "No English." She called over her shoulder to an older, heavyset man with hair popping out of his collar.

The man said nothing but just stared at him.

Wilner repeated the question.

The man shook his head. "No, don't know him."

Before Wilner could ask any follow-up questions the man slammed the door in his face.

THIRTY-SEVEN

Johann Halleck and his makeshift army had parked the truck off the soggy trail about a half a mile from the Zone River. Johann had one of the prisoners out of the truck and separated from everyone else off in the high weeds. The water was deep directly behind him and the man knew how vulnerable he was with his hands and feet tied, sitting next to a deep-water pond in the Everglades.

The man was smart enough to have heard the stories of how the alligators had adapted to the cooler temperatures, still active even in the near constant sixty-degree temperatures. They had also lost any fear of man. Although attacks weren't common, compared to the tiny human population, the percentage of attacks had skyrocketed. The same with snakebites. Without the encroachment of man the cottonmouth and rattler populations had soared.

The Zoner whimpered slightly as Johann just stared at him. That was another reason he had moved him from the others. He was prepared to do things his comrades probably wouldn't if this guy didn't talk.

Johann said, "Okay, my friend. Where's the house after we reach the river?"

"What are you gonna do?"

Without warning, Johann flicked open a folding knife. He made a quick slash across the man's forearm. Instantly blood leaked out down his wrists, over the synthetic ropes, and dripped into the water.

Then he said, "I'd worry what was going to happen to you. The blood will attract all kinds of predators and you can't do anything about it."

"Who are you, mister? You're not one of them settlers."

"I'm what bad men like you dream about at night. I'm someone who'll kill men who prey on others. Now you gonna talk?"

The man's lips started to quiver.

Johann played with the open knife in front of him. Then he heard the croak of an alligator close by.

The man flinched. "What the hell was that?"

"That was a good-sized gator."

"Okay, okay. The house is a mile south of the end of the trail. You cut along the river and he has a shitty wooden bridge that goes right into his backyard."

"Will they see us coming?"

"When you get close to the house the weeds thin out."

"How many men will be there?"

"Five, maybe six."

Something slithered around the man's leg.

"God, help me. I told you all you need, cut me loose." A tear ran down his dirty face.

Johann nodded. I'm gonna leave you in the truck then decide what to do with you and your buddy."

"What do you mean?"

"We can't have you coming back to the west coast."

"Mister, I swear I'll never leave the zone again. Just get me away from these snakes and gators."

Johann started to reach for the man when he heard gunfire near the truck. He sprang to his feet and raced back along the wet path, leaving the bound man at the water's edge.

Leonard Hall and his family had spent many years separate from the rest of the world.

Leonard's father had always called it the family's "secret" and it was the main reason he had kept Leonard isolated through most of his childhood. The secret had involved an unfortunate argument where Leonard's father had killed a female cousin in an argument. He'd choked her right in front of the rest of the family. No one panicked. No one called the police. She was simply buried in the back of their modest Pompano Beach home.

He had blocked out the incident as much as possible. Sometimes he'd dream about the day he watched his father murder Cousin Lilly. Once in a while it popped into his head during the day. He had never connected it to any of his own activities. Until now.

His aunt craned her neck to look out the back window and said, "There's a vehicle across the river."

Leonard barely noticed the big four-wheel drive as it cut to the south. A man ran ahead of the vehicle, but it was his aunt's neck that drew all his concentration.

Leonard reached into his pocket, relieved to feel his combat knife within easy reach.

Now the urge had taken hold and there was only one thing he could do.

Johann felt sick when he saw Sean dead on the ground behind the truck. A gash in his bald head and a bloody metal rod next to his long body told the story. Victor knelt beside him, sobbing over his dead friend.

"Which way?" called Johann when he saw the bed of the truck empty and knew the other prisoner had escaped.

Victor pointed toward the river and said, "I shot at him but missed. It all happened so fast."

"Where's Sewell?"

"He ran after him."

Johann didn't see anyone on the path, so he climbed up into the high cab of the truck and started the engine. He ignored a stump the big tires rolled over as he pulled onto the path and mashed the gas pedal.

He heard another shot then slowed the truck when he saw someone move ahead of him on the path. It was the escaped prisoner and he cut south into the swampy area where Johann couldn't follow in the truck.

He jammed the brakes when he saw a figure prone on the ground to the side. It was Jim Sewell.

He leaped from the truck, his feet sticking in the thick mud. This was turning into the disaster he had wanted to avoid.

THIRTY-EIGHT

Tom Wilner had narrowed down the possible houses where Janos Dadicek lived. The road along the Zone River held all types of different houses. From small, old-Florida one-bedroom shacks to near mansions. Of course, the mansions looked as run-down as the shacks with the lack of material and labor available for repair.

He hustled back to the car where Steve Besslia sat in silence with the two Simolits. Wilner opened the driver's door and said, "I think it's the big house about half a mile south. It looks like there's a bridge behind it."

Besslia nodded. "If it's not the house we walk away. This isn't the district. It's not like we can be sued or ruin a prosecution."

"That's fine except if it is the house we need to hit it hard. This family has a bad reputation down here." He cut his eyes to the two Simolits in the backseat. He wanted to see if they flinched at the comment. Anything to see if they were here because Janos Dadicek was, in fact, a member of their ancient family. They remained placid, ready to do what Wilner asked of them.

He looked back at Besslia and said, "Let me talk to one more house. The one down the street. Pick me up in a few minutes when I walk out. I don't want to spook anyone."

Besslia nodded as Wilner headed off toward the small yellow house. Wilner could see the rear end of a Honda parked in the rear of the house. He took a second to look around the porch once he was under the metal roof. He thought he heard someone inside.

He knocked on the solid wooden door that didn't match the house.

Mari Saltis had taught an English class for a teacher who had the flu. Down here in the Quarantine Zone, the flu wasn't always a simple matter of resting. Sometimes the flu turned into something worse and without the full access to medicines and the limited number of doctors people died of the flu. The other problem was the exotic diseases that mimicked common illnesses like the flu. That was one of the ways that the bioplague had spread so far before they figured out it was not an organic illness.

The class had felt like it dragged, partially because her mind was so preoccupied. She missed Tom Wilner and found herself constantly thinking of ways to see him. She was also worried about Leonard Hall.

He wasn't at work, which was odd considering the amount of time he usually put into the school since he started. He had been there every day when she got there, and stayed until after she left. He had been very quiet about his heroics in saving her and seemed to want to forget the whole incident.

She was also troubled by the idea that Leonard knew one of the prostitutes who had been murdered. Not that she thought he killed her. It was the Vampire. Just that he hung out with prostitutes. But he was a man. He could be lonely. She knew he lived with his aunt. Mari still didn't know how old Leonard was. His lean, muscular body gave the impression he was close to forty, but his face and graying hair made him look older.

She sat in the empty room as the girls headed off to another class. She gazed out the window, watching the light raindrops ping off the glass.

A young woman entered the room and stopped in surprise. "I didn't know anyone was in here."

"Just resting after an English class."

"I sit in here and read sometimes until my eleven o'clock algebra class." She took a seat on the other side of the desk where Mari sat.

Mari said, "What do you have to read?"

She held up a small, old paperback book. "I hate the electronic readers. There's a store on Market Row that has hundreds of these."

"What's the book about?"

"Just a crime novel but it's set down here before the changes. It shows Miami as a great center of commerce and some of the other cities as really upscale. Did you know there was a town named Aventura?"

Mari smiled at the woman who had not really known the zone as part of the United States except as a child.

Mari said, "Have you seen Leonard today?"

The woman shook her head and made a face.

"What's the look for?"

"He's weird. He gives me the creeps."

Mari wondered if she had been blind to Leonard because

he had been such a help to her. It was something to think about.

Johann Halleck kneeled down to the fallen Jim Sewell. But the former cop sat up quickly.

"He tricked me into an ambush. I don't even know what he hit me with." Sewell held a hand up to his head and it came away bloody. "I got a shot off on him."

Johann was up and in the truck quickly as Sewell scampered into the passenger seat.

The big truck shot forward and he turned to the right where the man had run. Quickly the soggy marsh turned to deeper water. A gigantic alligator cruised in front of them.

"He didn't go this way," said Johann.

"There's a lot of brush. He could've cut back in either direction."

Johann knew the man didn't have enough loyalty to save his friend, so that meant he was headed back to the house. Johann backed the truck out and headed toward the river. As he did the fleeing man sprang up from a low tangle of brush and started running in front of them.

Johann eased the truck in behind him, waiting for the man to tire from running so fast through the thick, wet terrain. He could see a small yellow house across the river and even someone in the rear room turn to look at the truck. He couldn't let the man get close enough to warn the Zoners they wanted to attack.

Leonard felt a tremendous relief as he looked at the shocked expression on his aunt's face. She had been looking at

the truck across the river and had said, "Why is that man—"
She never finished her thought as Leonard went with his urge
and instinct to drive his combat spike straight through her neck.

It was so fast and precise that she continued to turn her head
slightly and just stared up at her nephew as he maintained his
grip on the handle of the spike. Her body went limp.

He slipped the spike out quickly and stared at the precise
hole in the side of her lovely neck. The tiniest dribble of blood
spilled out. He eased her onto the side of the couch and placed
a hand on her shoulder, feeling closer to her now than he had in
all the years they had lived together in the zone. Her skin was
soft and youthful.

But she was dead. Because of him.

It was then that he realized he had crossed a line. He had
gone too far. His stomach churned as he considered the con-
sequences of what he had done.

Then a sharp knock on his front door startled him. It took
him several seconds to regain his composure.

He closed the combat spike back into the handle and shoved
it in his front pocket, crossing the room quickly to the front
door. There was no peephole; there was no need for one. He
couldn't remember the last time someone knocked on this
door. Not in the last ten years at least. People didn't mix in
this part of the zone.

He opened the door a crack and saw it was only one man. As
he pulled the door open the rest of the way he realized it was the
cop, Tom Wilner. Had he figured out what Leonard was up to?

The first thing the cop said was, "Can I ask you a question
about one of your neighbors?"

Leonard was so shocked he gave no reaction.

Then the cop said, "You look familiar. Do we know each
other?"

Leonard shook his head slowly.

The cop looked at him closely then asked, "Do you know the people in the big white house with the bridge across the river?"

Leonard started to think again. "I see them," he mumbled.

"Is the owner's name Dadicek?"

"Yeah, I think. A lotta people use the bridge." Then he realized what he should be saying: Why? Who're you?

The big cop hesitated. "Man, you sure seem familiar."

Leonard had stuck his hand in his pocket and gripped the combat knife. In his head he knew he'd have to be fast. He judged the cop's height and how he'd let the gravity-fed blade drop out then shove it up under Wilner's chin.

Wilner shook his head and said, "I need to talk to Mr. Dadicek." He looked over his shoulder.

Leonard thought this might be the moment to strike.

Wilner waved to someone and turned around to say, "Just a few friends with me."

Leonard looked to one side of Wilner's broad shoulders and saw the hive with three men sitting in it.

Wilner looked past him a little and said, "You live out here alone?"

"Uh, my aunt lives with me."

"She know the Dadiceks?"

"No, she's um, homebound. She's taking a nap right now." Leonard felt the sweat start to form on his forehead. He hoped the cop didn't pick up on his nervousness. He'd use the knife but the men outside would be here in seconds.

Then Wilner said, "Thanks," and turned back to the car.

Leonard shut the door and stumbled back into the other room. He looked at his still aunt and said, "Wow, that was close."

THIRTY-NINE

Johann Halleck looked down on the running man from the cab of the big truck. Jim Sewell bounced in the seat next to him. He knew he could not let this Zoner get close enough to warn the others at the house and he thought that a gunshot from this distance would be heard. He punched the gas and the engine revved as he tried to run the man down. It wasn't particularly sporting, but the settlement was counting on him ending the Zoner's reign of terror.

Before the bumper of the truck smashed into the man he pivoted on his right foot and dove off the path into the rough foliage near the deep water.

Johann slammed on the brakes, causing the truck to skid in the mud. He put a hand on Sewell's chest and said, "I'll get him. Back the truck out of sight of the house."

He was on the ground running after the prisoner in a matter of seconds. As he bounded through the brush he realized he had no weapon with him. It didn't matter, he had to stop the man any way he could.

The tracks were easy to find in the thick mud and he knew the man couldn't be more than a few yards in front of him. Johann cut through the thick brush with vines running up out of the murky water and through each separate bush like a trap. As he broke through one of the bushes deeper into the swamp he felt a searing pain in his shoulder, which knocked him to the ground. He turned his head to look over his shoulder in time to see a thick log glance off his head.

His face was knocked into the mud and his vision blurred, but he was conscious and not about to let this creep get away.

Johann rolled to one side as the man raised and then swung the heavy log again. It made a thumping sound as it hit the thick mud in a few inches of water.

The man hefted the log again and advanced toward the dazed Johann. He swung, catching Johann as he tried to slip the blow. It cracked against his jaw. But now Johann was standing and launched a hard kick to the man's ribs. As the man stumbled back, Johann threw his whole body into him.

The log dropped harmlessly to the ground and the man gave Johann a surprised look.

Johann knew that look well. He had no idea how Johann had survived the attack. The man continued to back away until Johann closed the distance and grabbed his chin and the back of his head. Johann twisted hard, sharply turning the man's head. His neck snapped and he sunk into the mud.

Johann didn't even think of the man as he raced back to the truck to start his assault on the Zoner's house.

Wilner felt like he was on an official raid by the UPF. He stood on one side of the door and Besslia stood on the other.

They had their heavy-duty pistols drawn and were listening to activity in the house.

They didn't have time to call in reinforcements even if they could come into the zone. Wilner had sent the two Simolits around to the rear of the house in case someone ran out the back. He didn't ask but knew both men were armed.

He had spent a lot of time narrowing down his suspect houses to this one. Janos Dadicek had to live here.

Wilner looked at his partner and nodded his head once. He tried the handle and found the door unlocked. He twisted it and shoved the door open. The two cops buttonhooked or looped around the door frame to the inside wall, their pistols up.

A man stepped into the hallway. Seeing the intruders, he yelled and fled toward the rear of the house. Wilner fell into pursuit. As he passed the first room in the hallway he heard a familiar and terrifying sound: someone had a flasher.

The weapon's discharge took out half the wall and set fire to the room across the hall. The blast knocked Wilner into the kitchen where the man was standing, raising a new M-20 assault rifle.

Wilner fired into the center of the man's frame. Just like in all the practice sessions with the marines and UPF. The man twitched and dropped the rifle as he fell back against the counter, then toppled onto the floor.

From the hallway he saw the man with the portable flasher as he raised it. Before he could fire, gunshots from behind him cut him down.

Wilner looked up to see Steve Besslia at the far end of the hallway, his pistol up.

Two more men rushed into the kitchen. Wilner screamed, "Freeze." He emphasized the point by holding his pistol on them.

One of the men was elderly and they both raised their hands.

From the backyard Wilner heard more shots and looked out the window. One of the Simolits had been shot in the arm but they both stood over a dead man with a new automatic pistol by his side.

It looked like this part of the operation was going smoothly.

Johann Halleck had Jim Sewell behind him in the bushes with a rifle they had taken from the Zoners. The rifle was one of the new German urban assault rifles that fired bullets made of all types of material. This one had a clip of ceramic material designed to injure one person at a time but not hurt others by passing though.

Sewell was still adjusting to all the advances since he had slid from his underground evidence hole. Johann worried what he might think if he wandered into the district or some other urban area. The way the former cop was talking, Johann thought he would stay with the settlers.

Johann had a U.S. Army M-20. A combat rifle with a short barrel but tremendous accuracy that was feared by most Middle Eastern countries. Produced on a massive scale, the weapon was familiar to virtually the entire world.

This one had a small optical sight, which allowed for sniper-like shots. Johann was in the low reeds directly west of the house with the small bridge that cut across the Zone River.

Something was going on at the house. He heard some shots and men shouting. Now he was in position to see the entire rear yard and porch of the large house. Two men were standing over a body.

Johann used the scope just to get a look at the men. Immediately he recognized them. They were Bejor Simolit's sons. He figured the Simolits might be involved in something as vile as trading in humans. If Bejor knew about this there was no telling how he had lied to Johann about the killer.

Johann knew what he had to do. If he put them each down with a shot to the head he could cross the bridge, deal with the others then go back and ensure each man was dead by pumping as many shots as he needed into their heads or hearts.

He took a deep breath of the cool air and raised the rifle to his shoulder. He sighted in on the taller of the two Simolits. The young-looking man's dark hair filled the small scope as he slowly released his breath and tightened the pressure on the trigger.

FORTY

Tom Wilner took his time clearing the rest of the house. He didn't want to be surprised by some hidden gunman after he started talking to all the occupants. Steve Besslia watched the two living prisoners in the kitchen and the Simolits had the backyard. All in all it was just like a raid in the district except technically this was legal and there was no warrant.

Wilner found a second rear door as he finishing searching the back rooms. He holstered his weapon, opened the door and called back to the Simolits.

"It's me, Wilner, don't shoot. You hear me?" He waited until he heard one of them say, "We hear."

He stepped into the soggy grass and onto a stone path that led to the rear patio.

"You guys okay?"

They just stared at him. It would be very difficult to hurt one of these guys short of a direct shot to the head.

Then he heard a gunshot from across the river.

———————

Johann was outraged that the Simolits would be involved with these raiders. He also knew that this action could very well lead to the all-out war between the families that they had somehow avoided for the past century. His fear was that if he did nothing the Simolit family would just deny any allegation and nothing would ever get done.

He continued his aim at the one with dark locks of hair. He saw them move to acknowledge someone else in the backyard but decided no matter who else was there this Simolit was going down. He knew he'd have to follow up because the single shot wouldn't kill him. But it would put him out of action for a while.

He took in one last breath then slowly let it out as he took final aim.

He saw someone with sandy-colored hair come from the corner of the house and his face flashed next to the Simolit as Johann pulled the trigger.

In that split second he realized the other man was Tom Wilner.

He jerked the barrel up as the bullet left the rifle.

He prayed it was enough.

Wilner and the Simolits ducked as they heard the shot but the bullet went high, striking near the roof of the house.

All three men had their pistols out and pointing across the river, searching for a target.

From inside, Besslia called out, "Who's shooting? What's wrong?"

"Stay down, Steve. We got a sniper across the river."

Then they heard someone shout from the thick brush. "Don't shoot, it's me, Johann Halleck."

Wilner watched as the tall, Nordic-looking man stood from the bushes. He held a M-20 over his head in one hand.

The Simolits spoke to each other in Serbian. Wilner stood and holstered his pistol. He waved and yelled, "Come on over, Johann." He kept an eye on the Simolits to make sure they didn't try anything, but they holstered their weapons as well.

He watched as Johann crossed the bridge and stepped up onto the porch.

Leonard Hall heard the shooting and knew it had to do with that hotshot cop, Wilner. He had his own problems. Like his aunt. He had to dispose of her body. He had never worried about disposal before. In fact, leaving the bodies to be found was part of the fun. Hearing someone talk about "the Vampire" gave him an additional thrill. No one had a clue.

Sometimes he didn't have a clue either. There was no telling when the urge would push him to act. Usually it was a slow progression when he saw a neck that interested him. Sometimes it faded and occasionally it disappeared all together. Whatever it was that pushed him to fixate on necks.

And his aunt had paid the price.

He had her wrapped in several blankets with thick waterproof tape secured around the carpet. In his car he had twenty feet of heavy chain he intended to wrap around her as well once all the strangers left the neighborhood.

Until then he had her stashed safely in the hall closet, standing upright. He thought the blankets would keep the smell down if she had to stay there a little while.

What he really wanted to do was get back to a normal life.

It was reassuring that Wilner didn't recognize him, but as smart as that guy was he'd figure everything out soon enough.

Then he heard one of his inner friends say, "It's too late now, Leonard. You're stuck in this hell. Now you've got all of us stuck too."

Tom Wilner sat at a large kitchen table with the two prisoners across from him. Johann Halleck and Steve Besslia were standing behind the prisoners still amazed at how the two issues—Zoners and the Vampire killer—led to the same place. They had the two Simolits outside standing guard while they questioned the men they had captured.

The prisoners had not spoken a word. Wilner knew they had to be shocked that anyone would assault their base of operations all the way down here in the zone.

Now the older man looked at Wilner and said, "Who are you?" He had a light accent but it was there all the same.

Wilner said, "My name is Tom Wilner and I'm a detective with the Unified Police Force."

"What the hell is the UPF doing down here?"

"Police work."

"What have I done to bother the UPF? I only deal with people in the zone. I don't go into the district. Mostly because of men like you."

From behind him Johann growled, "The western wilderness is out of the zone."

The old man twisted to see Johann. "But it's not the district."

Wilner said, "I'm looking for a man. I was told he lived here."

"Who are you looking for?" asked the old man.

"Janos Dadicek."

"I am Janos Dadicek. Why do you seek me?"

Wilner stared at him. "You can't be Janos Dadicek. You're an old man."

"It will happen to you one day. You'll see."

"How old are you?"

"Seventy-eight."

Wilner looked up at Besslia. This couldn't be right. This wasn't the man he saw the night of the killings in the district. This old fart couldn't outrun him.

Wilner reached into the inside pocket of his weatherproof jacket and jerked out the page with an enlarged copy of the killer's fingerprint.

He looked at the old man. "Let me have your right hand."

The old man hesitated.

Wilner snapped his fingers. "I'm in no mood to wait. Give me your goddamn hand."

The old man slid his hand across the table slowly. Wilner snatched it up and compared the middle finger to the picture of the print on the page. He concentrated and stared at both the finger and the paper.

Then he let go of the old man's hand and looked up at Besslia. "It's not him."

The old man, Dadicek, said, "I'm not what? Why are you here?"

"You were questioned by the Pompano police years ago."

Dadicek thought about it and said, "Yes, I remember."

"What'd they ask you about?"

"A girl that was murdered."

"Why you? What led them to you?"

"They knew I was a pimp. They thought I might have seen something."

"I thought you were a plumber."

"I was until I discovered my true calling. I love dealing in women and the zone is the perfect place for that."

Johann Halleck said, "Not anymore."

Dadicek twisted and said, "Why not? There is no law to stop me here."

Johann said, "I am here to stop you."

FORTY-ONE

Unified Police Force Detective Tom Wilner was exhausted. Physically, emotionally and spiritually he had nothing left to give. The raid in the morning and all the hard work that led up to it had meant nothing. He was no closer to finding the Vampire than he was the day he had chased him into the zone.

Steve Besslia sat quietly across the desk, just staring out the rain-streaked window. This was unlike his usual duties and Wilner was surprised how well Besslia had adapted to the demanding work of investigation. He had also come through for him when he needed the Hive-cycle cop to come through.

Wilner tried to scribble a note but the pen didn't write. He threw it so hard against the wall that it stuck. Then he shoved a pile of paperwork off his desk. It scattered onto the dingy floor in a symmetrical pattern around the desk.

Besslia finally said, "It's not a total loss. We did stop the Zoners and they were causing a lot of problems in the wilderness."

Wilner nodded, wondering what happened to the prisoners

he allowed Johann Halleck to cart back to the settlers. "But I was so sure the Vampire was Janos." He held his hand to his eyes. Images of the dead nurses came back to him. The prosthetic hand found in the furnace. The fact that Janos Dadicek was human. How could he have been so wrong?

Besslia said, "We start again on the list. This time with one less name."

Wilner looked at the other files still on his desk. "Why didn't the cops use the print to eliminate suspects back then? They had a list. It would be simple to check."

"You said they were good detectives."

"Yeah, and the handwritten note about Dadicek being a crooked freak was correct. The comment wasn't directed at this case."

"We'll see if there is something else hidden in the files."

"What about the info you brought back from Naples? What was the suspect's name on the community college identification card?"

"Leonard Dawson."

"Maybe we'll find a link to him somewhere." He looked at his friend. "Thanks, Steve."

"For what?"

"For not letting me feel sorry for myself."

Sammy Cyclops jumped at every sound or odd moving shadow. He was convinced the handyman was the Vampire that everyone was talking about. There were even rumors that cops had come into the zone from the district and jacked up a house on the Zone River.

Now Sammy sat in the bushes across from the school. He

had to know if the cops grabbed him. He couldn't think of another reason to raid a house down here. But everyone was talking about it.

He should have figured out who the Vampire was after the man ripped through his partners at the old North Miami city hall. Then to have him cut down his new gang was more than Sammy could take. He'd have to tell someone. But who?

All Sammy knew was if the handyman was still around so was the Vampire. And the zone wasn't big enough for the two of them.

Mari Saltis stood, looking out her office window. There was a lot of work to do for the school, she had some money to raise, bills to pay, textbooks to approve but all she could think about was Tom Wilner. She missed the handsome detective from the Lawton District. She missed him so much that for the first time in years she considered what it might be like to live in the district; to be part of the United States again.

There was a gentle rap on her office door.

She called out, "Come in," as she turned and was surprised to see Leonard Hall in the doorway.

"I was afraid we had lost you, Leonard."

He looked down. "My aunt died."

"Leonard, I'm so sorry." Mari crossed the room with her arms outstretched.

Leonard stood upright like a child and allowed Mari to hug him.

She said, "What happened? How did she die?"

"I don't know," he mumbled. "I think it was something in her throat."

She stepped away from him and motioned to the small couch at the rear of her office. They sat across from each other and chatted for a while. She felt like it was helping Leonard.

"Do you need anything?"

He shook his head.

"Would you like some time off?"

"No, I'd prefer to work. There is a lot I have to do here. It'll keep me occupied."

She smiled and patted him on his shoulder.

"Is everything all right here at the school?"

"Yes, nothing is new."

"Is your policeman friend coming down any time soon?"

"I hope so."

Leonard gave her a weak smile and mumbled, "So do I."

Johann Halleck shook his head as he looked up at the three men hanging by the limb of a giant tree on the trail between the zone and the western wilderness. The sun rising in the east poked through the clouds to cast a spooky light on the men. Their hands were tied roughly behind them and their necks were bent at sickening angles.

Johann had given the choice of what to do with the prisoners to the settlers. Victor surprised him by saying that they had to die and he didn't want anyone at the settlement to see it. Then he suggested hanging them and leaving their bodies as a warning to anyone else who had the idea of invading the wilderness and doing the same thing.

Johann didn't like to see an educated and caring man like Victor turn to dark decisions like that, but it was a sound idea. Then the settlers shocked Johann by insisting that they take the men onto the bed of the big truck, secure the ropes then drive the truck away. It left the men dangling, twitching and choking for more than a minute.

The two younger men cried and pleaded. The one Johann had tied and questioned near the water appealed to him for mercy. Old Janos Dadicek spit just before the truck pulled away. That defiant attitude might serve him well as he roasted in hell.

Now the settlers and Johann just looked up at the bodies, swaying in a slight breeze.

"That'll show people we're not easy targets anymore," mumbled Victor, sounding as if he wanted to justify what they had done. "Next time we'll fight."

Johann looked into the back of the truck that had a stack of weapons and ammo they had taken from the Zoners' house.

They piled into the cab of the truck and started their trip back over the rough trail to the western wilderness.

Johann watched the endless Everglades pass by the windows and hoped he hadn't corrupted the ideals of the settlers and set them on a different path. He'd leave them soon. He had made the settlement safe. At least from outsiders. It was time to get back to civilization.

Or, more accurately, the Lawton District.

FORTY-TWO

Steve Besslia thought he was dozing off when his tired eyes caught a sentence with three faded words. He read it again, then couldn't help shouting, "I got it."

He could see he made the drowsy Tom Wilner jump a little at his excitement.

The detective looked over to Besslia expectantly.

Besslia couldn't help but smile. "I know why the cops didn't try and print the suspects during the Mary Harris investigation."

"Why?"

"They found the print on a black hair clip that had been wedged in the seawall."

"So?"

"The lead detective, Butler, found it a month after the body and down from where the body was actually discovered."

Wilner sat up, staring at his partner.

"He was one hell of a detective. He must've been frustrated and walked the scene again. The report says the clip was protected in a crevice in the seawall. Then the lab guys must've thought he was grasping at straws and didn't get around to processing it for another four months."

Wilner added, "By then a lot of other things were going on."

Besslia said, "I know what really affected the case."

"What?"

"Look how Butler signed the report." He held up the yellowing old paper. "He was promoted to sergeant and moved out to the road."

"Just like we do it."

"A police tradition that's screwed up more cases than lawyers."

Wilner nodded and said, "Steve, you been bailing me out a lot lately. I appreciate it."

Besslia had to smile.

The two UPF officers spent another hour going over everything in the files that was still readable.

Besslia held up the list. "We can remove Janos Dadicek from the list. He was a creep and living in the area but those weren't his prints here or at the other crimes."

"And he wasn't the guy who ran from me."

"Of all the names here the one they seemed to have passed by at the time was this Lenny Nelson."

Wilner said, "Sometimes it's the guys you don't take seriously that slide by. Why wouldn't they take this guy seriously?"

Besslia stared at the old report. "This one is hard to read. It looks like he might have been some kind of student."

Wilner said, "Leonard Dawson, the guy questioned in Naples, was a student. Right here in the old Broward County."

Besslia said, "We may have another winner."

Before they could start to look into files more to follow up on their theory the emergency alert tone went off on both their V-coms at the same time.

Leonard Hall's day at work had dragged by. One of the factors making time slow down was the knowledge that he still had to get rid of his aunt's body when he got home. That made it hard to concentrate on replacing light sockets with ones he had salvaged from an old police station nearby.

Mari wandered into his small workroom off the courtyard in the center of the school. Her sweet smile and voice cheered him, but didn't make him feel too much better about all that had happened.

She said, "I was worried about you and wanted to make sure you were okay." She settled on the stool next to his workbench.

He nodded. He was about to answer when one of the voices made a rude comment and distracted him.

Mari placed a hand on his arm. "You sure you're all right?"

"Yeah, just tired."

"Maybe you should head out early today."

He was about to agree when he heard something. Just a wave of noise from a distance then some clear, precise gunshots.

Mari stood and cocked her head.

Leonard let his breath out. She had heard it too.

Mari said, "What's that?"

"I don't know." An explosion from far off ate up all the other sounds.

"Good Lord," said Mari, rushing off to do what a smart leader would do. Find out what she needed to do to protect the students.

———

Tom Wilner and Steve Besslia listened to the simultaneous broadcast over both their V-coms and the station speaker.

A male voice said, "All sworn personnel are to immediately assemble on Bob Graham Boulevard in the southern part of the district with full body armor and weapons ready to go."

The two cops stared at each other until Besslia said, "What the hell could this be about?"

Just then the commander came marching through the office. Two uniformed cops trailed him, slipping on their body armor, which no one ever wore.

Besslia stood and blocked the squat man's exit. "What's going on, skipper?"

"Some damn New Yorker newcomer started flapping his gums about how the new restaurant is serving human flesh as part of its burgers. As pissed off as all the newcomers are it gave them a reason to trash the place. Now it's a full-blown riot. Some of the guardsmen on the border already responded from a few blocks away and fired a couple of volleys high but it didn't scare any of them. Now we got work to do, boys. Follow me."

Wilner could see how the commander had inspired troops to follow him in the Philippine conflict. He knew how to talk but more important he wasn't afraid to move. Once a man like that started moving you couldn't help but be caught up in his wake.

Wilner let himself get caught up. It seemed like the commander picked up more and more followers until there were nine cops struggling to get into their protective gear by the time they hit the rear parking lot.

"Lets move out," shouted the commander as he slipped into his car and drove out of the lot.

Wilner was worried about what might happen if the border were unmanned and this riot spilled into the zone.

He'd do his best not to let that happen.

FORTY-THREE

In Iran, Wilner had been in some urban fighting but most of it was open desert, large force clashes. In Bosnia it was more of a mix as the U.S. soldiers fought to keep the peace more than anything else.

The scene in front of him now shocked him. It might have been the fact that this was not some foreign battlefield but only about ten miles from his house. It was clear the chaos had surprised the other cops as they arrived too.

This force of officers who had been with the UPF ten years or less had not seen anything like this. Florida had been nearly empty through most of their tenure. Crowds had never been an issue. At least not like this.

More than two hundred people—men, women and some kids—had taken over the restaurant and trashed it. Several cars nearby were burning. The crowd was armed with scraps of metal and baseball bats.

Wilner noticed there weren't too many guns. No one wanted

to risk the harsh penalties for carrying a gun. There hadn't been an armed robbery in years since punishment for gun crimes was sure, swift and severe. Who wanted to spend a lifetime fighting in some far-off land because you used a gun? The military made sure you got to see as many guns as you ever wanted.

The commander stepped up behind Wilner and several others and said, "We need this thing quiet and we need it right now. No way we want the media to get photos of this shit. Not with more new arrivals on their way." He shouted so all the cops in the area could hear. "Let's suit up and see what we can do to convince these people to go home."

It looked to be a long night.

Sammy Cyclops couldn't believe how easy it was to cross into the Lawton District. One National Guardsman was on duty and he seemed greatly preoccupied by something on his V-com. Sammy heard the corporal moan to someone on the other end of the communicator, "Man, I wish I could be there."

Sammy didn't say anything, he just kept walking quickly. If he had known it was this easy to slip into the United States he wouldn't have paid smugglers for all the things they brought down to the zone like real Budweiser beer or potato chips made with salt and preservatives, not the greasy ones fried up right there in the zone. Now the trick was finding his way around inside another country. This was his first time north of the Miami Quarantine Zone since the government had cut them off.

Another major concern was arrest. He had entered the country illegally. Even though technically he was born a U.S. citizen in the little town of South Miami, his family didn't move north when the government's warning of the pending new border was broadcast over and over.

Sammy's father had said nothing would change. He believed Miami and Dade County owed more to South America and the Caribbean than the United States. He was right in a way, but he had no idea of the problems coming down the road.

Once the jihadist movement threatened Latin America and the money wasn't flowing into Miami from the north, most travel dried up. The collapse of air travel added to the Quarantine Zone's problems. No one and nothing came into the area. Jobs and opportunities dried up and by the time anyone realized it, the border was sealed and the U.S. government had declared Miami a restricted area.

Sammy's father died of cancer a few years later. At least they thought it was cancer. Without any real doctors and working equipment no one could diagnose him properly. He died in their home with Sammy's mother and sister at his side.

Now the town of South Miami was empty. The few people who stayed after the Quarantine Zone was established moved north into the main population center just south of the border with the United States.

As he crossed the bridge and entered the United States he heard an odd sound like a sporting event. It sounded like the old soccer games where Brazilians would cheer until they dropped.

Without thinking he turned toward the sound even though he knew he had to find a cop to tell him what he knew.

Steve Besslia marveled at the chaos as it spread. He even appreciated the ingenuity of some of the weapons made by the rioters. One man had taken a piece of the giant broken front window of the restaurant and wedged it on a stick making a clear and terrifying battle ax. A woman used plastic food trays as shields. The crowd had turned from destroying the restaurant and nearby businesses to facing down the UPF and National Guardsmen.

The problem as Besslia now saw it was that there weren't very many of them. He was joined by thirteen UPF officers and there were nine National Guardsmen. They were armed but who wanted to open up on civilians? The cops and the guardsmen were not even coordinated. The guardsmen were down behind the cover of obsolete personnel carriers—the ones that got sent to a less important post like watching a quarantine zone.

Unlike most of the other cops, Besslia had never seen combat. This might be as close as he ever got. He hoped it was as close as he ever got, but he couldn't deny that he felt a certain level of excitement, a thrill of seeing a scene with so much potential for violence. He knew it was wrong and he wished he didn't feel it.

The cops stood out in front of the crowd, dodging the occasional rock or bottle. The UPF commander gathered them in a tight group and moved them behind the guardsmen.

Their squad leader sounded like the former army captain he was. "We gotta figure out who the leader is."

One of the patrolmen said, "Leader? It's a riot."

"There's always a leader. Someone who the people rally behind in the face of authority. We take him out and the rest fold."

"How can we identify him?"

"We could use optics to scan the crowd but it would take too long. I'm sure these numb-nuts National Guardsmen are getting the same shit as me. The government wants this ended. Like right now."

Then Besslia had an idea. He spoke up before he could stop himself. "I know a way, skipper."

The commander gave him a skeptical look.

Besslia plowed straight ahead. "What if one of us slipped into the crowd. You know, infiltrated it. Then communicate back to you who the leader is. It would be the fastest way."

"One of us?" asked the commander.

"I'll do it," answered Besslia without flinching.

The commander thought about it, a flush coming over the scar on his right cheek. He looked up at Besslia and said, "Good idea, get to it. But you might not be able to use your V-com in the crowd. It wouldn't look right and would attract too much attention."

"I'll shut it off and stash it before I join the main group. Once I find out who the leader is I'll go back, retrieve it and give you guys a call."

The commander said, "Besslia, you're full of surprises today."

Mari had the school officially closed and girls on their way home in a few minutes. Once she had heard about the riot and the spreading violence just above the border she acted quickly.

Now it was her and Leonard as he secured the rear gates and she waited for him before she locked up the front doors. She had seen too many little things go wrong to think that a riot in the district couldn't spread or inspire a similar event down here. Even as she scurried around to lock up she thought about Tom Wilner. She gave a silent prayer that he would be safe. His commitment to duty wouldn't keep him away from something like a riot in his own district. The thought of him and the small UPF force facing a dangerous crowd made her legs weak, but there was nothing she could do about it now.

Leonard hurried in from the courtyard. "All set. I put an

extra chain through the rear gate and all the outer windows are locked."

"Good. Thank you, Leonard. I don't know what I would've done without you."

He smiled and nodded.

"We should get out of here in case the riot spreads."

"Where are you going?"

Mari was surprised by the question. "To my home, of course."

"You live even closer to the border. You need some place safer."

She thought about that and without hesitating said, "Can I stay at your house?"

As she watched his face she realized her first idea was to keep him from being alone in the face of his aunt's death. But now he looked like he might be uncomfortable with the idea.

She said, "It's all right, Leonard."

"No, no. Of course you can stay at my place. It's just a little messy right now."

"Are you sure?"

"I'd like the company."

As they headed out the front door she realized she might be the one that was uncomfortable. The idea that he knew a murdered prostitute crept into her mind. But it was only until the riot blew over.

What could happen in a short period of time like that?

FORTY-FOUR

Steve Besslia was scared but not sorry he had volunteered for this assignment. He had slipped off most of his equipment and was now debating taking his big duty pistol into the riot.

Tom Wilner shook his head. "You need it in case something goes wrong."

"But it'll be too obvious. The mission is to identify the leader of the group."

"And stay alive."

"Look, you got your chances to be a hero in the war. You've done your bit, now I'm gonna do mine."

"You don't have to prove yourself, Steve."

Besslia thought about it and smiled. "I know I don't. That's why I'm doing it. It's the right thing to do. It needs to be done and it was my idea. That's why I'm doing it. It feels good not to have to do it to prove myself."

The UPF commander walked over to them. "You got balls, Besslia. I'll give you that." He tossed a white T-shirt to him. "That's my brightest, whitest shirt. It should make you easy to point out." He turned to Wilner. "Willie, you're gonna keep an eye on your buddy and let us know if there is a problem."

Wilner nodded.

Besslia liked the attention of the UPF commander. He pulled off his durafiber shirt and slipped on the wide T-shirt. It draped over him like a tent.

Besslia said, "No way I'm trying to hide a gun under this thing. I already look like a kid wearing my father's shirt."

"I'll be watching you like a hawk."

"You won't get distracted or bored, will you?" Besslia smiled.

"I'd still like you to carry a gun.

He looked at his partner. "You're gonna be watching me. What could go wrong?"

Tom Wilner peered through powerful binoculars with settings for night vision, infrared and three other settings on the visual spectrum. Now he was just using magnification and the light provided by the setting sun and streetlights. He had been searching the crowd to see if he could see anyone directing things, but the shell of the restaurant building blocked a lot of the action.

He flinched as one of the tall yellow arches started to rock and was finally pushed over. It crashed onto the street, trapping one man. Parts of the plastic covering shattered and spread across the black asphalt. No one moved to help the fallen man.

The crowd had grown in the last twenty minutes as more and more district residents heard about the disturbance. That made sense because many of the new arrivals were unhappy about their forced relocation and this was the most exciting thing to happen in the district in a long time. The added people made it harder to see but the newest rioters didn't seem to have their heart in the violence.

Besslia had made one last contact with Wilner when he was about to slip into the crowd. Now Wilner was on the alert to watch for him on one side of the crowd. As if on cue, Wilner saw the flash of Besslia's white T-shirt as he emerged from a street to the side of the restaurant.

Wilner got on his V-com to his boss and said, "He's in."

"Roger that," the commander's voice answered back. "Stay on him, Willie. He's too good of a cop for us to lose."

Wilner lost Besslia behind the building and took the binoculars from his face and stood up to get a better view of the crowd.

As he stood there a man's voice behind him said, "Can I talk to you?"

Wilner turned to see a man with an eye patch. Then he realized who it was.

The man said, "You remember me?"

Wilner just nodded.

Leonard Hall didn't push his steam-powered Honda to the full twenty-four miles an hour it could go. He didn't trust himself with Mari alone at his house. He didn't want to hurt her but he hadn't intended to kill his aunt either. It just happened.

He didn't feel right saying no to her request to stay with him during the emergency.

She chatted with him on the drive out to his house, asking a few innocuous questions about his childhood and how he grew up. He lied like he always did. No one would believe him anyway.

Then Mari asked, "Leonard, are you lonely?"

He snapped his head at the way she asked the question. "Why?"

"Well." She hesitated. "Someone said you might have known one of the dead prostitutes. I just wanted you to know that there are a lot of women in the zone who would be good for you?"

He fidgeted and felt the sweat buildup on his forehead. Leonard didn't answer but noticed one thing: Mari had a wonderful neck.

FORTY-FIVE

Wilner had stepped back from his observation post for a minute to listen to Sammy Cyclops's story. The shaken zone resident had risked a lot to come into the United States just to talk to Wilner. He knew he had a moment or two while Besslia was behind the building. Still he had another UPF officer pick up the field glasses and keep an eye out for him.

Sammy said, "I had to tell someone."

"Tell what?"

"I know who the Vampire is."

"How?"

"I saw him the day he killed some of my boys down at the old North Miami city hall."

Wilner remembered the day and also how the men died and he hadn't shot them. "You have my attention."

"Then he killed three of my newer boys. He stabbed two of them right in front of me. Used a big-assed spike right into their throats."

Wilner now focused all of his attention on the man. "Would

you be able to identify him? Did you get a good look at him?"

"Good look? I know him. I know where he is."

"Who is it? Where is he?"

"He's the handyman at the school for girls in the north end of the zone."

Wilner stared at him while he made the simple connection. He mumbled to himself, "Mari's school."

Sammy answered anyway. "That's right. We was shaking her down when the handyman come and interrupted us. He moved like a damn cat. He played with us. He was twice as fast and double as strong as any of us. It's like he's a double human, the things he does."

Wilner grasped his shoulders and said, "Gray hair, average height and weight?"

"Yeah, I guess."

"Did you hear his name?"

"Larry or something white like that."

"Leonard?"

"Yeah, that's it."

Wilner felt a rush of fear as he thought about Mari so close to a killer.

Steve Besslia dodged a rock thrown indiscriminately. The noise seemed less intense inside the crowd than it did from across the wide street. He could see why the meager force of cops and military border guards had not scared the crowd into dispersing. When he looked toward them he could hardly tell if anyone was even watching the growing riot. The National Guardsmen were crouched behind one of their heavy vehicles and the UPF men weren't numerous enough to seem threatening at all.

Many of the rioters were more interested in stealing food and equipment from the destroyed restaurant and trashed warehouse next door. A woman ran by with an armload of meat patties. Apparently she didn't listen to rumors.

The crowd flowed from the rear of the restaurant where he noticed a concentration of people, then saw a man standing on a crate and addressing them. This seemed like the logical place for him to start looking for a leader. The problem was that he knew if he ventured toward the building he'd be out of view of Wilner.

So far no one had shown any aggression toward him. The excitement of the assignment had given way to a cooler assessment of what needed to be done. Was this a sign that he was maturing and becoming a professional? He took a minute to get an estimate of how many people were in the crowd. He looked for avenues to surprise them if the UPF needed to assault the rioters. He also kept out a tactical eye for where he could escape if things turned ugly.

He stored the information like he was reading someone else's battle plan. He knew that when he briefed the commander he'd be able to go through each aspect of his recon. But he still had to determine the leader and right now there was only one candidate.

He eased toward the rear of the building and out of the safety of Tom Wilner's view.

Wilner felt the anxiety build in him as he continued to sweep the crowd with the binoculars in an effort to find Steve Besslia. Sammy Cyclops had moved farther back and was sitting, waiting for Wilner to escort him back into the zone. The crowd had grown larger but not more aggressive.

The UPF commander approached Wilner.

"Who's the pirate?" he asked, pointing a thumb at Sammy.

"He just told me who the killer is."

"The neck guy?"

"Yeah, the Vampire." Wilner wanted to ask to go get him in the zone but he knew his duty was to watch Besslia. It ate at him that Mari might be down there with the killer close by but he rationalized that Leonard had been there all along and not harmed her.

He felt his stomach tighten just at the thought of it and it made him realize how much he cared for the schoolteacher from the Quarantine Zone. She wasn't just beautiful, she cared about the people down there and saw the value in running her school.

Wilner started to silently pray for Besslia to come out of the riot. Laying prone on the street, he had caught a couple of glimpses of his partner as he worked his way through the crowd.

A discussion, which was getting louder, erupted behind him. Wilner lowered the binoculars and twisted, looking over his shoulder. His commander was leaning in close to a National Guard captain.

Wilner saw other guardsmen hefting a large but portable flasher. A large-caliber machine gun mounted on their personnel carrier swiveled toward the crowd.

Wilner stood to back up his boss. As he stepped up behind him he heard the young captain say, "We have orders to shut this thing down right now."

The UPF commander snarled, "This is my problem right now."

"It was until the government decided they couldn't let this drag on. There's too much at stake."

The commander pointed at the flasher on a tripod. "You gonna use that on civilians? American civilians?"

The captain ignored the commander and ordered his men into position.

Wilner stepped up and said, "There's a cop in the crowd undercover."

"Then get him out, fast."

"We don't have communications with him. At least give a warning and wait for a response."

The captain turned to face Wilner. "The warnings to disperse have been ignored. You guys have made no impact. Now it's our turn. We're going to end this riot and give future rioters something to think about."

The captain went back to his preparations. He called over his shoulder to the UPF commander, "Get your men back behind us. We don't want to nail a cop by mistake." He chuckled. "Too much paperwork." His men started to laugh too.

Wilner looked back at the crowd hoping to see Besslia heading back to his V-com or out of the riot altogether, but all he saw were angry transplanted people throwing anything they could at the cops and military on the perimeter.

Wilner looked at his boss to see what the commander had in mind. It was apparent the commander was at a loss as to how to stop the approaching tragedy.

Wilner knew he might need to do something drastic.

Mari thought Leonard's little house on the edge of the Zone River was cute. Small and old, but nice for two adults with no children. The river ran the length of the zone and had a number of tributaries that were all called the Zone River. It gave a number of houses on the western edge of the zone the chance to be on a nice flowing body of water.

Leonard had mumbled several times to himself as they drove out here. He sounded as if he were talking to someone and twice Mari said, "Excuse me?" Leonard just brushed off her inquiries by shaking his head.

He had started to twitch occasionally too. Mari had never noticed it before and wondered if it was a reaction to his aunt's death.

She paused on the front porch as Leonard worked an ancient lock and then held the door open for her.

Inside the house was furnished with pre-zone pieces that would've seemed out-of-date anywhere. A dusty haze covered the living room.

Leonard turned on a couple of lights, which were powered by a stored ambient light cell. She had become an expert at telling how a house was powered. No generator noise, no windmill out front, so the only alternative was the less-powerful cells. It meant he had no air-conditioning or other high-powered appliance.

Leonard excused himself to change while she settled into the couch in the rear of the living room. Behind it was a big bay window with a view of the river and the Everglades beyond. After sitting and enjoying the view for a moment her mind drifted back to her concern for Tom Wilner. She missed not having access to news as quickly as she once did.

Then she noticed an odor. She sniffed the couch. It was dank but not the source of the strong, unsettling stench.

She stood and tried moving to other parts of the room to see if she could detect where the smell was originating from.

After a minute of trial and error she stopped where the odor was strongest.

The closet.

FORTY-SIX

Wilner felt his eye twitch the more the National Guard captain barked stupid orders.

The young captain turned to the senior UPF man and said, "You don't understand, Commander. This is bigger than you or me. There are trainloads of new arrivals set to come down here and something like this could ruin those plans."

"So could a massacre of residents," the squat commander replied.

Both men had attracted their subordinates behind them like a couple of gangs preparing to rumble.

The younger captain looked out over the crowd. "This is a lot like Tehran toward the end of the Second Iranian War. I don't want another Tehran."

Wilner looked at the young man and said, "Were you in Tehran?"

"Well, no, but I've read about it."

"I was there. This is nothing like that. Those rioters were the Iranian army in civilian clothes. They were armed and their plan was to retake the key government buildings. Have you ever seen combat, Captain?" He made it more of an accusation than he meant to.

The captain ignored the question, which meant that he had not seen any combat. He turned and started to deploy his men.

Wilner said, "There's a UPF officer in there. You can't shoot."

"I have my orders. I don't give a damn about some cop in there. What good could he do in there anyway?"

"He's trying to figure out who the leader of this mob is."

"Won't matter when he doesn't have a mob to control."

Wilner watched as the soldiers fanned out with their weapons ready. The three men on the flasher started charging the weapon.

Wilner had had enough. He reverted to the impulsiveness he had as a younger man in the marines. In one motion he drew his pistol with his right hand. At the same time he grabbed the captain by the collar with his left hand. He jerked the smaller man to him and had the pistol up to his cheek in a flash.

"There's a change of operational plans, Captain." Wilner had to use restraint not to blow this creep's face off right that second.

Besslia listened to the man shouting to the crowd gathered behind the restaurant for a few minutes. He also worked his way out from behind the building occasionally so Wilner could see he was okay. He also wanted to ensure he wasn't rushing to judgment on this man addressing the crowd.

He was about thirty, wearing an L.A. Cowboys football jersey.

Besslia inched into the smaller crowd with the riot surging around them. He could hear the man clearly.

"They moved us here against our will. This is the only way to get back to our homes. We must make a statement even if it means destroying every business in the district." He waved toward the line of cops and soldiers. "They don't have the men to stop us." He stepped down from the plastic crate he had stood on. He led the group to the edge of the building. "Look, there are only a few of them. They can't do anything. If we rush them we can have guns too."

Besslia listened but his instinct was to rush back and warn his partners. Then he tried to look past the words and see if he could pick up other details that might help in his report.

The speaker's dark complexion and black hair made him look Hispanic but the three guys who were standing behind him made Besslia recognize that this was an organized effort. The other men followed the speaker as he led the group to view the police line.

Besslia inched up to the front of the group and focused on the three men supporting the speaker. Their alert eyes scanned the crowd and beyond. One man looked to the roof of the building. Besslia followed his eyes and saw another man on the roof with binoculars. These guys were more than they seemed.

He heard one man call back to yet another large man who was watching some crates behind them.

Then Besslia put it all together: they were jihadists.

Leonard Hall stepped out of his bedroom into the hallway just in time to see Mari with her hand on the knob to the closet where his aunt was stored. Before he could shout for her to stop, a voice in his head cackled, distracting him. The slight hesitation was all it took. He watched, helplessly, as Mari twisted the knob and opened the door.

He saw her body tighten and then jump back as his aunt's corpse, wrapped in a blanket with duct tape and wedged in the closet upright, came tumbling out onto Mari.

She tried to catch it, not realizing that the old blanket held a cadaver. The weight pushed her back and both she and Leonard's aunt landed on the floor. The blanket had drawn back from his aunt's head.

Mari looked like she wanted to scream but no sound came out of her mouth. She scooted away from the body, her eyes never moving from his aunt's pale, but still pretty, face.

Leonard could clearly see the wounds on her neck and knew Mari could too.

She looked from the body up to Leonard. "Her neck." She sobbed a couple of times and took in a gasping breath. "You killed her. You're the Vampire."

Leonard squeezed his eyes shut a few seconds, then he looked up and quickly moved toward his aunt's body. Mari was gone.

Then, out the bay window, he saw Mari as she ran out behind his house toward the river.

Now he had to deal with her too.

FORTY-SEVEN

Steve Besslia took a few minutes to retrieve his V-com but no one answered when he called. He started jogging back toward the UPF officers along the edge of the riot.

Now he saw them closely grouped with the National Guardsmen. He eased to the rear of the group, nodding to one of the cops that was watching the crowd.

He said, "Hey guys, what's up?" Then, as they turned toward him he saw what everyone was looking at. Wilner had his gun to the face of a National Guard captain.

Wilner saw him and immediately lowered his pistol. He actually smiled and said, "Hey, pal. You got it under control for us?"

"There really are just a few guys running the show in there."

The UPF commander stepped up. "What'd you get, Besslia?"

He pointed toward the restaurant where the crowd got thicker. "See the guy in the L.A. Cowboys jersey?"

The commander and Wilner nodded.

"He and the others are speaking Arabic. They're coordinated. I think they might be jihadists."

The National Guard captain said, "He'll be hit in our first volley."

Wilner gave him a hard look. The captain immediately backed down and eased away from them.

Wilner turned his attention back to the man in the blue and silver football jersey. Someone handed him a set of binoculars and he zeroed in on the man. He was shouting to the rioters.

Besslia said, "He's not alone. There are three guys behind him and one on the roof watching us."

Wilner checked the statement and immediately saw it was true.

The National Guard captain said, "Stand back, men, we're going to open fire."

"Hang," yelled Wilner. "Do you have a couple of soldiers who are good shots with their assault rifles?"

The captain hesitated and then nodded his head.

"Bring them up to take out five men at once. Then see what happens."

The captain stared at him.

"C'mon, Captain," started Wilner. "You might avoid a lot of trouble if this works."

The captain thought about it then pointed to five riflemen. "Move up and listen for targets."

Wilner watched as Besslia carefully pointed out the instigators. The National Guardsmen took a few minutes to each designate a target. Then they flipped up the short optical sight.

A sergeant coordinated the soldiers. He was a little older and looked like he might have seen action.

"All right, fellas." He kept a calm voice. "Sight in on target." He waited. "Aim." He waited a second then said, "Three, two, one, fire, fire, fire." He never shouted and the men responded like professionals. The shots weren't in perfect unison but all the targets were hit.

The man on the roof toppled off and fell somewhere behind the restaurant. The man in the Cowboys jersey had time to look up before the rifleman assigned to him fired. The bullet caught him square in the face, sending him straight to the ground. Two of the support men were down but moving. The last one tried to flee away from the riflemen and the riot only to be cut down by several rounds of fire as they all concentrated on him.

Immediately there was a different mood in the crowd. The sight of fellow rioters being killed, as well as the main leader's head exploding in front of spectators, caused a mass exodus of people.

The UPF commander looked at the National Guard captain. "Good shooting, Captain. Now let's see what the crowd does."

The captain's eyes flicked over to Wilner and his big duty weapon.

Mari took a chance when Leonard spaced out and shut his eyes. She had fled immediately through a rear door out into the backyard. The setting sun and rising moon, both reflected in low clouds, provided a surprising amount of light. She could make out a footbridge behind a field near Leonard's house.

She calculated her chances of reaching a neighbor or of fleeing across the bridge where Leonard would be less likely to think she ran. The hollow sound of her hard shoes over the wooden bridge made her slow slightly to sound less obvious. The water under the bridge flowed steadily with a light, easy sound.

She crossed the grassy slope on the far side of the river. The sounds of the swampy lowlands seemed to envelop her as she sought the darkest shadow to hide in.

There was still no sign of Leonard. She slowed, thinking she had escaped.

Wilner was amazed at how quickly the crowd had dispersed after the short volley from the National Guardsmen. Three UPF men ventured into the fleeing crowd and captured one of the men wounded by the rifle fire. The other four were already dead.

The man bled from one wound in his shoulder. His dark skin was turning pasty as they waited for a medic to show up.

Wilner listened as the UPF commander kneeled down next to him. The combat veteran wasn't in the mood to follow guidelines laid out by policy.

"Son, if you want help, you better start talking."

"I want help but there's nothing I can say."

"We know about you and your buddies starting this thing and keeping it going."

The young man's dark eyes moved around the crowd of men watching him.

The commander grabbed him by the arm and shook him. "Should I just let you go and tell the rioters they had been used by a jihadist? You think they'll understand?"

The man still didn't answer.

The commander looked up and said, "Make an announcement over the loudspeaker of who was responsible and let's let this one go back." He didn't even look at the prisoner.

The man immediately started to panic. "Wait. What do you need to know?"

"Who sent you guys in here?"

The man hesitated.

The commander stood up "Get this asshole outta here. Let's see what they do to him. Should be funny."

This time the man spoke right up. "We're from Jordan. We've been in the United States since the Crescent War."

"Who told you to stir up this shit?"

"The head of the intelligence services. He said that they had to stop the repopulation of Florida and isolate you. I don't know why."

The commander looked toward two uniformed officers. "Transport this man to the district hospital and stay with him until relieved. I believe the feds need to hear what he has to say."

Wilner liked his boss's style. He slid next to the squat commander and said, "Boss, I need to go."

The commander turned and looked at him.

"The killer. I know where to look in the zone now."

"Okay, okay, Willie, you can go, but I need Besslia here."

Wilner looked and saw his partner swell with pride at the idea the commander needed him for anything.

Wilner nodded. "No problem, but I'm gonna take a car down there."

"Go ahead and be careful. We got it here."

Wilner was in a UPF hive racing south in a few seconds.

FORTY-EIGHT

Steve Besslia stood next to the commander as they watched the last of the crowd quickly run back to their homes. The restaurant was trashed and the street covered in debris and a few bodies. But there were no active fires, and the houses surrounding the scene were all intact.

The commander said, "Okay, here's the plan." He pointed at the two uniformed cops. "You two get up on the interstate near the Northern Enclave and make sure no news crews are coming down. If they are stop them and send them north again." He turned to another patrolman. "Frank, get some help and recover every body out there. We want just trash and debris when the maintenance crew comes to clear the road."

"What about the restaurant?" one patrolman asked.

"Once we got everything cleaned up, the restaurant is gonna have a fire. Nothing special just a regular fire."

Besslia looked at the boss. "What about me?"

"You're gonna supervise the cleanup."

"Supervise?"

"Sure, you're a detective now. You need some responsibility."

Besslia tried to act cool but couldn't hide his smile.

Tom Wilner flew over the bridge into the zone so fast the lone guardsman didn't have a chance to protest. The streets of the zone were empty. He figured people heard what was going on and fled to safety in case things got out of control.

He pulled up to the little house where Mari lived. Before he was to the front door the Jamaican lady that lived next door called from her porch, "She ain't home."

"Do you know where she is?"

"Might be at the school but she ain't come home since she left for work this morning."

Wilner nodded his thanks and hopped back in the big hive. He was at the school in a few minutes, pulling up to the curb in front of the closed building. He still jumped out and ran up the front yard to the locked main door.

He pounded, hoping that Mari might answer. But no one did.

Checking his pockets he felt his small handheld light with a radium battery that would last a lifetime. Then he felt his locking combat blade in his rear pocket. Flipping it open, he slid the hard steel blade between the double doors and worked it up until he felt the latch. Losing all patience he shoved the knife handle hard to the side like a pry bar and popped the doors wide open.

He ran through the hallway calling Mari's name.

He wasn't sure what he might find but darted into Mari's office. He looked over her desk for a note or some hint where she had gone. There was nothing. He slammed a fist into the desk and stood up.

As he headed out the door he noted a series of photographs on the wall. He used his hand light to illuminate them better. The first one was Mari, the second one was an older black woman and the third one was a man in a workshirt by a workbench. He looked at the man with graying hair and knew it was Leonard. He also recognized him as the man who he asked where the Dadicek's house was. He knew exactly where the Vampire lived.

Leonard Hall walked deliberately out his back door and followed the exact path that Mari had taken. Her sunken footprints in the soggy ground were easy to follow. He realized she had crossed the small pedestrian bridge and was surprised she would elect to go back into the wilderness like that.

She couldn't be allowed to tell everyone who he really was and what he had done. He pulled out his German army knife and worked the spike out into position.

He crossed the bridge slowly, using what little light remained to see if he could spot the terrified teacher.

Mari's whole body had started to shake when she crouched in the shadow of a sprawling cypress tree. She wasn't cold or even completely wet yet. She was scared and knew it. Who wouldn't be with a killer searching for them? She could clearly see the house and Leonard as he casually walked out and started following the same route she had. He hesitated at the bridge. How did he know where she had gone?

She watched in horror as he pulled out a tool and unfolded it. It didn't take a telescope to see it was a weapon of some kind. How could she have been so wrong about someone? She thought God had sent Leonard to help her run the school and keep her safe. God had not sent Leonard.

She debated fleeing deeper into the Everglades as Leonard crossed the narrow footbridge. The only issue was if she could stay hidden in the dark shadow or if Leonard would see her when she started to move.

She looked around for an escape route. When she turned back around she saw the outline of Leonard against the rising moon and clouds.

Without thinking, she screamed.

FORTY-NINE

Tom Wilner burst into the house where Leonard Hall lived. He had his pistol up and was moving through the house quickly to use what element of surprise he had.

He stopped in the living room when he saw a body on the ground. A quick look told him it wasn't Mari and that the woman was dead. He continued through the house before coming back to the body.

He stooped and examined the corpse. She was an attractive woman but he couldn't tell her age. He took a close look at the wound on her neck. It was definitely the work of the Vampire and now he was certain Leonard Hall, or whatever his name, was the killer the locals called the Vampire. His next question was if he was a Simolit or Halleck. Fifty years was a long time.

But before any of those questions could be answered he had to find the man.

There were lights on when he arrived and the door was unlocked. Someone had just been here. The way he parked and approached the house didn't give them a chance to see him coming. But where had they gone?

As he looked around the kitchen behind the living room he heard a woman's scream. He jerked his head up and just caught a glimpse of someone across the river. He knew the scream came from Mari.

Mari had pushed through the thick brush into the ankle-deep water at the edge of the Everglades. She had lost sight of Leonard but knew he was close by. The sounds of the great swamp made her jump and flinch as she changed directions several times. Finally she realized the depth of her disorientation.

The deep, ominous croak of a large alligator made her freeze. Something slithered across her foot. She jumped and let out a quick yelp. She was mad at herself. She knew she couldn't afford to give away her position to Leonard. It was dark enough back here but every step splashed water and she had no idea how to escape. The idea of being grabbed by one of the aggressive gators terrified her as much as Leonard.

Mari found solid ground and realized it was a path up to a wider open field. She trudged up the path and once on higher ground she could look down the wide path and see the back of Leonard's house. Now she knew where to go. She hoped Leonard was still searching for her in the brush.

Mari started to run back toward the house, her heart pounding. Then, about twenty feet in front of her, she saw the outline of a man and slid to a stop.

It was too late to dive back into the bushes and water. She was trapped and knew it. She felt sick to her stomach. She now knew what it meant to be frozen in fear.

———————

Steve Besslia looked over the scene as a crew of district maintenance men moved a big truck that vacuumed up most of the trash and debris in quick, easy passes. Aside from the destroyed structure of the restaurant and three burned-out cars there was no way to tell a riot had ever occurred. The bodies of the jihadists and the four people killed in the riot had already been through the medical examiner's office and then incinerated. The border crossings were all fully manned by the National Guard again.

Now his mind could focus on his friend Wilner and his mission inside the zone. He knew the combat marine with experience in two wars could take care of himself but he still worried about him.

A black hive pulled up next to Besslia and the UPF commander appeared on the driver's side. He called to Besslia as he hustled around to him. "You did one hell of a job here, Besslia."

"Thanks, boss."

"Why don't you sound happy about it?"

"I'm worried about Wilner."

The UPF commander surprised him as he considered the comment then said, "Yeah, me too."

"Things are almost wrapped up here, you want me to check on him?"

"I've tried to raise him on the V-com but the shielding over the zone won't let the call through."

"I'll go check the school and poke around for him if you want."

The commander shook his head. "I can't risk my best men down there at the same time. He's a big boy. He'll be fine."

Besslia stared at his boss. He didn't know what surprised him more; the praise or leaving Wilner on his own

Mari regained her wits as she kept her eyes in front of her. As she was about to dart into the swamp to her right she heard the croak of an alligator again. This one was close. Right about where she had intended to jump into the brush.

Then she heard, "Mari!"

It wasn't Leonard's voice.

"Tom," she shouted as she ran toward him. She felt his embrace and started to weep.

He hugged her then released it. She stepped back and saw he had his pistol in his hand.

"How'd you find me?"

"Long story, I'll impress you with it later. Now let's get back to my car."

"So you know about Leonard?"

"He's the Vampire."

"I am impressed."

Wilner took her hand and started to lead her back. He had his pistol out in front of him and swung it in all directions as they carefully moved forward.

The alligator croaked again.

Then, as they passed a thicket of brush and trees, a figure burst out toward them. Mari could see a flash of metal in the weak light.

Wilner shoved her away from the attack.

She heard him grunt and saw that he had squared off with the attacker.

They moved and she could see Leonard with an odd-looking knife in his right hand. Tom Wilner had retreated a few steps and was holding his right arm, trying to stem the flow of blood from his forearm.

In the attack, Leonard had cut Wilner's arm and caused him to drop his pistol. Now Wilner was doing everything he could to stay between her and the killer.

FIFTY

Tom Wilner crouched with both hands out. The gash on his right arm was bleeding freely so he had lost most of his grip, but the arm could be used to fend off another blow from the heavy combat knife in Leonard's hand. Behind him he could hear Mari gasping each time the blade swished through the air. Then something flew past his shoulder, causing Leonard to leap to one side.

Mari was throwing rocks to distract the killer. That girl could think under pressure, an ability that Wilner greatly admired.

Wilner had retreated so far from the first attack that he couldn't even see where his pistol had landed. Now he needed time to reach for his own knife in his front pocket. He turned quickly to Mari and said, "Keep throwing things at him."

He waited until another rock whizzed past him then reached for his pocket.

Leonard expected the rock this time, dodged it, then managed to gouge Wilner in the right arm again.

The UPF detective returned to his defensive posture. As he

backed up the ground became less stable and he could feel his feet start to splash in shallow water.

A tree limb swung past him then Mari stepped up, swinging wildly. This time Wilner stuffed his aching right hand into his pocket, felt the folding combat knife but was unable to close his hand around it.

Leonard slipped a strike with the tree limb and got his left hand around it. He jerked it hard out of Mari's hands.

Wilner looked at the man's face and realized that he was enjoying this. He didn't want to rush things. He could've slashed Mari but didn't. Instead he stood there grinning at the two of them like one of the alligators in the swamp eyeing his next meal.

Wilner took the break to confront him with the truth

"I know who you are, Leonard Nelson. Or is it Dawson?"

Leonard froze. He considered the accusation and answered, "I forgot I was them too. That's some good detective work."

"I know what you are too."

Now Leonard smiled and said, "I'm not really a vampire, that's just what those people call me."

"But you're a Simolit."

"A what?"

"A Halleck?"

"Huh?"

Wilner wondered if Leonard didn't realize what he really was. Perhaps he was like Wilner's own children; raised by humans and unaware of his own abilities.

Leonard lowered his knife and said, "What are you talking about?"

Wilner could see Mari creeping up to hear the whole conversation. Somewhere close by an alligator croaked and splashed in the water.

Then Wilner asked, "How old are you?"

Leonard didn't hesitate. "I'm sixty-five."

Wilner thought about that and suddenly everything became clear. "That's why the Pompano cops didn't question you much. You were only a kid."

Leonard cocked his head. "Only a kid when?"

"When you murdered Mary Harris."

Leonard was silent.

Wilner let his right hand ease toward his pocket while Leonard seemed so distracted.

Leonard said, "The girl on the seawall."

Wilner nodded.

"I was fifteen. No one suspected me. They just asked questions because I was down at the water a lot. I did it before I knew what was happening."

"What about the others since?"

"Those I did on purpose."

"For the last fifty years?"

Leonard didn't respond.

"Then you're human."

"Yes, of course. What else could I be?"

Before Wilner had to formulate an answer, Mari said, "A demon who preys on people."

Wilner now had his right hand in his pocket again. "You were just a kid. You could've gotten help."

"I could've, but no one cared. All my father wanted to do was keep the fact that he and my mom were brother and sister quiet. I wasn't allowed to socialize with anyone. Turns out I'm better off for it."

Wilner could see how agitated the killer was becoming.

Leonard said, "I've never been arrested and I'm not going to be tonight."

All Wilner said was, "I know," as he drew and flicked open his own knife.

Leonard had to listen to the cop and his gibberish about being something other than human. Was this guy crazy? It was confusing.

As Leonard was about to raise the knife again and go after the cop and Mari with renewed purpose, the cop scooted backward and flicked his hand, making a folding knife open to a long, deadly looking combat blade.

This was a new wrinkle but it excited Leonard.

Wilner felt like he had a chance now as he shifted the combat knife from his right to his uninjured left hand. He left his right hand up for defense. Blood dripped and spewed down his arm, dribbling off his elbow as he feinted and dodged in a deadly game.

Now the water was deeper but Leonard was bogged down in it as well.

Wilner blocked a blow with his right forearm and was able to lay a solid slash across Leonard's side. Instantly blood stained the man's T-shirt and started dripping into the murky water. Wilner didn't rejoice much since he had lost a lot more blood than Leonard.

The crazy dance of feints and jabs continued with Wilner landing two slashes across Leonard's right thigh. Even at dusk

Wilner could see the man's jeans darken as blood pumped out of the deep wound.

Leonard rushed Wilner and they locked in a mutual embrace, empty hands holding the other man's knife hand.

They tumbled into the deeper water and thrashed around. Wilner tried to dunk Leonard and hold him under the water. Leonard managed a light slash across Wilner's left arm as they separated and squared off again.

Wilner had lost track of where Mari was but he hoped she was safe and using the time he was buying to flee back to the house.

Wilner also noticed how winded he was getting sloshing around in the water. He knew it was a combination of loss of blood and extra effort. He could only hope Leonard felt the same way.

Wilner backed away from swipe after swipe of Leonard's long, sharp blade. Suddenly he felt the ground slope sharply and realized they had fought to the precipice of a deep pond here at the edge of the Everglades.

Leonard followed until he lost his balance on the sloping pond bank.

Wilner had crept around until he was in knee-deep water and Leonard was in deeper water, almost to his hips. The UPF cop saw his advantage and knew he had to keep Leonard in the deeper water where he couldn't maneuver as well and expended a great deal more energy. Wilner also hoped his wounds would start to catch up to him.

The water was red with the blood from both men and Wilner dodged from side to side, keeping Leonard in the deeper water. Something hard and heavy slipped over Wilner's foot, then a second later, it clipped his ankle.

As he tried to process what kind of animal could've just brushed him, the water erupted in white splashes as a giant alligator's head broke the surface of the water like a missile and clutched Leonard's arm, twisting him around completely.

Then Leonard was free and reaching for help from the taller cop.

Wilner stumbled backward, trying to get away from the area.

As Leonard started to wade forward the water behind him swirled and Leonard was yanked hard off his feet. He was jerked underwater and the water bubbled and started turning pink.

By the time the alligator's death roll was over and the water quiet again, Wilner was back up near the trail and saw no hint of the man that many just called the Vampire.

FIFTY-ONE

Tom Wilner had never liked hospitals. During the Second Iranian War he had visited too many buddies who never got out. But after all he had been through he didn't mind the quiet room at the district's main hospital. It had been a long time since he watched video broadcasts other than news.

In the last two days he had seen a couple of newer movies, a lot of old movies, as well as more news than he ever thought he could stomach.

Sandwiched between seemingly endless reports on the Urailian ship and the negotiations with Germany about withdrawal, was a short, inaccurate story on a freak fire at the southern edge of the district that had left several dead. No mention of the civil disturbance was ever made.

Over the past few days Wilner occasionally saw images of the violence or of the alligator snatching Leonard whenever he closed his eyes. Just like the violent images of war had faded from his dreams over time he felt sure the same would happen to his current plague of nightmares.

He was safe and would make a full recovery with only some scars on his arm and chest. His children were safe and Mari had not been harmed by the deceptive and prolific killer who had been named, the Vampire.

He had just picked up a magazine that covered current events when the door to his room opened a crack.

He looked up, then smiled at the face of his daughter, Emma, poking around the open door. Then Tommy stepped out from behind her.

They raced to his bedside, Tommy jumping up and jostling the stitches in his chest. He didn't care.

Steve Besslia stepped in behind them with a broad smile on his face. He lifted his arm to usher in someone and Mari Saltis appeared as if by magic.

Wilner visited with his children as Mari watched until a nurse asked if they wanted to see the pet sheep the hospital staff kept in an open side of the hospital. The nurse explained that sick children liked touching real sheep since there weren't many around anymore.

As soon as they had followed the nurse out, Mari stepped up and clasped Wilner's hand. Besslia stood on the other side of his bed, still smiling.

"How'd you get her across, Steve?"

"I'm a detective now. Those border guards do whatever I say." He looked out the window at the dull sky. "Hey, I'll be back in a little while. I haven't seen a real sheep in years." The newest UPF detective headed out the door, shooting a thumbs-up to Mari and Wilner.

Mari smiled as she looked down at Wilner. She stood holding his unbandaged hand for a full ten minutes without saying a word. That suited Wilner fine.

Finally he said, "I really can't think of anything to say except that I'd do anything for you to move up here."

"I'd love to be closer to you but the people in the Quarantine Zone need me as much as ever. You can see we're making progress. It won't last if the residents flee."

Wilner nodded. "I just want to see more of you."

"You could move to the zone. You're a hero down there. That's all anyone can talk about. The UPF cop who stopped the Vampire."

Wilner let out a laugh.

"No, really, you could set up the first police department. A real police force would change a lot of things."

"Chief Wilner. I kinda like the sound of that."

Mari leaned down and gave him a long, deep kiss. "The perks would be great."

Just then the door burst open and the kids rushed in with news of the sheep that was living like a king downstairs.

Wilner looked up at Mari and said, "I love your idea but for two obvious reasons, I have to decline."

The disappointment on her face stayed with him longer than the dreams of Leonard being eaten alive.

Olive Lolley had been born on the island of Jamaica when it was a destination for tourists from the United States and England. Moving to Florida had been easy when she married a retired U.S. Army sergeant. Then after they had settled in the town of Homestead, south of Miami, everything changed. She had always been gifted in languages and her Spanish was excellent, which made her popular with her Cuban neighbors. She had moved to this little house on the Zone River six years ago and planned for it to be her last home. Although she had been lonely since her husband died in the first terror attack in Miami, she had made a slow, quiet life for herself.

Then a few months earlier she had found a man who had washed down through the various tributaries of the main river and had been stuck on a cypress knoll behind her house.

She couldn't believe the burned, bloodied, shattered man was still alive. She had cared for him using the basic skills she had learned as a long-term care nurse. She had managed to find gauze and antiseptic to clean and bandage him.

She had sung Spanish songs to him every evening.

She prayed to her beloved Jesus that infection wouldn't kill him and her prayers were answered. Although he could do little other than move his dark eyes, he had seemed to make some improvement over the past weeks.

Today he had startled her as she unwrapped his face. The melted and scarred flesh had healed dramatically.

Then her patient said, "You have done me a great service." His voice was clear and strong. She noticed the accent and careful pronunciation.

"My name is Tiget Nadovich and you speeded my recovery by years."

Olive fanned her face as she felt a little faint. She couldn't believe the mess of flesh she had fished out of the water would ever be able to talk or look so good.

"You're a good woman," he said.

"I never thought you'd look so . . ." She searched for a word.

"Human?" offered her patient.

"Yes, I suppose so. I'm so glad you're feeling better. You may have no fear, Mr. Tiget. You can stay as long as you wish."

"I appreciate your offer but I have things to do."

"Such as?"

"First I must retrieve my children. Then the world is open to me."

JAMES O'NEAL is a native Floridian who spent his youth exploring the ever-shrinking wild areas of his home state. The changes he's seen over the past four decades pushed him to write this series of novels set in the near future of Florida. He has written extensively about Florida history.

After graduating from Florida State University, O'Neal started a career in law enforcement. He was a special agent with the United States Drug Enforcement Administration (DEA) and has spent the past twenty years as a special agent with the Florida Department of Law Enforcement. He has seen the evolution of police work and made logical choices for the novels of where police procedure will be in the near future. His research included conferring with armorers about future calibers and projectiles as well as speaking with biologists about the underlying theories of the novels regarding human development and related issues.

O'Neal has created a series of videos highlighting books of different genres. The videos feature appearances by writers such as Michael Connelly and W. E. B. Griffin. The videos have been featured on television news shows and in publishing industry newsletters. The videos can be found at www .jamesonealbooks.com.

He is a lifelong fan of science fiction and has read widely, from Robert Heinlein and Philip José Farmer to his contemporary favorites, Harry Turtledove and John Scalzi. After a visit to Seattle's Science Fiction Museum and Hall of Fame, O'Neal started his first science fiction novel, *The Human Disguise.*

O'Neal currently lives on a quiet lake in Florida with his wife and children. He spends his free time windsurfing, running, and diving in the warm waters of the Atlantic. He also continues his practice of martial arts, which he has pursued for thirty years. He holds a black belt in Shotokan karate and a black belt in Isshinryu karate.

O'Neal writes under the pen name of James O. Born. As James O. Born, he has written five police thrillers. He is a recipient of the Florida Book Award. In 2009, he won the Barry Award for his short story "The Drought," which appeared in Michael Connelly's *The Blue Religion.* He was also named as one of the Twenty-one Most Intriguing Floridians by *Florida Monthly* magazine.